Kebbi, feeling an intoxication much more of impending triumph than of drink, faced his single opponent across the blanket-covered table. The tall man's shadowy companion, as if she meant to protect his back, moved up close behind him, where she remained standing.

And now, moving slowly, the hand of the unknown brought forth from somewhere inside his cape a truly magnificent jewel, holding it up for all to see. The stone was the shape of a teardrop, the color of a sapphire's blood. His large, strong fingers held it up, turning it in the lamplight for Kebbi to see and admire. Still, the man's attention was entirely concentrated upon Kebbi, as if he were totally indifferent as to anything that other folk might see or do.

Unhurriedly the tall man said: "I will stake this gem against the Sword you wear."

Tor books by Fred Saberhagen

A Century of Progress
Coils (with Roger Zelazny)
Dominion
The Dracula Tape
Earth Descended
The Holmes-Dracula File
The Mask of the Sun
A Matter of Taste
An Old Friend of the Family
Specimens
Thorn
The Veils of Azlaroc
The Water of Thought

THE BERSERKER SERIES

The Berserker Wars
The Berserker Throne
Berserker Base (with Poul Anderson, Ed Bryant,
   Stephen Donaldson, Larry Niven, Connie Willis,
   and Roger Zelazny)
Berserker: Blue Death

THE BOOKS OF SWORDS

The First Book of Swords
The Second Book of Swords
The Third Book of Swords

THE BOOKS OF LOST SWORDS

The First Book of Lost Swords: Woundhealer's Story
The Second Book of Lost Swords: Sightblinder's Story
The Third Book of Lost Swords: Stonecutter's Story
The Fourth Book of Lost Swords: Farslayer's Story
The Fifth Book of Lost Swords: Coinspinner's Story
*The Sixth Book of Lost Swords: Mindsword's Story**

*forthcoming

THE FIFTH BOOK
OF
LOST SWORDS

COINSPINNER'S STORY

FRED SABERHAGEN

TOR
fantasy

A TOM DOHERTY ASSOCIATES BOOK
NEW YORK

THE FIFTH BOOK OF LOST SWORDS

Copyright © 1989 by Fred Saberhagen

A TOR Book
Published by Tom Doherty Associates, Inc.
49 West 24th Street
New York, N.Y. 10010

Cover art by Jim Warren
Cover design by Carol Russo

ISBN: 0-812-55286-5

Library of Congress Catalog Card Number: 89-39878

First edition: December 1989
First mass market edition: September 1990

Printed in the United States of America

0 9 8 7 6 5 4 3 2

ONE

I swear to you, most royal and excellent lady," declared the handsome and distinguished visitor, "I solemnly pledge, most lovely and farseeing Princess, that if you can save the life of my Queen's consort and end his suffering, her royal gratitude and his—not to mention my own—will know no bounds."

Princess Kristin sighed. Over the course of the past two days, she had already heard the same statement a score of times from the same man, sometimes in very nearly the same words, sometimes in speech less flowery. Now once more she forced herself to attend with courtesy and patience to the representative of Culm.

As soon as the distinguished and handsome visitor had concluded his latest version of his plea, she turned half away from him, trying to frame her answer. Over the past two days she had endeavored to give the same reply in different ways. This time the Princess began her response in silence, with a gesture indicating the view beneath the balcony on which they stood.

Below the Palace, sloping away toward the sea, rank on rank of the neatly tiled, multicolored roofs of Sarykam gleamed in the bright sun of summer afternoon. Halfway between the Palace and the harbor, the mass of crowded buildings was interrupted by a tree-lined square of generous size, which held at its center the chief White Temple of the city. This structure, a pyramid of stark design and chalky whiteness, contained among other things two shrines, those of the gods Ardneh and Draffut.

Of greater practical importance to most people was the fact that the pyramid also contained, within a special coffer, the Sword called Woundhealer.

Today, as on almost every day, a line of people seeking the Sword's help had begun to form before dawn in the Temple square. Now in the middle of the afternoon that line, easily visible from the Palace balcony, was still threading its way into the eastern entrance on the harbor side of the white pyramid. The line was still long, and new arrivals kept it at an almost constant length. The people who made up the line were suffering from disease or injury of one kind or another. They were the ill, the crippled, the blind or mad or wounded, many of them needing the help of nurses or close companions simply to be here and join the line. Some of the sufferers had come from a great distance to seek Woundhealer's aid.

Even as the Princess gestured in the direction of the white pyramid, a pair of stretcher-bearers, lugging between them an ominously inert human form, were being ushered by white-robed priests toward the front of that distant queue. The priests of Ardneh who served this particular Temple were accustomed to making such decisions about priorities, thus assuming momentarily the role of gods. From the balcony there was no telling whether the body on the stretcher was that of a man, woman, or child. The Princess thought that no more than a minimum of protest would be heard from those whose turns were being thus preempted; she could see that today's line was, as usual, moving briskly, and no one in it should have to wait for very long.

Meanwhile, the most recent beneficiaries of the power of the Sword of Healing, many of them accompanied by their relieved nurses and companions, were emerging in a steady trickle from the Temple's western door. People who only moments ago had been severely injured or seriously ill, some even at the point of death, were walking out healthy and whole. From experience Kristin knew that their bandages and splints would have been left in the Temple, or were now being removed and thrown away. Stretchers and crutches, indispensable a few minutes earlier, were now being cast aside by vigorous hands. Only a few of those who had just been healed still needed help in walking, and to them strength would return in time.

For the Sword of Mercy to fail to heal was practically unheard of. As a rule every supplicant who limped or staggered or was carried into the eastern entrance of this White Temple soon came walking out, with a firm step, from the western exit. Today, as usual, some of the cured were waving their arms and shouting prayers of gratitude audible even to the two watchers on the distant balcony.

The Crown Prince Murat, tall emissary from the land of Culm, having gazed dutifully upon the distant scene as he was bidden, chose to ignore whatever inferences the Princess had meant him to draw from the sight. Instead he promptly resumed his arguments. "If, dear princess, it is a matter of some necessary payment—"

"It is not that," said Princess Kristin quickly, turning back to face her visitor fully. Kristin was about the same age as the Crown Prince, in her early thirties and the mother of two half-grown sons. But she looked a few years younger, with her fair hair, blue-green eyes, and fine features.

She said to her eminent guest: "When you paid your own formal visit to the White Temple yesterday, Prince Murat, no doubt you noted that most of those who benefit from Woundhealer's power do make some payment in the form of offerings. These funds are used to maintain the Temple and to pay its priests and guards. Others who benefit from the Sword are unable to pay; and a very few refuse to do so. But none are denied treatment on that account. If your

Queen's unfortunate consort can travel here to Tasavalta, the powers of the Sword of Healing will be made available to him under the same conditions."

"Regrettably that is not possible, Princess." In the course of his brief visit Murat had already offered this explanation at least a hundred times, or so it seemed to both of them, and now it was his turn to repeat a statement slowly and patiently. "A condition of nearly total paralysis afflicts the royal consort, combined with the most fearful arthritic pain, so that even the movement required to go from one bed or one room to another is a severe ordeal for him. An overland journey of more than a thousand kilometers, only half of it on roads, is, as you can appreciate, quite out of the question. Ten kilometers would be impossible."

"Then I am truly sorry for him. And sorry for your Queen, and for all her realm." And it seemed that the Princess was speaking her true feelings. "But I am afraid that the Sword stays here, in Tasavalta. That is my final word."

A silence fell, broken only by the occasional noise, a rumbling cart or a raised voice, rising from the thronged city below. Kristin half expected her visitor to raise yet again the point that sometimes the Sword was taken out of the city of Sarykam, and carried on tour in a heavily guarded caravan that visited the outlying portions of the realm, bringing healing to those unable to reach the capital. If he did choose to raise that point again, she had her previous answer ready: Woundhealer was never allowed to go outside the borders of the realm. Her patience held; she could sympathize with Murat, though she would not yield to him.

But the persistence of the Crown Prince, not yet exhausted, this time took a different tack. He said: "Still, the journey to Culm and back with the borrowed Sword could be quickly accomplished by my troop—accompanied, of course, by any number of representatives you might choose to send with us. Our mounts are very swift, and we are now familiar with the way. My master's healing once accomplished, the Sword could be on its way back here the very same day. Within the hour. I would be willing to pledge my honor to you on that."

The soft urgency of his voice was unexpectedly hard to resist. But Kristin still said what she had to say. "I understand your arguments, Prince. I am willing to believe that you mean your pledge, and I respect it. But once your realm found itself in possession of such a treasure as Woundhealer, convincing arguments would soon be found as to why the Sword should stay there, as a policy of national health insurance."

"No, Princess, I must—"

"No, Crown Prince Murat, your request is quite impossible to meet. The Sword of Love stays here."

Before the Crown Prince could devise yet another argument, the conversation was interrupted. The door leading to the balcony, which had been standing ajar, burst open violently, and a small form came running out.

Startled and angry, the Princess turned to find herself confronting the younger of her two sons, who at ten was certainly old enough to know better than to behave in such a way.

"Well, Stephen? I hope you have some just cause for this interruption?"

The boy, as sturdy as his father had been at the same age, though somewhat darker, was flushed and scowling, evidently even angrier than his mother. But now he drew himself up, making a great effort at self-control. "Mother, you once said that I should tell you at once if I knew of anyone practicing intrigue within the Palace."

"And I suppose you have just now discovered something of the kind?" It was easy to see that the Princess was not inclined to accept the alarming implication at face value.

"Yes, Mother."

"Well?"

Stephen drew a deep breath. His anger was cooling, and now he seemed reluctant to go on.

"Well?"

Another deep breath. "It's my tutor, Mother. I believe he is about to come to you with false stories concerning my behavior."

And indeed the Princess, raising her gaze slightly, discovered that very gentleman now hovering inside the balcony door, irresolute as to whether he should match his pupil's daring and interrupt what looked like a state conference, simply to defend himself.

Sternly Kristin ordered her younger son to go to his room and wait there for her. The command was delivered in an incisive tone that allowed no immediate argument; it was obeyed reluctantly, in gloomy silence.

Then the Princess silently waved the tutor away, and turned to apologize to the ambassador for the interruption.

The tall man smiled faintly. "I have two children of my own at home. Youth needs no apology. And a fiery spirit may be an advantage to one who is born to rule. Indeed I suppose it must be considered a necessity."

"As are self-control, and courtesy; and those virtues my son has yet to learn."

"I'm sure he will acquire them."

"You are kind and diplomatic, Murat." The Princess sighed again, quite openly this time, and spoke for once unguardedly. "I wish his father were here."

There was a pause. It was common knowledge that Prince Mark had spent no more than ten days at home during the last half year, and that the timing and duration of his next visit home were problematical.

Murat bowed slightly. "I too wish that. I had looked forward to meeting Prince Mark. His name is known and respected even in our far corner of the world."

"Not that my husband would give you any different answer than I have given, on the subject of loaning out the Sword of Healing."

The visitor bowed again. "I must still be allowed to hope that the answer will change."

"It will not change." After a pause, the Princess added: "If you are wondering about my husband's absence, know that he is in the service of the Emperor; he is the Emperor's son, you know." In the minds of many, the Emperor was a half-mythological figure; and that a prince should believe he owed this legend service was an idea sometimes hard for outsiders to grasp.

And sometimes even the Princess, who had never seen her mysterious father-in-law, found the situation hard to understand as well.

The Crown Prince said: "I was aware of Prince Mark's parentage."

Suddenly Kristin heard herself blurting out a question. "You don't—I don't suppose that any news has come to you recently regarding his whereabouts?" A month had now gone by in which no winged messenger had brought her news of her husband. Unhappily, this was not the first time such a period had elapsed, but repetition made the stress no easier to bear.

"I regret, Princess, that I have heard nothing." Murat paused, then made an evident effort to turn the conversation to some less difficult subject. "Young Prince Stephen has an older brother, I understand."

"Yes. Prince Adrian is twelve. He's currently away from home, attending school."

Again there came interruption, this time more sedately, and welcome to both parties. It took the form of a servant, announcing the arrival of the other members of the Culm delegation. These folk had been sight-seeing in the streets of Sarykam this afternoon, and some of them had visited the White Temple down the hill.

And now good manners required that the Princess and her companion come in from the balcony, to join the Culmian visitors and other folk inside the Palace.

One of the junior members of the Culmian delegation was Lieutenant Kebbi. This was Murat's cousin, a red-headed, bold-looking, and yet unfailingly courteous youth, who now showed his disappointment openly, when he heard that the Princess was standing fast in her refusal to loan out the Sword.

Lieutenant Kebbi looked as if he might want to raise an argument of his own on behalf of the Culmian cause. But Kristin turned away, not wanting to give the impetuous youth a chance. None of the arguments that she had heard so far, and none that she could imagine, were going to sway her, sympathetic as she was.

Others still importuned her. At last, beginning to show her impatience with her guests' pleading, Kristin demanded of them: "How many of my own people would die, while the Sword was absent from us?"

For that there was no answer. Even the eyes of the bold young lieutenant fell in confusion before the Princess's gaze when she turned back to him.

Once more she faced the delegation's leader. "Come, good Murat, can you number them, or tell me their names?"

The tall man only bowed in silence.

One of the several diplomats on hand quickly managed to change the subject, and talk went on until eventually the delegation from Culm withdrew to their assigned quarters. In there, servants reported, they were conversing seriously and guardedly among themselves.

In the evening, when the sun had set behind the inland mountains, the visitors from afar were once more entertained with Tasavaltan hospitality. There was music, acrobats, and dancers. To Kristin's relief the subject of the Sword had been laid to rest. This was now the third day of the Culmians' stay, and they expressed a unanimous desire to depart early in the morning.

During the evening, more than one Tasavaltan remarked to the Princess that the guests from Culm seemed to be taking their refusal as well as could be expected. Certainly they had now said and done everything they honorably could to persuade Princess Kristin to change her mind.

With some of the guests pleading weariness, and with the necessity for an early start hanging over them all, the party broke up relatively early. Before midnight the silence of the night had claimed the entire Palace, as well as most of the surrounding city.

At about dawn on the following morning—and, through a strange combination of unlucky chances, not before then—Kristin was awakened, to be informed by an ashen-faced aide that the Sword of Healing had been stolen from its place in the White Temple at some time during the night.

The Princess sat up swiftly, pulling a robe around her shoulders. "Stolen! By whom?" Though it seemed to her that the answer was already plain in her mind.

Awkwardly the messenger framed her own version of an answer. "No thief has been arrested, ma'am. The delegation from Culm reportedly departed about two hours ago. And there are witnesses who accuse them of the theft."

By this time Kristin was out of bed, fastening her robe, her arms in its sleeves. "Has Rostov been aroused? Have any steps been taken to organize a pursuit?"

"The General is being notified now, my lady, and I am sure we may rely on him to waste no time."

"Let us hope that very little time has been wasted already. If Rostov or one of his officers comes looking for me, tell them I have gone to the White Temple to see for myself whatever there may be to see."

Only a very few minutes later she was striding into the Temple, entering a scene swarming with soldiers and priests, and aglow with torches. With slight relief she saw that her chief wizard, Karel, who was also her mother's brother, was already on hand and had taken charge for the moment.

Karel was very old—exactly how old was difficult to determine, as was often the case with wizards of great power, though in this case the figure could hardly run into centuries. He was also fat, spoke in a rich, soft voice, and puffed whenever he had to move more than a few steps consecutively. This last characteristic, thought Kristin, had to be more the result of habit—or of sheer laziness, perhaps—than of disease. For Karel, like the more mundane citizens of the realm, had had the benefits of Woundhealer available to him for the past several years.

Karel reported succinctly and with deference. After a few words the Princess was in possession of the basic, frightening facts. Last night, as usual, the Temple had been closed for a few hours, beginning at about midnight. Ordinarily a priest or two remained in the building while it was closed, ready to produce the Sword should some emergency require its healing powers; but last night, through a series of misunderstandings, none of the white-robes had been on duty.

An hour or so past midnight, the chance passage of a brief summer rainstorm had kept off the streets most of the relatively few citizens who might normally have been abroad at such a time. And so, incredible as it seemed to Kristin, apparently no one outside the Temple had witnessed the assault, or raid.

Kristin at first had real difficulty in believing this. There was always someone in that square. "And what of the guards inside the Temple?" she demanded. "Where were they? Where are they now?"

The old man sighed, and gave such explanation as he could. Inasmuch as White Temple people were notoriously poor at guarding such material treasures as came into their hands from time to time, the rulers of Tasavalta had never trusted the white-robed priests to guard the Sword. Instead, a detail of men from an elite army regiment protected Woundhealer.

At least two of these soldiers were always on duty inside the Temple's supposedly secure walls and doors. But last night, at the crucial hour, one guard of the minimal pair, though a young man, had collapsed without warning, clutching his chest in pain, and died almost at once. A few moments later the victim's partner, reaching into a dark niche to grasp the bellrope that would summon help, had been bitten on the hand by a poisonous snake, and paralyzed almost instantly. The soldier's life was still in danger. The snake was of a species not native to these parts, and so far no one had been able to explain its presence in the Temple.

Scarcely had Kristin finished listening to this most unlikely story when more news came, a fresh discovery almost as difficult to believe. A lock on one of the Temple's doors had accidentally jammed last night when the door was closed, effectively preventing the door from being secured in the usual way. The defect was a peculiar one—highly improbable, as the locksmith kept insisting—and it must have seemed to the woman who had turned the key at the hour of sunset that the door was securely locked as usual.

Karel gave a slight shrug of his heavy shoulders. "The theft was accomplished by means of magic, Princess," he said in his soft voice. "There's no doubt of that."

"And a very powerful magic it must have been." After a momentary hesitation, she asked: "A Sword?" Already she thought she knew the answer; and it would not be hard, she thought, to guess which Sword had been employed.

"Very likely a Sword." The old man nodded grimly. "I feel sure that Coinspinner has been used against us."

Once more their talk was interrupted. Now at last a witness had been discovered, one besides the poisoned guard who could give direct testimony. A shabby figure was hustled before the Princess. One of Sarykam's rare beggars, who had spent most of the night huddled in a doorway on the far side of the square, and who now swore that at the height of the rainstorm he had seen a man wearing the blue-and-orange uniform of Culm carrying a bright Sword —it had certainly been no ordinary blade—carrying it drawn and raised, into the White Temple. Meanwhile, the beggar related, others in the same livery had stood by outside with weapons drawn.

"This man you saw was carrying a Sword *into* the Temple, and not out of it? Are you quite sure?"

"Oh, oh, yes, I'm quite sure, Princess. If I'd seen a foreigner taking something out, I would've raised an alarm.

Thought of doing so anyway, but—you see—I'd had a bit too much—my legs weren't working all that well—"

"Never mind that. Did you see him come out of the Temple again?"

"Yes, ma'am, I did. And then he had two Swords. I tried to raise an alarm, ma'am, like I said, but somehow—somehow—" The ragged man began to blubber.

After hearing this testimony of the sole witness, Kristin made her way into the inner sanctuary, and carried out her own belated inspection of the actual scene of the crime. There, on the very altar of Ardneh, she beheld the crystal repository in which the Sword of Healing had been kept, a fragile vault now standing broken and empty under the blank-eyed marble images of Draffut—doglike, but standing tall on his hind legs—and Ardneh, an incomprehensible jumble of sharp-edged, machinelike shapes.

The actual breaking of the crystal vault and carrying away of the Sword would have been simple, and staring at this minor wreckage told her nothing.

Leaving the Temple now, the Princess went to survey the status of the Swords still kept in the royal armory, beside the Palace and only a short walk distant.

If the Princess and her people were able to speak of Coinspinner with a certain familiarity, it was because the Sword of Chance had reposed for some time within the stone walls of the armory's heavily guarded rooms. But about seven years ago that Sword had vanished from the deepest and best-watched vault, vanished suddenly and without explanation. Under the circumstances of that disappearance there had been no need to look for thieves. One of the known attributes of the Sword of Chance was its penchant for taking itself spontaneously and unpredictably from one place to another. Forged by the great god Vulcan, like all its fellow Swords, Coinspinner scorned all obstacles that ordinary human beings might place in opposition to its powers. Coinspinner was subject to no confinement, and to no rules but its own, and exactly what those rules were no one knew. By what progression, during the last seven years, the Sword of Chance had passed from the Tasavaltan armory to somewhere in Culm would probably be impossible to determine, and would be almost certainly irrelevant to the current problem.

Deep in the vaults Kristin encountered the senior General of her armed forces. Rostov was a tall and powerful man in his late fifties, whose curly hair had now turned almost completely from black to gray. The black curve of his right cheek was scarred by an old sword-cut, which his perpetual steel-gray stubble did little to conceal.

Rostov was taking the theft personally; he was here in the armory looking for weapons of particular power to take with him in his pursuit of the thieves, who had several hours' start. A number of people could testify to that. Everyone in Sarykam had been expecting the delegation from Culm to leave this morning anyway, so no one had thought much of their moving up their departure time by a few hours. It had seemed only natural that after their unsuccessful pleading they would want to avoid anything in the nature of a protracted farewell.

Now, as Kristin ascertained with a few quick questions, three squadrons of cavalry were being made ready to take up the pursuit, which Rostov intended to lead in person. As far as she could tell, her military people were moving with methodical swiftness.

The Princess informed her General that Karel the wizard planned to accompany him; the old man had told her as much when she spoke to him in the Temple.

"Very well. If the old man is swift enough to keep up. If his wheezings as we ride do not alert the enemy." Rostov was staring at the three other Swords kept in the royal armory, and his expression showed a definite relief that these at least were still in place. Dragonslicer would probably be useless in the kind of pursuit he was about to undertake, but he now asked permission of the Princess to bring Stonecutter, and thought he would probably want Sightblinder as well.

Kristin, after granting the General her blessing to take whatever he wanted, and leaving him to his preparations, returned to the Palace. There she gave orders for several flying messengers to be dispatched from the high eyries atop the towers. The winged, half-intelligent creatures would be sent to seek out the absent Prince Mark and bear him the grim news of Woundhealer's vanishment.

By the time she had returned to the Palace, the sun was well up, but veiled in clouds. She could wish that the day were brighter. Then it would have been possible to signal ahead by heliograph, and there might have been a good chance of intercepting the fleeing Culmians at the border. But the clouds that had brought rain last night persisted, and if Coinspinner was arrayed against the realm of Tasavalta, today was not the day to expect good luck in any form.

At about this time, staring at the gray and mottled sky, Kristin began to be tormented by a truly disturbing thought: Was it possible that Murat's whole story regarding a crippled consort had been a ruse, and that the Sword was really now bound for the hands of some of Mark's deadly enemies?

The Princess's only comfort was that no evidence existed to support this theory. The fact that no attempt had been made to steal Dragonslicer, Stonecutter, and Sightblinder, or do any other damage to the realm, argued against it. Apparently the Culmian marauders had been truly interested only in obtaining the Healer.

The rain was still falling when the pursuit was launched, a swift but unhurried movement of well-trained cavalry, flowing out through the main gate of the city, every man saluting his Princess as he passed. A beastmaster with his little train of loadbeasts, carrying roosts and cages for winged fighters and messengers, brought up the rear of the procession. General Rostov and the wizard Karel rode together at its head.

TWO

At midday, under a partly cloudy sky and far from home, Prince Adrian, the twelve-year-old heir to the throne of Tasavalta, was standing at the top of a truncated stairway, a broken stone construction that curved up the outside of an ancient, half-ruined, and long-abandoned tower. A brisk wind blowing from the far reaches of the rocky and desolate landscape ruffled Adrian's blond hair. He carried a small pack on his back, and wore a canteen and a hunting knife at his belt. His slim body, arched slightly forward, wiry muscles tense, leaned out from the upper end of the stairs over the broken stones meters below.

The boy, tall for the age of twelve, was gazing intently, with senses far more discerning than those most folk would ever be able to call into use, across a threshold so subtle that it was all but invisible even to him. He was trying to see into the City of Wizards, inspecting the way ahead as carefully as possible before advancing any farther.

The curving stairs on which Adrian was standing came to an abrupt end halfway up the side of the moss-grown and abandoned tower. Once the steps had gone up farther, but not now. They terminated at this point in abject ruin, giving no hint to ordinary eyes of any reasonable or even visible goal that they might once have had. An observer equipped with no more than the usual complement of senses, and standing in Prince Adrian's position, would have seen nothing ahead but a bone-breaking drop to the nearest portion of the forbidding landscape.

In fact, the only other human observer on the scene had perceptions that also went beyond those of ordinary human senses—though not so far beyond as Adrian's.

Trilby, the Princeling's companion and fellow student in the arts of magic, was only two years older than he, but physically she was much more mature. With a pack on her back and a wooden staff in hand, she now came climbing the curved stairs to join him.

Reaching the top step, Trilby stood beside Adrian in momentary silence, gazing ahead to see if she could determine exactly what it was he found so fascinating; she knew that his extraordinary vision was almost always able to see more than hers. Having now shared approximately a year of study and occasional rivalry under the tutelage of old Trimbak Rao, the two young people had reached a plateau of mutual respect.

Trilby was coffee brown of skin, with straight black hair, full lips, and dark eyes that displayed a perpetually dreamy look, belying her often acutely practical turn of mind. Her shapely and rather stocky body, dressed now like Adrian's in practical traveler's clothing—loose shirt, boots, and trousers—was physically strong. A more experienced student, she was still marginally superior to Adrian in one or two aspects of magic, though after a year of cooperation and competition she suspected that he had the potential to be ultimately and overall the greatest wizard in the world.

"What d'ye see?" she asked him presently.

"Nothing special." The Prince almost whispered his reply. Then he withdrew his gaze from the distance, relaxed his pose somewhat, and spoke in a normal voice. "Just wanted to check everything out as well as I could, before we go in."

Trilby took a long look for herself. Then she said: "The

road is there, am I right? Just about at the level of our feet?"

"Right." Adrian sounded confident. "As far as I can tell, it starts here, right at the place where we'll be standing when we step through to it from the top of this stairs. Then it runs in a kind of zigzag way, but free of obstacles, for a couple of kilometers, until it gets close to the tall buildings."

"That agrees with what I see." The girl paused for another careful look before continuing. "The next question is, do we go in immediately, or take a break first?" They had already hiked for half a day since leaving the studio of Trimbak Rao, early in the morning.

Adrian hesitated, not wanting to appear reluctant to get on with the test they faced. But it was uncertain what problems they might encounter immediately on entering the City, and Trilby's suggestion of stopping for food and rest soon won out in his mind.

Both of the young people were carrying canteens, as well as a modest supply of food. And each of them, if pressed, would have been able to create food by magical means. But that kind of magic was costly in time and energy; it would be much wiser to conserve both of those resources against a possible later need.

Sitting near the foot of the ruined stairs, they opened up their packs, retrieving sandwiches and fruit. There was no need for a fire, and neither explorer suggested making one.

Trilby and Adrian had taken their last meal early in the morning, before setting out on foot from the studio and workshop of Trimbak Rao. They had hiked a good number of kilometers since then, but the required path through the desolate terrain had included many turns; now, sitting at the foot of the half-ruined tower and looking back along the route they had come, they could just descry the buildings of the wizard's complex halfway up a distant hillside. These were fairly ordinary-looking buildings—now, and most of the time. But appearances here, as in

much else, could be deceptive. In fact, these structures had
the habit of changing their appearance drastically, depend-
ing upon the viewer's distance and angle, as well as the
quality of his or her perception.

Chewing slowly on a sandwich, Adrian remarked: "I
don't think we'll have any trouble actually getting in. Do
you?"

Trilby shrugged. "I don't see why we should." She was
not as totally confident as she sounded—she thought that
perhaps Adrian wasn't either—but they had discussed the
situation many times before, and she had nothing new to
add at the moment.

This field trip was part of an examination marking the
end of their first year of study with Trimbak Rao. Trilby
and Adrian had been assigned the task of entering the
chaotic and mysterious domain called the City of Wizards,
obtaining a certain object there, and bringing it back to
their teacher.

The object desired by Trimbak Rao was an odd-shaped
ceramic tile—rather, it was any one of a number of such
pieces that were to be found uniquely in the pavement of
one small square in a certain parklike space within the
City.

Probably—the master had been vague about background and history—the space had once been part of a real
park, the grounds of some great palace perhaps, originally
built in a distant location somewhere out in the mundane
world. By some unspecified power of magic a portion of the
palace grounds had been transported to its present location. And in the process—like most of the other compo-
nents of the City—it had probably been altered drastically.

Trimbak Rao had repeatedly warned his two students,
before they set out, about several potential dangers. The
chief of these, if the emphasis of his warnings meant
anything, was the Red Temple that adjoined the present
site of the park:

"The main room of that particular Red Temple was
dedicated to a particularly abominable vice. But now it

should be safe enough for you to pass nearby. If you are reasonably careful." The magician hadn't clarified the statement.

Also, before he dispatched the two apprentices upon their mission, the Teacher had called their attention to the east wall of his study. Hanging there, carefully mounted in a reconstructed pattern, were a series of tiles, dull brown and unimpressive at first glance, similar to the one they were to obtain. Only the pattern, still just beginning to emerge with the growth of that series, was interesting. It seemed to depict a human body, or more probably more than one.

The number of tiles, twenty or so, already collected by the Teacher might be taken as evidence, thought Adrian, that some substantial number of Trimbak Rao's earlier students had successfully concluded missions similar to their own.

Now, while Trilby and Adrian ate some food, and rested on the bottom steps of the stairs encircling the old tower, the young Prince wondered aloud whether there might be some special reason why Trimbak Rao himself was not allowed to, or chose not to, make repeated journeys to this mysterious City park, and bring back the whole paved square if he desired it.

"And I wonder what'll happen when he has the entire pattern completed on his wall?"

"There must be some magical reason why he can't go himself," Trilby decided. She didn't know what that reason might be, and she had no opinion to offer on the subject. It was better to keep one's mind on practical matters. As the older and more experienced of the two students, she had been placed in command of this mission. But, as usual when teams were sent out, there had been a strong indication from the Teacher that all major decisions should be shared if possible.

Trilby had developed an ability to incinerate small amounts of garbage magically, and now she put that particular talent to use. Not so much a squandering of energy, she told Adrian, as a last trial to make sure that her powers were in working order.

Now, as the two advanced students busied themselves with the trivial chores of cleaning up after their meal, Adrian found he had to make a conscious effort to keep himself from reaching out with his magical perceptions to try to see what was going on with his parents and his brother at the moment.

His natural ability to maintain such occult contacts, once very strong, had been fading naturally over the past few years as he grew older. And on this subject his Teacher had counseled him: "Your parents have been making their own way in the world for some time now; you are almost old enough to do the same, and the cares of state with which they are now chiefly concerned will be yours soon enough. Right now your primary responsibility is to complete your schooling here, and to avoid unnecessary distraction."

Trilby now talked with Adrian about her parents. Her father was a middle-class merchant, her mother's family farmers in the domain of Tasavalta, with little or nothing in their background to suggest that one of their children would be extremely talented magically.

And Adrian talked of his family, and expressed his wish that he could see more of them.

Trilby assured the Prince, and not for the first time, that she did not envy him his royal status. In many ways prosperous commoners, like her own people, had things easier.

"Are we ready to go on?" the girl asked.

"Ready!" Adrian shouldered his pack again.

"On into the City, then."

Adrian, because of the superior sensitivity of his magical vision, was one step in the lead when the pair climbed again to the top of the broken stairs.

But Trilby, as the senior member of the expedition, did not forget to remind the boy that it was her duty to go first when the time actually came to cross the threshold.

This time when they reached the top of the stairs, Adrian stopped, took one more look and nodded, then let her go ahead, both of them muttering the words that Trimbak Rao had taught them.

Neither apprentice fell or even stumbled when they stepped beyond the last stair and over the subtle threshold. Both had successfully made the transition, at that point, to a somewhat different plane of existence. Both were able to establish solid footing upon the road that went on into the City, away from the tower—Adrian, turning to glance back at that structure, discovered that it existed in both planes. Here in the City it looked somewhat shorter, and did not appear to be so badly ruined after all.

The narrow road on which they now found themselves led forward crookedly, angling in long dogleg turns, toward the distant silhouette of the tall buildings clustered about the center of the City proper. The road was unpaved, of hard-packed earth, dry and yellowish, and at the moment it bore no traffic except themselves. The softer earth on either side of the way was reddish brown, stretching away in gentle undulations to a great smear of grayish dust that formed the whole circle of the horizon. Above that, the bowl of sky began as lemon yellow at the edges, and rose through shades of blue and green toward a small, gnarled cloud, quite dark and somehow hard to look at, around the zenith. The sun, thought Adrian, if it was anywhere, must be in concealment behind that cloud. The time of day, at least, had not changed greatly.

The young explorers kept walking.

"Well," said Trilby in a quiet voice when they had covered a few score meters of the road, "here we are. Looks like we've done it."

Adrian only nodded.

The explorers had now reached a point from which they could see that the thoroughfare on which they walked indeed led, after many turns, into the heart of the City proper.

And in that urban heart, which still appeared to be at

least a kilometer away, they were now able to perceive in some greater detail the physical outlines of the City's crowded structures. They were a strange collection indeed, of divers styles and shapes, as if they might have been gathered here from the far corners of the world. Close behind those silhouetted buildings the peculiar sky seemed to curve down to meet the dusty earth. And Adrian thought there was a strange richness, akin to electricity, in the very air that he and Trilby now breathed.

Trilby was nudging him with an elbow. She said: "Looks like a slug-pit over there."

He followed the direction of her gaze, to a place of disturbed earth some forty or fifty meters away on the right side of the road. "Yes, I see it."

They walked on without trying to investigate more closely. Both young people had been made well aware by their Teacher of certain perils in the City that had to be avoided; structures within it whose mere entry would almost certainly be fatal; snares that had to be watched for, and modes of travel that within its shadowy boundaries had to be strictly prohibited for reasons of safety. Just as Trimbak Rao had taken care to caution his advanced students about all these dangers before they set out to take their test, he had also reassured them that he considered them capable of successfully avoiding all the hazards.

Ordinary human eyes, viewing the City of Wizards from within, would have had this much in common with the eyes of the most perceptive magicians—both would perceive their surroundings as a vast jumble of ruins and intact buildings, strangely lighted under a changeable and often fantastic sky. The City's central region was streaked by open vistas of barren and abnormal earth, and marked by some grotesque and extravagant examples of whole architecture. Inside the City, or so Trimbak Rao had instructed his apprentices, sunrise and sunset were sometimes visible simultaneously, along opposite edges of the sky; and sometimes there were two moons in the sky at the same time, one full, one crescent, though otherwise looking identical to the familiar companion of Earth.

There were many viewpoints of the subject that might possibly be taken. Looking at the matter one way, the City of Wizards could scarcely be called a city at all—or, if the phenomenon was looked at in another way, it consisted of portions of several cities, and of portions of the rural world as well, normally separated in space and time, but here blended by conflicting and persistent magics into a confusing juxtaposition.

Generally, folk devoid of the skills of wizardry found it impossible to discover an entrance to the City at all—or to enter it even if they should manage to locate a threshold. People unskilled in magic might have journeyed all the continents of the mundane earth from north to south and east to west in search of the City and never have seen its gates. But to the skilled and properly initiated, many ports of entry were available.

Wizards of vastly different character and varying classes of ability came here to the City. So had they come from time immemorial, sometimes only to amuse themselves, sometimes to duel, sometimes to train their more promising apprentices. And here in the City, by the general agreement of their guilds, the more responsible among the workers in enchantment carried on many of their more dangerous experiments, researches that might otherwise do damage to some portion of the generally habitable world.

Sections and shards of the outside world, samples from a number of real cities and countrysides, had all been incorporated into the City from time to time. Houses and temples of every kind, even whole fortifications, had sometimes drifted or been hurled here, places wrenched out of their proper space-time locations by the contending or experimental forces of magic. Surprisingly, at least to Adrian, there had even been a substantial amount of original construction in the City over the centuries of its known existence, some of it carried out by human hands to the designs of human architects. But most of this deliberate building was badly designed. Much of it was never completed, and little of it endured for long.

As the Teacher had explained, both things and people judged unendurable by normal society were sometimes banished from the normal world, to end up here. Among the human inhabitants were the mad, the desperate, the fugitives, the utter outcasts of the world.

And also among the inhabitants were many who were not, and never had been, human.

THREE

W est of the city of Sarykam the sky grew clear before midday, and then promptly began to cloud again with a speed that suggested the possibility of some cause beyond mere nature. The sun had moved well past the zenith, and into a fresh onrush of gray scud lower than the nearby peaks, when the Culmian Crown Prince, now riding near the rear of his fast-moving cavalcade, halted his riding-beast and turned in his saddle to look back. From this position he was able to observe a great deal of the landscape, mostly a no-man's-land of barren mountains with which his small force was surrounded. The domain of Tasavalta was physically small and narrow, and the border in this area was ill-defined. But the leader of the fleeing Culmians felt confident that he had already left it behind him.

Four or five of Crown Prince Murat's comrades in arms, all of those who had been riding near him, now stopped as well, glad of the chance of at least a brief rest for their mounts. Farther inland, the bulk of the small Culmian force had already vanished behind jagged hills. At the moment, somewhere in that direction, another trusted officer was carrying the Sword of Love steadily toward Culm.

Another Sword, Coinspinner, that Murat had secretly

brought with him to Tasavalta rode openly now at his belt.
And up to this point, in the adventure of Sword-stealing,
the Sword of Chance had performed flawlessly for the man
who wore it.

So far, all was going according to plan. It was necessary
to assume that by now the theft from the White Temple
had been discovered, and a determined pursuit launched.
But until now none of Murat's people had actually seen
anyone coming after them.

An hour ago Murat had detailed one scout to ride far in
the rear for just that purpose. And he was pausing now to
let that scout, Lieutenant Kebbi, catch up to report.

His timing seemed excellent. For even as the Crown
Prince and his companions watched, a single rider appeared at a bend in the rearward trail, a couple of hundred
meters back. The small figure in its orange-and-blue uniform waved its arm in a prearranged signal meaning that
there was news to tell. Then the distant scout urged his
mount forward at a good pace.

Murat, followed by the handful of people with him,
spurred his own riding-beast forward along the narrow
trail, and in a few moments met the scout. The lieutenant,
reining in as he drew near his compatriots, reported in a
somewhat breathless voice that the expected enemy pursuit had only just now come into sight.

"How far back?" the Crown Prince demanded.

"We've half an hour on them yet," said Kebbi. Then the
lieutenant had a question: "Sir, what do you think will be
done with the Sword of Mercy after the Royal Consort has
been healed?"

Murat, mildly surprised, blinked at his relative. "I don't
know," he said. "Not our problem." Then he paused. "I
was quite sincere, you understand, cousin, when I pledged
that Woundhealer would promptly be returned to
Tasavalta." The more Murat thought about it now, the
more he wondered if the lovely Princess Kristin had been
right, and Woundhealer would never be returned, would
never have been returned in any case.

Kebbi persisted. "I understand, sir. But I thought that your pledge was made on the condition that the Sword should be loaned to us willingly, which it most certainly was not."

"Well, as I say, it won't be our problem to worry about." The Crown Prince looked at his men gathered about him. "Ready to move on? Someone else can take a turn tail-ending."

But Kebbi spoke up quickly. "Sir, let me ride back once more—I'll be better able to judge if they're truly gaining on us or not."

"Very well, that's a good point. If your mount is tired, pick a spare." And one of the small group of riders was already leading a spare mount forward.

With several men to help, changing the lieutenant's saddle and the rest of his equipment from one animal to the other was the work of only a moment.

Meanwhile there was more information to be gained. "Can you estimate how many there are in the pursuing force?"

"Haven't got that good a look at them yet, sir. But I can let them get a little closer this time. That way I should be able to form an estimate." On a fresh steed now, Kebbi looked boldly ready to take risks.

"Wait," said Murat suddenly, and drew Coinspinner from its sheath at his belt. "This should go with the man in the position of greatest danger and greatest need."

The lieutenant stared at him wordlessly for a moment, then nodded. "Thank you, sir." In another moment, handling both the sharp blades gingerly, he and Murat had exchanged Kebbi's mundane though well-forged sword for Coinspinner.

Wasting no time, Kebbi saluted sharply with his new weapon, and turned his mount away. He appeared to be on his way to drop back again and check on the enemy's progress.

But once he had ridden away a few meters with Coinspinner still unsheathed in his grip, and had looked it over, as if he were making absolutely sure of what he had, he stopped his mount and turned back again, showing a broad grin.

Something in the posing attitude of his cousin sent the beginning of a foreboding chill down Murat's spine.

In a voice considerably louder than would have been necessary to make himself heard, the Crown Prince called out: "What are you doing, Kebbi?"

The Sword-wielder, his every movement showing confidence, edged his riding-beast back a little toward the others, as if to make sure that what he said was heard distinctly. What he said was: "I'm looking out for myself. For my own future."

"What?" demanded Murat—though in his heart he knew already. Already he understood the horror of what was happening. Certain episodes of Kebbi's childhood were replaying themselves relentlessly in Murat's memory.

His cousin smiled at him, almost benignly. "I think you understood me the first time, sir. You who have the disposal of such matters at court have pretty well arranged it that I won't have much of a future unless I do take matters into my own hands."

The little group of Murat's countrymen who sat their steeds around him were muttering now. He yelled: "What are you talking about? Have you gone mad?"

"Not in the least mad, sir." Kebbi shook his head. He had a clean-cut face, and a habitual expression that somehow managed to suggest he was supremely trustworthy. "There's just no prospect of advancement for me in the normal course of events, that's what I'm talking about. Yes, *now* I see that you look thoughtful. *Now*, with a little effort, you can remember how the case for my promotion went, when you sat on the board of review. I'm sure it was a mere detail to you, the career of a very junior officer. Oh, an extremely reliable junior officer, one who could be chosen to participate in a mission like this, and even entrusted with a Sword. But also one who could be passed over with impunity when it came time for promotions.

"No, I'm not the least bit crazy, cousin. In fact, if you stop to think about it, you'll see that my behavior makes a lot of sense. I now have a matchless treasure in my hands." He paused to swing the Sword, taking a cut or two at the air to try the balance—which was of course superb.

When the lieutenant spoke again his voice was changed, lower and calmer. "It is the real thing. We proved that beyond any doubt in the White Temple. And now that I've got this Sword in my hands, I simply prefer to keep it for myself—the matter is as uncomplicated as that."

A moment later Lieutenant Kebbi had inserted Coinspinner into the sheath at his belt. He kept his right hand comfortably on the black hilt afterward.

Murat, sitting his mount helplessly, had the feeling that his own life, his career, his sanity, were all draining out somehow from the toes of his boots, through his stirrups, to the ground. Knowing it was useless, he still had to shout again.

"Kebbi, I warn you! If this is some joke, some stupid attempt to force me to admit that you are valuable—"

The younger man was shaking his head. "That would indeed be stupid, and I'm not stupid. That's something you, dear royal cousin, are finally going to have to realize. No, no joking, cousin. I am now going to turn my steed and ride away—it would be stupid on your part to try to stop me, as I am sure you realize. Instead I would suggest that you catch up with those loyal people who are carrying the other Blade for you, and hurry home as fast as you can with that one. You can still be at least half a hero there, in royal eyes, if you arrive with a useful Sword to replace the one you've lost."

"If you are serious—then what are you attempting to do?"

"My dear Crown Prince, I am not *attempting* to do anything, as you will have to admit sooner or later. What I'm doing is an accomplished fact. I'm taking this Sword away from you, just as we took the other one from the Tasavaltans."

As Kebbi spoke, he continued to sit his mount facing the others from a distance of thirty meters or so. Now one of the Culmian sergeants, outraged beyond measure by the treachery in progress, spurred his own riding-beast forward to pass Lieutenant Kebbi, moving to cut off the unspeakable traitor's line of retreat.

That, at least, must have been the tactic the sergeant had in mind. But he was never able to perform it. He passed within half a dozen strides of his target, turned, and was just beginning to raise a mace with which to threaten or to strike when the rear hooves of his mount slipped from the narrow trail. The cavalry beast, normally surefooted, screamed in an almost human-sounding noise before it fell. A moment later the sergeant's mount had disappeared over the edge of a minor precipice.

The man himself managed to leap from his stirrups only just in time to keep from going with the animal. Instead he fell forward, awkwardly, and in landing struck his forehead on his own spiked mace. Once fallen, he lay facedown, without moving, except that the muscles of his back twitched convulsively.

"You see?" demanded Kebbi, who had been watching, as he turned back to face the others. There was a quiver of triumph in his voice. "You see? I am well protected."

The Crown Prince had nothing to say. He could only hope that he might soon awaken from this hideous dream. The only comfort he could find in the situation was the knowledge that the main body of his small force, carrying with them the Sword of Mercy, were still moving away on the road to Culm, putting distance between them and their pursuers as rapidly as possible.

As long as the band of volunteers, no more than two dozen in all, had remained closely united on this mission, then the luck carried by one man might have served to protect them all. Now the luck of the Sword of Chance was gone from them. But with the start Coinspinner had afforded, the people who were carrying Woundhealer might still be able to get away to Culm. They had their orders, and no matter what happened to Murat and his rear guard of half a dozen, they would press on.

But what was he going to do about Kebbi? It was unthinkable that the young man could simply be allowed to ride away now that he had revealed his treachery. But what could be done against a Sword?

Another officer in the small group broke the brief silence. His voice, controlled with a great effort, still quivered with his helpless fury. "What will you do now, Kebbi? Where will you go? We'll hunt you down, you know, sooner or later."

The lieutenant made a gesture, shrugging with his arms spread slightly, as if to say: *if you would hunt me, here I am.* He did not appear to be in the least perturbed by the threat. "What will I do? Why, to begin with, I believe I'll get myself out of your way here, and allow you to set up your rearguard defense—this looks like a good place to arrange an ambush. The Tasavaltans will certainly be here within half an hour. I suppose you still have some kind of a fighting chance against them, even without Coinspinner—a better chance than I had when I came up for promotion that last time."

"Traitor! Vile traitor!"

The man who was now carrying the Sword of Chance ignored the denunciation. It appeared that he could well afford to do so. In no hurry to escape, he paused to look around at the configuration of the land. "Yes, cousin, you definitely have a chance, though they must know these mountains better than you do—farewell, then." With that the treacherous lieutenant turned his mount and departed.

He was forty meters away, riding with his back to his former comrades, when one of the volunteer troopers, a dead shot with the longbow, gritting his teeth at seeing this scoundrel jog away unpunished, drew, aimed, and loosed a shaft aimed true at the center of the traitor's spine. Just at the crucial moment the renegade, who never looked back, happened to bend aside to make some minor adjustment to his right stirrup strap. The arrow missed him by several centimeters. The man with the Sword continued to ride away, superbly unaware of death's close passage. But of course the truth was that the arrow had put him in no danger of death at all.

At that same moment, no more than half a kilometer away in the direction of Tasavalta, General Rostov, having halted his advance for the moment, was grinding his teeth. All day long the General and his Tasavaltan cavalry had been suffering from bad luck, and it did not help that he knew the cause, and knew that matters were very unlikely to improve. Several landslides—none of them brought about by any sentient agency, Rostov was sure—had come down just in front of his troops, in places guaranteed to create maximum obstruction. Problems with broken harness had multiplied unbelievably for equipment that was well maintained, and a sudden attack of severe bellyache had felled one trooper who had to be left behind.

And now a rain that promised to be heavy had begun. Not that Rostov was entertaining any thought that he might be beaten. That was not his way. Nor were any of the men or women he had chosen for this pursuit resigned to defeat—at least none of them had yet been ready to admit such a thought in Rostov's hearing.

The General, knowing of a shortcut alternative to a portion of the route that the fleeing Culmians had doubtless taken, had naturally enough led the Tasavaltan force that way. Had it not been for the landslides and other delays, they would have been in time to cut their quarry off. Even as matters stood, he thought that they had gained several hours on the Sword thieves.

Rostov had not been able to catch a glimpse of the enemy since leaving Tasavalta. But during the last kilometer or two of the pursuit, fresh animal droppings and other signs indicated that the Culmians were now very close ahead.

Karel the wizard had ridden for the most part in grim silence, but certain subtle signs indicated that he was not idle. The few words uttered by the old man suggested that he was having very little luck with any of his spells today; he was not accustomed to failure, but given the overwhelming nature of the magical opposition, anything except failure would have been surprising.

Now one of Rostov's officers halted his mount beside the General's. "Sir, I wonder if the thieves will be arranging an ambush for us? There's a place just ahead that's so ideal I doubt they'll pass it up."

The General grunted. He had been thinking along the same lines, and in fact that was why he had chosen this spot to halt. So ideal was the terrain ahead for such a tactic that Rostov's instincts informed him that a Culmian ambush *must* be there, though there was no way to confirm its presence until the point was reached. A wind had sprung up in the last hour, fierce enough to ground the little flying beasts he would otherwise have used as scouts.

Having foresightedly brought Stonecutter with him, the General, after surveying the landscape more thoroughly, now put the Sword of Siege to work to open up a new trail. His intention was to bypass the probable ambush site narrowly, and, if at all possible, take the ambushers from behind.

One source of worry was the fact that Stonecutter invariably produced a pounding noise as it worked. But on reflection he thought this was not likely to prove a fatal difficulty. Out here in the open, Stonecutter's working noise would probably be unheard by people who might be waiting on the other side of a thick wall of rock. And the same howling wind that was keeping the winged scouts out of the air would tend to rush the sound away.

The wizard, for whom nothing had worked properly since setting out on this pursuit, was now beginning to adopt a fatalistic attitude. "I fear that if Coinspinner is arrayed against us . . ." Karel, with a shrug, let his words trail off.

But Rostov, as usual when going into action, was ferocious and implacable. "You tell me that the enemy has powerful weapons. I say so do we. And I also say damn their weapons. If we are in the field against them, we must find some way to attack." Almost as an afterthought, he added: "All of them won't have stayed to entertain us in an ambush. Part of their force almost certainly is bearing Woundhealer on ahead—and it's a good bet that those people will have taken Coinspinner too."

Working with Stonecutter in the driving rain, a pair of the General's men were already hacking an incline into the side of a cliff that would otherwise have been utterly impassable. They were incorporating stair-steps at the steeper parts, and making the whole wide and gentle curved enough for riding-beasts to use. Naturally they had begun their labors at a spot out of sight of the enemy above. One man wielded the Sword of Siege, cutting limestone like so much butter, digging stairs rapidly out of the side of a cliff, while his helper slid the freshly carved blocks away and over the edge.

A few shock troops, with Rostov himself and Karel among them, were to climb the newly created stair and take the enemy from the rear, while the bulk of the General's three squadrons waited, mounted, ready to attack the ambush frontally at the proper moment.

And Rostov had one more weapon to bring into action. Calling a well-guarded pack-animal forward, he reached into one of its cargo panniers and pulled forth Sightblinder. The Sword of Stealth looked an exact duplicate of its god-forged brothers, save for the different symbol, in this case the sketch of a human eye, that it bore on its black hilt. At least it looked so to the one who held it; gazing at the reactions in the faces of his people looking at him now, Rostov knew that each of them was seeing something or someone even more awesome than their General.

A few moments later, halfway up the newly created path with Sightblinder still in hand, waiting for the stonecutting to be finished, Rostov was beginning to wish that he had brought dogs, to help pick up the scent when other indications of a trail were lacking. Well, it was too late to worry about that now. Beside him, Karel had his eyes closed and was muttering—trying to ward off Coinspinner's imminent counterblow, perhaps. That stroke was coming, no doubt, in some form, if the Sword of Chance was still in the possession of the ambushers. But there was nothing Rostov could do about it, and so he refused to let it worry him.

In a matter of only a few minutes the necessary rough stairs had been completed. The chunks of rock removed, sliced loose as easily as so many bits of melon, had been pushed tumbling into a depth so great that there was no need to worry about the sounds of their falling alerting the foe.

And now Rostov, disguised by the Sword of Stealth, and his handful of picked men, moving close past the pair of rock-cutters, wind and rain blasting in all their faces, were at the top of the new pathway.

No one in sight, as yet. But there was another little plateau not far above. The General, climbing ponderously and carefully, motioned sharply with his arm, and a young scout, much more agile than Rostov, clambered past him.

After peering cautiously through a notch at the top of the cliff, the lithe young soldier turned his head back and whispered: "No one in sight."

That, as Rostov understood, could mean that he had chosen exactly the right spot for his outflanking movement; or of course it could mean that no ambush had been set here after all, and he and his men were only wasting time.

Silently he gestured a command, and in silence his small party of picked men moved rapidly forward, until all were solidly established upon level ground. Armed with the Sword of Stealth, he moved ahead of them. The actual location of the supposed ambushers was still above them and in front, but each side was now shielded safely from the other by an intervening wall of rock. From the point where Rostov had now got his men, however, the supposed enemy strong point could be outflanked by an easy climb along a natural formation.

At the next level place they reached, one of the men just behind Rostov, a good tracker, paused and murmured: "A lot of hoofprints. They seem to have split up here, General. One of them at least—yes, I think only one—rode off in that direction, to the west. And what's this? An arrow, definitely Culmian, broken against a rock. It hasn't been here long, but it wasn't shot in our direction. I think it must have been aimed at the man who rode alone. Can it be that luck's deserted them?"

Rostov squinted westward through the shreds of driving mist. "Well, that western trail lies open to us if we want to follow it. But I don't think we do. Not just yet at least. No ambush there, so it's not the route they're fighting to defend."

Karel, puffing with the climb on foot, but so far keeping up, asked him: "Can it be they're splitting up in an effort to confuse us?"

"If so, it seems unlikely they'll succeed. Let's move on up the rest of the way, as quietly as we can. Then we'll be behind their ambush if there is one. We'll see how many of 'em are ready to stand and fight."

A few minutes later, the Crown Prince Murat of Culm had seen the failure of the ambush he had so carefully and, as he thought, so cleverly arranged. Howling fiends in blue and green, only slightly outnumbering his own small rear guard, but with the great advantage of surprise, had fallen upon them from the rear. And at the head of the attackers, almost crushing resistance by sheer visual shock, had moved a perfectly lifelike image of the very Queen of Culm herself. At least two of Murat's men had thrown down their weapons at the sight.

As the Crown Prince lay trying to regain his senses, after being felled by a blow to the back of his head, he could not at first understand how he had been overcome. His trap had been bypassed by people who must have somehow made their way up a sheer cliff, where he had thought that even a mountain goat would be helpless. And then, the seeming presence of the Queen—

Only when Murat saw a Sword in one of the attackers'

hands, and the thought of Stonecutter occurred to him, followed by that of the Sword of Stealth, did he begin to realize the truth.

In their planning for this mission, the Culmian intelligence had failed—they had never guessed that Stonecutter and Sightblinder would still be available to their new enemies.

Victorious Rostov, proven right in his tactical predictions, was still in a grim mood. His own men had suffered only minor wounds. Five Culmians were dead, and one, their commander, was taken prisoner. But neither Coinspinner nor Woundhealer was here with the vanquished enemy.

The Crown Prince's head wound proved to be not serious. He was conscious in time to watch Rostov's cavalry squadrons come pouring relentlessly through the narrow passage he had almost died trying to defend. And presently he had recovered sufficiently to mutter a few words of anguished defiance.

Rostov, grim-visaged and surly, made little of the fact of his sole prisoner's high rank. At the General's orders, the captive was treated much as any other prisoner would have been, and as soon as he was able to stand again, he was tied into the saddle and stirrups of a captured mount.

"Where are the Swords?" Rostov then demanded of him. "I know that two at least were with you."

Murat sighed. "Woundhealer is on its way to my Queen."

"We'll see about that."

Karel, frowning, signed that he wanted to ask the prisoner a question. "And Coinspinner, Prince? I have good reason to believe that it is no longer with the other Sword."

Rostov frowned in surprise on hearing this.

Murat shook his head. There dawned on him a vague hope that these men, whose outrage and fury he could understand, and who came armed with Swords of their own, might possibly be able to avenge the treachery of Kebbi.

He drew a deep breath. "The Sword of Chance is now in a traitor's hands," he said. Briefly he confessed how he had foolishly handed over Coinspinner, with his own hands, into those of Lieutenant Kebbi, and what his cousin had done thereafter.

The fierce winds that Coinspinner had somehow caused to arise were abating now, and it had become possible for the Tasavaltan beastmaster to get his winged scouts and messengers into the air. One flyer, a magical cross between bird and mammal, was sent home to Sarykam with word for the Princess on the progress made thus far. Others were dispatched to try to locate the fleeing Culmians.

Taking several items from his mount's saddlebags, Karel went to work. Soon he was able to confirm to his own satisfaction that Coinspinner was now somewhere to the west of here, while Woundhealer lay to the south.

Wizard and General conferred briefly, and then the scar-faced Rostov turned back to his prisoner. "Well, Crown Prince. Can you ride?"

"Bound into this saddle as I am, it would seem that I have no choice."

"That is correct. Prepare to do so."

It was going to be a grim and uncomfortable ride back to Sarykam, Murat thought to himself. Though once there in the Tasavaltan capital, he vaguely supposed, things might not be too bad. Doubtless, once he was there, he would in some way be accorded special treatment because of his rank. Even a room in the Palace could be a possibility.

And whatever else happens to me, he thought, I am going to see more of that lovely, lonely Princess. Murat and his own wife had been for some time now on bad terms. Some part of him was curiously pleased that he was soon going to see Kristin again, even though she could hardly greet him with anything but the anger reserved for a treacherous enemy.

After the wizard and the General had taken counsel again, they dispatched most of their force, under Rostov's military second-in-command, armed with Stonecutter against further ambushes, in pursuit of the Culmians carrying Woundhealer. None of the Tasavaltans had much more to say to Murat for the time being. But he was not slow to realize that he was not being taken back to Sarykam, at least not immediately. Instead the two leaders, armed with Sightblinder, with himself as their prisoner, and no more than half a dozen troopers as escort, were setting out upon the trail of Lieutenant Kebbi and the other stolen Sword.

FOUR

Who holds Coinspinner knows good odds
Whichever move he make
But the Sword of Chance, to please the gods
Slips from him like a snake.

Kebbi was singing the words of the old song to himself, in a strong tenor voice, whose musicality would probably have surprised the majority of his former comrades of Culm. Meanwhile he was allowing his riding-beast, a fast and sturdy cavalry animal, to carry him along another mountain trail, under a cheerful morning sun.

Yesterday, upon taking his leave of the Crown Prince and his small doomed force, Kebbi had traveled on until well after dark, maintaining a moderate pace in a generally northwesterly direction. He had trusted to the godly magic that he carried to guarantee that his mount was not going to step over an invisible precipice, or halt on the brink of one so suddenly that it threw him from the saddle. But the animal, doubtless unaware that it had any magical assistance to depend on, had managed but slow progress. Nor was weariness in beast or man to be cured by good fortune. Eventually, when he had fortuitously happened upon a sheltered spot beside a small stream, Kebbi had decided to make camp for the night.

He had been up with the sun and on the road again. Now, today, everything was going well—of course. And naturally—as it now seemed to him—there were no signs of pursuit.

He'd hardly bothered to make any effort at covering his trail since acquiring the Sword, but an hour ago the unexpected minor thunder of a small avalanche behind him had confirmed his expectation that his tracks were somehow going to be effectively wiped out, without any effort on his part. Or, if they weren't wiped out, it wouldn't matter. Neither the Tasavaltans nor any outraged Culmian loyalists were going to be able to catch up with him—or if they did manage somehow to overtake him, they'd no doubt wish they hadn't.

The morning was bright and promising. Kebbi rode on, singing, with one hand resting easily upon the black hilt at his waist. He owned no land and had no real family in Culm, and most of his worldly possessions were now tied up in a modest bundle behind his saddle. Having Coinspinner, what else did he need to carry? Whenever he needed something, it would somehow be provided, he was confident.

The Sword of Fortune was now his. And unless he, like Murat, was fool enough to place it willingly in the hands of someone else, fortune was going to be his also, from now on—at least until such time as the Sword decided to take itself away.

He knew enough of Coinspinner to realize that it could be expected to do that sooner or later. Supposedly it had once rested for a few years in the Tasavaltan treasury—and then, without giving notice, the Sword had abruptly moved itself out. Simply, easily, and inexplicably it had passed through all the physical and magical barriers with which such a repository must be equipped. No one had even realized that it was gone until they came to look at it again.

So Kebbi couldn't say with any assurance how long he was likely to have the Sword, but with any luck at all—he grinned a twisted grin as that phrase passed through his mind—with even a minimum of luck, he'd possess it long enough to establish his fortune in the world. Then someone else would be welcome to take a turn at a charmed life. Kebbi wouldn't be so greedy as to object to that.

There crossed his mind the question of where he was going to rest tonight. Well, he would leave that to the currents of fortune also. Before he'd actually stolen the Sword, Kebbi had entertained, at least in passing, the idea of taking Coinspinner back to Tasavalta and thereby becoming a hero to the Princess and her people there. But when he had calculated all the possibilities as best he could, he doubted that such a double traitor could stay in very high regard elsewhere.

Oh, of course, the Sword would take care of him in Tasavalta, just as well as it would anywhere else. It was only that there were a great many other places where he would prefer to spend his future, rather than in that cool and unexciting land.

Besides, he thought, it would be harder for the Culmian folk to trace him if he took Coinspinner somewhere else, somewhere very far away most likely, for his reward. And sooner or later, whenever the Sword left him, he would become vulnerable to their revenge.

And now, even as Kebbi rode and grinned and sang, a nagging suspicion began to grow in him that he shouldn't be relying totally on the Sword's good fortune. It was never good to rely that heavily on anything outside yourself. He'd have to start using his brain again, at least. Kebbi ceased to sing, and gradually began to be more alert.

Thus most of the day passed uneventfully for the deserter. During its course he began, almost in spite of himself, to take serious thought on the subject of what his destination ought to be, if it was not to be Tasavalta again. Kebbi's plan to steal the Sword of Chance had taken form quite suddenly, only after the expedition to Sarykam was under way, and until now it had seemed to him enough, once he had his prize, to travel to some great distance from the land of Culm.

Vaguely Kebbi came to have in mind two or three cities, only one of which he had ever visited, all distant places where he thought he would be able to sell his treasure at a great profit if he chose, or where he could use the Sword somehow to obtain some of the wealth with which he would there find himself surrounded. He supposed in an uncertain way that if the Sword, or the powers behind it, just knew what he wanted, he would somehow be provided with the necessary means to reach his goal.

He took thought on the subject now, as he rode steadily along, but no better plan presented itself. Well, there was no hurry.

Toward evening he came to a place where his trail intersected another one, the latter almost large enough to be called a road. Here the fortunate traveler spied an isolated building, big enough to be more than a simple house, in front of which a dozen or more people were gathered.

In the glow of the setting sun the place looked like the poorest kind of inn. If there had not been people to be seen in front of it, he would have doubted that the dilapidated structure was in regular use. Certainly it was badly in need of maintenance and probably not far from collapse. Kebbi's first impression was that this place might well be a den of bandits. What might have been an inn's sign had fallen into ruin some time ago, and there was no deciphering it now. A couple of large tables, and some chairs and benches, all badly weathered, stood in front of the place.

Ten or twelve thuggish-looking men were standing idly about in a few small groups. Kebbi's imagination suggested that they might be only waiting for the fall of night before revealing their true identities as some breed of nocturnal monsters. As he drew nearer the men in turn looked him over quietly, for the moment having nothing to say.

In a place a little apart from the men, a few women were also waiting, for what it was hard to guess. By the look of them they might have been the dregs of Red Temple outcasts. One was lighting a fire in the open.

Kebbi, feeling the inevitable stiffness of a long day's ride, and knowing that he must show it, stopped in front of the inn and dismounted—there was no way to disguise the fact that he was riding a good and valuable animal, and he would not have been surprised to be told that some of the loungers were already trying to guess what his riding-beast might be worth if they could get it away from him.

Well, let them try it. Somewhere he'd heard that Mark, before he became Prince of Tasavalta, had been wounded —scratched, at least, and probably not too inconveniently —while carrying Coinspinner in the thick of a ferocious battle. Well, maybe that light scratch had somehow been lucky for the man who was to rise from commoner to prince—maybe it had even brought him his exalted rank. Anyhow, fate, working through the Sword of Chance, had brought Mark out of obscurity into a great position in the end, hadn't it? He, Kebbi, was ready to accept a light wound for a similar result. The gods knew he'd already had some bad ones for much less reward.

One of the younger loungers was coming toward Kebbi now, indicating with a servile smile that he was ready to act as groom for this obvious gentleman-soldier. And now, from somewhere inside the building, a villainous-looking landlord materialized to wonder aloud if the new arrival was seeking food and lodging.

"I'll take a drink first," Kebbi told the man. "Ale, if you have it. And some care for my mount. After that, we'll see about the rest." He was thinking that, magically protected as he was, he'd rather take his chances sleeping in the open at trailside than endure the bugs and noise and stench that were undoubtedly provided to every guest at this inn along with his room—or his share of floor space. The Sword's power would doubtless keep him from being murdered as long as he slept with it at his side; but he doubted whether Coinspinner's activity would condescend to reach so far into the inconsequential as to protect its owner from all vermin.

Surprisingly, the beer brought to him was pleasantly

chilled, and its taste not all that bad. By the time Kebbi had swallowed a third of his first mug, a game of chance involving dice was beginning to get under way around one of the outdoor tables positioned in front of the ramshackle building. A worn blanket, once issued in someone's army, had been smoothed over the table's rough wooden surface, and on this cloth the dice were dancing. Kebbi had hardly turned his gaze in that direction before several of the players invited him, with false heartiness, to take part.

Kebbi's first impulse was to refuse—ordinarily he didn't think of himself as a gambler. But then, this would hardly be gambling, would it? And in truth he was very short of coin.

When the invitation was repeated, he nodded his head in acceptance. As he moved to take a seat on one of the curved benches that ringed the table, he noted that some of the players were aiming curious glances at the black hilt of his Sword.

"Unburden yourself, why don't you, stranger, and sit down."

Acknowledging the invitation with a smile, Kebbi shifted the burden of Coinspinner into a comfortable position. He rubbed the sheath of his weapon familiarly, with one hand. "It brings me luck," he told the company, and saw their answering grins. No one alluded to his Sword again. He wondered if any of them could possibly have recognized it for what it was. Certainly no one here would think it odd that a stranger playing in this game would want to keep his weapons handy. Perhaps, he realized suddenly, one or more of his fellow players were also using some kind of gambling magic. Well, let them try.

As might have been expected from the general appearance of the company, there was as yet no great amount of money in evidence on the blanket-covered tabletop, where now the landlord, bending over carefully, was setting down a pair of flickering and flaring lamps. The table itself was wobbly—as Kebbi had also expected—and groaned and tilted whenever someone leaned on it. The local rules, as the landlord now proclaimed, required the dice on each throw to be bounced off the rectangular base of a lamp—which lamp the thrower used was his own choice—an ancient and reasonably effective prescription against mundane manipulation.

With Kebbi sitting in, there were now six participants in the game. The remaining male loungers and the women—who for the most part remained somewhat more distant—formed a casual audience. From among the women there came the desultory sound of tambourine and drum, and eventually two of the least repulsive of them began to dance. None of the men paid much attention to the show.

When the dice came around to Kebbi, he cast them out casually, taking care only that they should strike the base of the nearest lamp. He won his first throw.

On his second throw, which followed immediately, he won again.

According to the commonly accepted rules of this game, he now had the option of letting the dice pass on, and so he chose to do.

The play went around the table, others winning or losing in their turns. So far only trivial amounts were being wagered. The rules were somewhat complicated, but every soldier knew them, and every bandit and wastrel as well.

Betting on every throw was not required. So far Kebbi had made no losing bet—he doubted it would be possible for him to do so, as long as he had Coinspinner strapped on—and the modest winnings on his first two throws remained intact.

Still, he could not manage to develop any great enthusiasm for the game. No matter what happened, Kebbi was sure, he was not going to win any important amount of money here, not from these poor-looking men. But luck had led him to this inn; and doubtless Fortune, as directed by his Sword, had some great plan for him that started in this inauspicious way. Well then, let Fortune indicate to him what she wanted him to do next.

At last he drained his mug—it had been refilled only

once—set it down on the edge of the blanket with a decisive thump, and got to his feet. "Well, gentlemen," he announced cheerfully, "the road waits for me."

His announcement was greeted with unanimous scowls around the table. "Not yet it don't," a large man grumbled immediately.

"That's right," chimed in another. "How 'bout giving us the chance to get some of our money back?"

Kebbi, who had been half expecting such protests, had already decided in the interests of peace to give in to them the first time they were offered. The next time matters would be different, and no one could say he hadn't given them a chance to recoup their trivial losses. Perhaps when the protesters had lost more, they would be willing enough to see his back.

"As you wish," he said, shrugging, and resumed his seat.

"This time," announced the physically largest of his adversaries in a challenging voice, "we use my dice."

"That's all right."

A few moments later, the owner of the crooked, probably magical dice was staring at them in disbelief. His pet artifacts had obviously betrayed him; whatever spell or other trick he'd used had been overridden as if it did not exist. The pattern of the pips represented a very ordinary combination, but obviously it was not a pattern the owner had expected from these particular dice on one in a million throws.

And naturally it was a pattern that won for Kebbi yet again.

A series of muttered remarks among the locals, only partially audible to the stranger, revealed that their opinions had now begun to differ sharply. One faction was definitely ready to let the overlucky stranger go his way in peace. But another faction, fast becoming dominant, was entertaining quite different ideas.

The biggest of the local men stood up. Glowering at Kebbi, he proclaimed: "We don't need any wizards in this game."

The Culmian shook his head. "I should think your friends would pay more heed to your protest—if it didn't come from a man who brought crooked dice into the game."

As he finished speaking, Kebbi pushed back from the table and stepped free of the encumbering bench. From that position he backed away, intending to get his back near one of the scrawny trees in the inn yard. Not that he doubted the power that protected him, but somehow he saw no need to make things unreasonably difficult.

One or two players remained at the table, waiting for the interruption to be over. The rest of them came after Kebbi, unhurriedly, methodically. Now they were beginning to surround him, and some of their hands were reaching toward weapons. Their proposed victim had his right hand on the black hilt of his own blade, though he'd not actually drawn it yet.

There was a pause. So far the air of confidence displayed by the stranger was holding the others back. But none of them seemed to recognize a Sword, and Kebbi understood that in a matter of moments things were going to get really ugly.

Before the storm could break, there came an interruption.

Kebbi, his attention warily on his fellow players, was among the last to notice the arrival of a tall and handsome man, who now appeared silently, standing at the edge of the firelight, with a shadowy and much smaller attendant poised just behind him. It was as if the two of them had just arrived by walking—there had been no sight or sound of any animals they might have ridden—along the lightless road. Coinciding with the arrival of the pair, the moon emerged from behind a fragmentary cloud, and in the change of light the two figures took on a spectral look.

The tall newcomer was richly dressed. Putting up a hand, he threw back the hood of his sumptuous cape, revealing golden curls and a healthy beard to match. Simultaneously he advanced slowly toward the gaming table. The lamplight fell on clear blue eyes, muscular shoulders, large hands, and a handsome face. A long sword of some kind was belted at the newcomer's waist.

His much smaller companion followed him closely, but maintaining a certain distance like a respectful servitor. A few steps closer to the lamps and it was easy to see that she was a woman, as fair as the man, and with a delicate feminine beauty of face that more than matched his masculine good looks. Her beauty was combined with an aura of power and self-confidence, enough of both that Kebbi heard not a single mutter of lechery from any of the scum present. He thought that even had her escort not appeared so formidable, the result would have been the same.

"I hope that the game is not yet finished." The voice of the tall newcomer was powerful, and strangely accented, and he was looking steadily at Kebbi as he spoke. "Come, I am sure that it must not be finished. For I intend to play." His smile showed perfect teeth.

Kebbi said nothing in reply to this. Nor did the men who had almost surrounded him. They were leaving him alone now, and beginning to drift back in the general direction of the table. The tall blond man moved in the same direction now, and their group shattered, softly and silently, and began to disperse into the background.

The music of drum and tambourine, which had faded away when the threat of violence loomed large, now resumed slowly. Very gradually the tempo began to pick up again.

The new arrival still smiled at Kebbi across the battered table, where two lamps still flared upon brown cloth. The dice, the original dice belonging to the landlord, lay at one end unattended.

"Shall we?" The newcomer gestured toward the abundance of empty chairs.

"Why not?" As he stepped forward Kebbi had his hand on the hilt of his Sword, and he could feel the immense power so subtly playing there. Fortune had somehow found a door to open for him, even in this almost uninhabited wilderness. He returned the stranger's smile.

The former participants in the game were now drifting back again a little toward the table. Not that they had any intention of sitting down; they were glad to excuse themselves from this particular contest, but they did not want to miss seeing it, either.

The stranger was as indifferent to what these men did as he was to the indifferent women who had now resumed their dance.

Kebbi and the newcomer, as if by unspoken agreement punctiliously observing some rule of courtesy, seated themselves simultaneously.

Kebbi, feeling an intoxication much more of impending triumph than of drink, faced his single opponent across the blanket-covered table. The tall man's shadowy companion, as if she meant to protect his back, moved up close behind him, where she remained standing.

And now, moving slowly, the hand of the unknown brought forth from somewhere inside his cape a truly magnificent jewel, holding it up for all to see. The stone was the shape of a teardrop, the color of a sapphire's blood. His large, strong fingers held it up, turning it in the lamplight for Kebbi to see and admire. Still the man's attention was entirely concentrated upon Kebbi, as if he were totally indifferent as to anything that other folk might see or do.

Unhurriedly the tall man said: "I will stake this gem against the Sword you wear."

All Kebbi could think was that Fortune, the Sword's Fortune, was working even more swiftly and powerfully than he had dreamt was possible.

"One roll of the dice?" he asked.

"One roll."

"Fine. I accept."

Satisfied, the stranger nodded and looked away. Now his long arm went out to scoop up the dice where they lay at the end of the table; and now he was putting them down on the cloth in front of Kebbi.

Now, at the last moment, Kebbi felt a twinge of reluctance to stake his Sword in any wager. But Coinspinner would not, could not, have led him into this situation only to have him suffer such a loss.

Unless this could be the Sword's method of taking itself away from him? But no, according to the stories Coinspinner used no human agency for that.

Another musician, he thought vaguely, had joined in. It now seemed to him that he could hear the sound of a third drum, tapping a jarring counterpoint to the first two.

And Kebbi threw the dice against a lamp—an eight.

Now it was the stranger's turn. His large right hand cupped the landlord's dice, and threw them out with careless impatience.

Seven.

The rich jewel that Kebbi had just won came arcing toward him through the lamplight, tossed by the stranger. Kebbi automatically put up his hand and caught the bright pebble in midflight.

"Now," said the stranger, to all appearances unperturbed by such a loss. "Now, we are going to play again. Double or nothing." And between the fingers of his gloved right hand appeared two more gems, each looking exactly like the one he had just lost.

Kebbi's breath hissed out between his teeth. "I accept." His doubts had been foolish. Whatever might happen next, he was protected.

This time the stranger threw first.

Four.

Yielding to a mad twitch of bravado, Kebbi threw left-handed this time. As he did so, three fingers of his right hand were resting lightly on his sheathed Sword's hilt, and the great, strange jewel he had just won was clenched securely in the remaining two.

But there was something wrong with the result, and

Kebbi could only stare at it without comprehension.

Three.

The dice read only three. A single pip on one ivory cube, two on the other. And that meant that this time, he—he and Coinspinner together—had lost.

Such a result could not be true. It could not be true. It could not be possible, or—

Struggling to make sense of the impossible, Kebbi did not notice that again only two drums beat in the background.

There had been some mistake, some error in the way the world was working. The Sword of Chance could not be beaten, least of all in a game of chance. But he could not bring himself to utter a word. How could his luck, how could the power of the Sword, have suddenly deserted him? The Sword itself was still with him. He could still feel its silent energy, seemingly unimpaired.

Kebbi was too stunned to make any effort at resistance when the tall stranger, giving up an effort to talk to him, came moving lithely around the table. He was jerked to his feet. Strong hands undid his swordbelt and pulled it away, carrying its priceless contents with it. A moment later the great jewel that had been his so briefly was torn from where his fingers still clenched it, mindlessly, against the palm of his hand. Then Kebbi was cast aside, staggering, like some emptied and discarded vessel.

A moment later the tall stranger and his diminutive attendant were in retreat, vanishing almost as suddenly as they had appeared. And already the local men, the losers in the first game, were closing in on the fallen Kebbi, determined to reclaim the few coins he had won from them.

Still too shocked to do anything, the most recent loser could already hear them arguing over who would get his riding-beast.

The tall blond man in the sumptuous cloak, hurrying away from the poor tavern with his companion and his new-won prize, had not far to go down the dark road before he was met by a griffin, a mount bigger than a warbeast, winged like a giant eagle and taloned, fanged, and muscled like a lion. The creature crouched before the man in the attitude of a submissive pet.

In the next moment the man's diminutive helper, the tiny woman of great beauty, moving like an active child, hopped aboard the beast. Then she looked down at him where he still stood gloating over the Sword he had just won.

He had drawn another Sword that looked identical to the first and was exulting with one blade in each hand.

"Master Wood?" she called, deferentially puzzled.

"One moment. With Coinspinner now in hand, I have some spells to cast. Trapping spells. Before I do anything else."

"Against Prince Mark?"

"Against his whelp. The elder one, the heir. A softer target, dear, by far."

FIVE

As Adrian and Trilby continued their steady advance into the City of Wizards, the landscape through which they passed became even less like that of the normal world outside. Within the domain they had now entered, a glow of extra magical potential, perceptible to their trained senses, touched and transformed almost everything.

As they approached the center of the City, the architecture around them grew ever more extraordinary too. Hovels and monuments stood side by side. Segments and quarterings of palaces, disconnected from their rightful places in the outside world, loomed over shanties. Mausoleums carved with incomprehensible inscriptions bulked next to fishermen's huts, far from any water.

And that center was somewhat closer to the travelers than had at first appeared. The bizarre urban skyline ahead of them, not really as tall as they had thought, was rapidly separating itself into distinct structures as they walked toward it. And at the same time the individual structures grew more distinct, in both their normal and magical outlines. In all this the two apprentice magicians found nothing overtly alarming. But still, despite the study and preparation that had led them to expect such phenomena, the intrinsic strangeness of the place was awesome.

As the two adventurers advanced, looking around them

alertly, each reminded the other at least once, in a low voice, that the most efficient way to accomplish their objective would be to obtain the desired paving tile and return to the compound of Trimbak Rao before midnight.

Their pace slowed somewhat as they found themselves, almost before they had expected it, moving right in among the taller buildings. Here the descriptions given them by Trimbak Rao continued to prove accurate. Their dog-leg road had turned into a broad paved street, not quite straight, wide in some places and narrow in others, crossed at short intervals by other thoroughfares, most of which were more distorted than itself.

Presently the explorers reached a distinctive intersection, marked by a triple fountain in the center. To reach their goal from here, if what their Teacher had told them was correct, it would be necessary to walk about a kilometer on a circuitous route. They could expect serious difficulties in ever reaching the park they were attempting to enter, Trimbak Rao had warned them, unless they approached it from the proper direction.

So far they had seen no living presence, human or otherwise, in the City besides themselves. The buildings around them appeared to be completely uninhabited, by humanity at least, and yet they certainly were not silent. At intervals there was music—of a kind. It was so unlike anything that Adrian had ever heard before, that he was unable to find words to describe it. He could tell from Trilby's expression that she was puzzled by it too. These sounds issued from unseen sources among certain of the buildings as the visitors passed. At other moments strange voices could be heard, some crying out as if in pain, some laughing, others singing or reciting gibberish. Trimbak Rao had not warned his students about these voices, and the explorers exchanged glances. But then, they had known that the City was in some sense inhabited, and there had been no reason for the Teacher to warn them of every harmless oddity they might encounter. Small waves of magical disturbance came washing across the cityscape with the voices, but still Adrian thought that most of them at least sounded human.

When he and Trilby had gone on a hundred meters from the square of the triple fountains, their pace slowed again, as by some unspoken agreement. Now something, some instinct, seemed to be telling Adrian not to hurry. Caution was essential here. Again and again he could hear the Teacher's voice, in memory, warning against undue haste.

The steps of his booted feet dragged on the cracked pavement.

Trilby appeared to be having somewhat similar thoughts, for her steps were slowing too; her eyes looked troubled when he glanced at her.

Moving at an ever more slothful pace, the explorers presently came in sight of a small, briskly flowing stream that appeared to have cut its course haphazardly between buildings. Most streets stopped abruptly at its banks, but a few had somehow acquired bridges.

Following the stream's bank, Adrian and Trilby soon entered the parklike plot of land that was their goal. At his first sight of the patch of thriving greenery, Adrian experienced a sense of anticlimax, though he was not sure how it was different from what he had been expecting.

The park was basically an expanse of grass that appeared to still be well maintained. Here and there a bank of hardy-looking flowers had been placed, as it seemed, by some gardener much given to random choices. Trees and bushes appeared in pleasingly unplanned positions, and narrow walks of fine gravel curved among them. The whole occupied not much more than an irregular hectare of land, and just beyond its hedged borders the structures of the City stood as before.

There on the park's left side stood what must be the Red Temple the Teacher had warned them about, looking very much as Trimbak Rao had described it, yet somehow not exactly as Adrian had expected. The customary Red Temple colors of red and black dominated what he could see of the structure's outer walls, which were also decorated with many statues depicting the joys of the senses.

"We'd better take a look around the perimeter of the park," said Trilby. "Before we start digging up tiles. Just to scout things out."

"Sure."

Beginning a clockwise circuit, the two young people walked closer to the Temple. As the angle from which they viewed it changed, the building began to take on a look of considerable deformity. From within the Temple's several doorways, all dark but wide open, issued sounds that made the young Prince think vaguely of some huge spinning mechanism, and also of a crowd of humanity all speaking in low and urgent voices.

Not that there was any crowd to be discovered when Trilby and Adrian peered over the hedge bordering the park, trying to see into the Temple's main entrance. Where once, no doubt, some eager throngs of customers and worshippers had passed, unmarked dust had drifted on the pavement, and small plants were growing here and there. There was no visible trace of human presence.

In the direction of the Red Temple, the indications and auras of magic, subtle and faintly ominous, were even more numerous than elsewhere in the City. But all the traces were weak and old; there was nothing that suggested clear and present danger.

They paused to study the statues and carvings on the Temple wall, showing the usual copulations and debauchery.

Adrian's companion, her head on one side, was taking time to consider the art critically.

"I intend to remain a virgin," said Trilby at last, speaking as if more to herself than to her companion. "For the foreseeable future."

Maintaining virginity was a frequent goal, Adrian knew, among both males and females who intended to devote their lives, or at least their youth, to magic. He was still a year or so too young to have to confront this as a personal decision; now he only nodded and moved slowly on.

"We'd better go slow," said Trilby, rather unnecessarily, as they turned away from the border hedge, back into the innocent-appearing parkland.

"Right. Take out time to scout this place, and do it properly." Adrian felt vaguely reassured that Trilby now shared his growing reluctance to be hurried into any aspect of their mission before they could think it out thoroughly in advance.

The park was more or less centered on a pool formed by the small river's encounter with a low dam. Over this barrier, no more than a couple of meters high, the water rushed with a continuous if muted roar.

"That's not as loud as it might be," Trilby commented.

"Magic?" Adrian asked.

"Magic?" repeated Trilby. Then with a shake of her head she answered her own question. "Well, of course it's magic. At least to some extent. Like everything else we've come across today."

Bordering on the pool was the paved square from which they were expected to remove a tile. Again things were not quite as Adrian had thought to find them. It was as if the soil had somehow been extracted from underneath, and the surface from which the tile would have to be removed was concave, with its lowest central portion under half a meter or more of standing water, at about the level of the surface of the nearby pool. This encroachment of the pool was evidently not a purely recent or temporary development. Furry-looking green plants of various sizes, thriving in this damp environment, grew over much of the exposed pavement and through the water, adding at least one more minor obstacle to the job of tile removal.

"Wow!" said Adrian suddenly, ceasing to be a coolly detached investigator.

"What is it?"

Probing with his powers as best he could into the earth directly beneath the pavement, Adrian confirmed what he had just detected there. "What a pool of energy. Could I ever raise an elemental here!"

Trilby looked at him with interest. "Are you going to try it?"

"No, not now. There wouldn't be any point. But wow, what a potential," he murmured, letting his perception range farther among the strained and troubled rocks and soil many meters beneath this fancy pavement.

Trilby was frowning lightly now, with more than concentration, Adrian thought; and he himself felt an undercurrent of slight uneasiness. Well, it was hardly astonishing if land in the vicinity of an ancient Red Temple, which had been transported magically into the City at some time in the past, should prove to be inhabited or infested by beings, powers, that seemed strange even to magicians. Perhaps yet another plane of existence, containing yet other inhabitants, was nearby.

"Well," said Trilby at last, and sighed like one unable any longer to avoid facing a distasteful job. "I suppose we ought to see about digging out our tile."

"I suppose," the Prince agreed doubtfully. "But listen, Trill—"

"What?"

"Are we really sure that this is the right place? The Teacher didn't say anything about the pavement being sunken in like this. I thought the place we wanted was going to be square and level."

"Good point. I wonder?" Trilby scraped with the toe of her boot at the green-scummed tiles of the visible portion of the floor.

And now, to Adrian, the tiles in this pavement were indeed beginning to look different than the ones he remembered in the study of Trimbak Rao. Because of the flood, the only tiles he could see clearly here were those around the edge. These were of an abstract pattern, containing no erotic figures, whereas those in the study had portrayed a scene, or several scenes . . .

"I don't know," Trilby was saying. "Remember those tiles we saw on Teacher's wall? Didn't some of them make up a scene, a figure of a woman, giving birth?"

"Yes. I can remember that. And some of them were just porn, like the Temple wall."

"No, that's not right."

The two explorers stood looking at each other in moderate puzzlement. Not that they were really concerned. Neither of them saw anything in their situation to worry about.

"The main point," said Trilby, giving her dark hair a shake, "is that we shouldn't rush things. We must make sure of what we're doing." The air seemed to be growing warmer, and she fanned herself with the hand that did not hold her staff.

Adrian had to agree. "Yes, you're right. The Teacher told us not to rush things. Over and over he told us that."

"Maybe we should scout around the area a little more."

"I think we should."

Without really thinking about it, they had turned their backs on the square of tiles, and were now standing side by side on the edge of the little pond. Its water looked deep and was almost calm, mirror-like until it began to curl into a white roar at the very edge of the dam. A small pier, wooden and moss-grown, projected from the near shoreline out into the pond, and a dugout canoe was tied at the pier's far end.

Trilby knelt down suddenly and thrust her hand into the water. "Feels cool."

Slipping off his pack, Adrian knelt beside her, cupping water in his own palms. "Sure does." Then he raised his eyes suddenly, staring at the canoe. There was something unusual about it, besides the fact that it had been carved from a single log, and finished smoothly, with exquisite skill. But for the moment he couldn't quite pin the oddity down.

Yes, something unusual, with overtones of the festive and the unpredictable . . .

"The sky's changed," Trilby informed him suddenly.

And indeed the day had now become almost normal. A bright and normal-looking sun, not too hot, was clearly visible over the building that adjoined the little park on the side opposite the Red Temple. Adrian made a mental note to himself to be sure to observe the way the sun moved as the day advanced He still had no idea of the proper directions in this world—if indeed such an idea had any real meaning here.

At the moment, apart from the twisted architecture surrounding them, and the occasional inexplicable sounds that issued from those structures, there was hardly any indication that they were in the City at all. Or so it seemed to Adrian.

The little river maintained its muffled roar. The hot sun shimmered on the brown and gray of the pavement tiles, and glared on the surface of the pond.

The vessel resting almost motionless in the calm water drew his attention once again, and he remarked: "We have some canoes very much like that one at home. But I never saw one so neatly finished."

"We should be getting on with our job." Trilby's sudden protest began in a tone of considerable urgency, but before she had uttered half a dozen words her voice once more lacked conviction.

"I suppose we should," agreed Adrian, after taking some time to think the matter over. But even as he spoke he felt a reluctance to hurry, or to be hurried.

By now the two of them had slipped off their packs, and were sitting quietly, contentedly beside the pool, contemplating the water and the canoe that drifted lightly on its tether. It was as if they were waiting for they knew not what. All around them, beyond the borders of the park, the City seemed to have grown quieter, except for the ceaseless roaring of the stream. Even the strange sounds proceeding from the buildings came less frequently. All hints of dangerous magic were in abeyance.

Methodically, unhurriedly, Trilby pulled off her boots,

and lowered her feet into the cooling water, wiggling her brown toes. The riparian ledge on which the explorers sat was just at a handy height above the pool for this maneuver.

Adrian imitated her actions. "That feels good."

"It sure does."

Trilby poked aimlessly at the water with her hiking staff, then laid it beside her on the ledge. "I wonder if we have time for a swim. I'd like a chance to really cool off."

"That sounds even better." And it did, it sounded great, except maybe there was something else they ought to be doing . . . but the thought refused to complete itself just now. Later he would come back to it . . .

Now the girl, frowning slightly, had turned her head toward him. "Adrian, I know you're not, well, you're not grown up yet, but . . ."

"Oh, sure. If you want a dip, I can take a walk." In Adrian's experience most people were fairly casual about nudity; he felt faintly surprised, and vaguely complimented that Trilby did not want him to see her with her clothes off.

She stood up. "Then it'll be your turn to swim. Or maybe we should toss to see who goes in first?"

"No, you go ahead. I'm not in any hurry."

Adrian turned his back on Trilby and started to take a walk. The hedged border of the park was only a short distance ahead of him, and beyond it rose the distorted bulk of the mysterious Red Temple, an interesting goal for exploration.

There were several openings in the boundary hedge, where little paths had been worn through, and the prince chose the nearest one. Only when he had begun to climb the broad stone stairs leading ultimately to the Red Temple did he realize that he had left his pack, canteen, and boots back at poolside. Oh, well. He climbed on barefoot, becoming interested in the configuration of the structure before him. Toward one end of the Temple, on his left, the carved figures and other elements of the design were all grotesquely flattened in one dimension, elongated in another, as if the perspective of the space in which they existed had been changed by the magical forces that had brought them to this exotic place and forced them into coexistence with other elements from elsewhere.

A selection of dark doorways, all leading into the Temple's interior, stood open ahead of him. And now that he was alone, he began to be troubled by the feeling that there was some trick, some clue, regarding their surroundings that ought to be of concern to him and Trilby but which they had not yet discovered. It wasn't a strong feeling, only a slight irritation. And it wasn't really a matter of danger, not as Adrian perceived it now. In fact he wasn't thinking of danger at all. But there was something forgotten or overlooked, maybe something that they were going to need . . .

Having progressed at a leisurely pace fully halfway up the stairs that ascended toward the distorted building, the prince on impulse stopped and turned to glance back. From here he could see over the hedge bordering the park into its interior. There was the narrow dam, the water rushing over, its muted roar still audible. And there, sure enough, was Trilby, forty or fifty meters away now, standing naked on the edge of the pool. Her brown skin was gleaming wet, and she was getting ready to dive in again.

And so he had got to see her that way after all.

She was unaware that he was looking, and indeed it didn't seem of any great importance. Yet Adrian stood very still, continuing to watch the girl. He told himself that he had a good reason for watching, that he was carefully making sure that she was still all right.

Her figure poised for a dive, and then arced out of sight. The faint sound of the splash was swallowed by the steady heavy murmur of the stream falling over the barrier. The canoe, beside its dock, bobbed gently with the waves the dive had made.

Very soon, before Trilby had resurfaced, the prince walked on, conscious of a vague feeling of uneasiness.

The nearest of the Temple's dim doorways widened around him, and he passed through it. Inside, once his eyes had adjusted from the direct glare of sun, he could see well enough. Entering the first hall he came to, Adrian discovered many empty tables and chairs, most of them tipped over now—once the instruments of gluttony, he supposed. He gave the place a perfunctory inspection upon entering, but all his senses assured him that these surroundings were perfectly safe. There was simply no danger here. Anyway, Trimbak Rao wouldn't have sent two of his favorite tender young apprentices into a place where there was real danger, would he?

Would he?

No, of course not!

Coming aimlessly outdoors again, Adrian paused, squinting upward, to check the position of the sun. By leaving the pool he had certainly changed his own position relative to the neighboring building, but there was the sun, the same angular distance above its rooftop as before.

Something to think about. Well, all in good time. He moved back into the Temple's dimness.

This time he took a different turning. Certain of the interior doorways were completely blocked, or their openings impossibly constricted, by tiers of masonry that seemed, through whim or ignorance, to have been built in the wrong place. Progress was difficult but not impossible.

The interior of this Temple was laid out according to a plan shared by a great many of its sister Temples around the world. Not that Adrian, at twelve, had ever been in any one of them before. Nor was he well acquainted with any cult of adult pleasures—but here and there he had heard stories.

This great chamber, containing a few large and strangely

decorated tables, had to be the House of Luck. One wall was entirely dominated by a huge gaming wheel, wall-mounted so that the numbers as they came up could be seen clearly from any part of a large room. A number of gaming tables were in the room also.

The wheel, big enough if not sturdy enough to run a sawmill, for some reason started to turn by itself just as the boy entered the gambling hall. He paused, looking at it attentively. Music from invisible instruments, played by no human hands, was suddenly loud and clear. Adrian, turning his head in response to a different, half-heard sound, observed a pair of semi-transparent forms, of vaguely human shape, ascending a stairway. One form, now exaggeratedly female, seemed to turn back to glance at him before disappearing at the top of the stairs. Upstairs, if the stories he had heard were true, was where the House of Flesh would be.

The wheel ratcheted to a halt, at the number zero.

He continued his exploration of the ground floor. Along with the steadily increasing euphoric sense of confidence, tranquility, and well-being, though in definite contradiction to it, the undercurrent of anxiety now came back more strongly than before. It was an apparently baseless feeling that something was beginning to go wrong, something that seemed the result at least in part of sheer bad luck.

He was picking up plenty of things to think about. Yes. Well, all in good time.

But his vague uneasiness guided him outside again. As if reluctantly, shuffling on bare feet, he made his way back toward the parkland and its pool. Pausing halfway down the broad steps, at the place where he had taken a secret look at Trilby, he looked for her again. But the girl was out of sight. If she was in the pool he couldn't hear her splashing, not above the steady background roar of falling water.

Adrian moved on, still walking deliberately, heading back into the park to rejoin his companion.

* * *

Arriving at the pool, he found nothing surprising. The canoe bobbed idly, its presence suggesting . . . something. But what? And Trilby, dressed once more in shirt and trousers, was sitting where she had sat before, again contemplating the water.

She raised her head almost languidly at Adrian's arrival. "Where were you, in the Temple? Discover anything new?"

"No. Not really." He sat down beside her, just where he had been before, dipping his feet in the water again. He wondered what to say. "How was your swim?"

"Fine. Cool. The water's nice and deep, you can even dive."

"My turn, then."

"Sure." Trilby got to her feet. "And my turn to take a walk around."

"I looked inside the Red Temple, but there wasn't much. A couple of spooky-looking figures, and a gaming wheel moved. No real interaction. Maybe you can find something interesting."

Left alone, Adrian became interested in the canoe. Carved in one piece, very skillfully, from a single log of gray-brown wood, it was thin and light-looking and graceful.

But first, he felt hot and the water beckoned. In a moment, Adrian was standing, and in another he had stripped off his clothes.

The first plunge was a clean joy. Coming up from the surprising green depths, the prince drifted on his back, in water marvelously cool. Now, he thought, to see about the canoe. A few strong kicks brought him to its side.

Pulling on a gunwale to peer in, he observed a single wooden paddle, neatly carved, lying in the bottom. Yes, he was going to have to try the canoe out.

Small boats of every kind were common enough in Tasavalta, and Adrian considered himself something of an expert. Starting in deep water, you couldn't simply scramble in over the side of a canoe. He climbed first to the pier, then got himself aboard the little craft and untied the cord that held it to the dock. As he did so, he abruptly realized what was so unusual about this boat—of all the objects in sight, here in the middle of Wizards' City, it was the only one devoid of any magical aura at all.

That ought to mean something, but he wasn't sure what.

For the time being he let the paddle stay where it was. The canoe, left to its own devices, showed no immediate tendency to be carried out of the pool and over the dam.

There had been a very little water, hardly more than damp spots, in the bottom of the canoe, before he climbed in dripping. He thought it might have trickled from Trilby's naked body—she might have investigated the boat too, played around in it between swims. And when she sat in it, her bare bottom would have rested just about where his was now.

Adrian eased himself from the middle seat and lay back, stretching out as much as possible, raising his knees over the middle thwart. He let his eyes close. The sun-heated wood would have felt the same, almost too hot for comfort, on her body as on his.

. . . on her soft, smooth, brown skin. On her flesh that was so very different from his, rounded but firm with unobtrusive muscle underneath. Her big breasts, as he had seen them from a distance, bulging in the sun, their broad dark nipples seeming to turn up a little in its heat.

The canoe bobbed lightly, for no discernible reason. Adrian remembered the female figure he'd glimpsed in the Temple. With his eyes closed he could imagine he saw her walking toward him.

Opening his eyes, the boy looked down at his own bare body, wiry and immature. Most of his skin was pale, seldom touched by the sun. But his body wasn't going to stay childish much longer. Soon, in a year or two, he'd be growing, developing real muscles. And something else too.

Like the male statues carved on the Temple wall. His body would be as much a man's as any of them.

Time passed.

At last, driven by some subliminal warning, Adrian sat

up abruptly. He could feel that his face was red, his ears burning, his body uncomfortable as if it had been used by alien powers. The canoe was drifting, bumping against a little bar that fortunately ran along the dam. Fortunately, because otherwise he and his boat would have gone right over. He still might, if the craft drifted only a little sideways. Grabbing up the wooden paddle, he backed water none too soon.

He had paddled back to a place near the middle of the pond, and was wondering in confusion what to do next, when he had a strong sensation that he was no longer alone. Inhuman creatures that he took at first for incubi and succubi from the Temple were standing semi-transparent on the very edge of the pool, the females clutching their transparent garments coyly round them. There were six of them, eight, ten. No, more. Numbers beyond counting. Many of the shapes were strange and indecipherable, but all were evil. Now Adrian understood that some of them might have come out of the Red Temple, but most had issued from somewhere else, only the gods knew where.

Heart pounding, throat suddenly a dry knot, the prince realized that he was surrounded by ferociously antagonistic powers, forces of hostile magic. So subtle had been their approach, so arcane the spells that shielded them from his view, that he had never perceived them until now. For hours, for days perhaps, they had been closing in on him, walling him subtly but powerfully away from the outside world.

Now he could see, he could feel, that they were on the brink of some climactic action that might destroy him. He had no time or nerve for careful thought. Acting instinctively in self-defense, his mind and his perception reached deep beneath the surface of the earth. As a drowning boy might have clutched at a log, so Adrian reached for and seized the energies of earth, molding them, prodding them into detonation.

The result was an elemental.

This particular elemental, born among the strains and

heat of rocks many meters below the surface of the earth, was very powerful even of its powerful kind.

Whirling and dancing in the circle of Adrian's enemies, there were no demons, but a foul host of other hostile powers. These at first jeered at his efforts to create a counterforce, taunted him with what they supposed must be his feebleness.

It was not a matter of the Prince's unleashing the elemental at them—for he had made no effort to restrain it in the first place. This was no comparatively gentle derivative of sky or water. Rather an earth-elemental, vast and imbued with the power of gravity. Suddenly granted sentience, this creature battled its way toward the surface, sending before it from the body of the planet a deafening eruption of shattered rock, geysering water, splattering fountains of mud.

Havoc resulted. All other forces of magic blurred, within the narrow locus of the elemental's influence. This zone contained the enemy powers surrounding Adrian. Their ring was broken, the ground reshaped, and the local course of the small river temporarily disrupted.

The essence of its being invisible, having no form but that of the earth from which it had been born, the elemental reached the surface and there jerked to a stop. The canoe, with Adrian still in it, was hurled into the air, to splash back violently. Somehow, clutching hard at both gunwales, he avoided being thrown out into the water.

The small dam had already burst, or rather it had been obliterated. The water contained in the deep pool was hurled downstream, the flood carrying the boat with it.

Adrian in his canoe was carried away upon this miniature tidal wave of water, propelled by a buckling and heaving landscape. He was borne downstream, through the broken ring of the powers that would have confined and perhaps destroyed him.

The elemental, still full of life and ferocity, drove dumbly on behind its creator, and tumult swept along the riverbed. Behind its passage the crash of falling buildings partially blocked the stream, which fought a new channel through the wreckage almost at once.

Stretched out in the bottom of the canoe, clinging for his life as waves and mud poured in on him, the Prince could only close his eyes and wait. At last the thunder of the erupting earth was quiet. He could only keep clinging to the thwarts and gunwales, and allow himself to be borne along. Drained by the great effort he had made in raising the elemental, he drifted into a semiconscious state.

None of the creatures evoked by his enemy's hostile magic pursued him; for one thing their formation had been shattered, and for another they had been given no such orders. They were constrained to soothing and trapping and holding.

Still the canoe continued to be borne forward, although now at a gradually diminishing speed. The elemental was following the craft downstream, but by slow degrees the creature was ceasing to propel it forward.

The dazed boy, being swept downstream, muttered the name of Trilby once or twice. But Adrian had no way of knowing what might have happened to her. Nor, if he had known, would he have had any means of turning back to try to help her.

Once raising his head, groggily, to look back, he saw shapes of blackness, as if the shadow of the whole earth, the City's skyline visible in silhouette, were being cast upon clouds high in the sky by some great sun-light in the center of the planet. And then he slumped into unconsciousness.

On regaining full consciousness at last, and bringing his head up out of the bottom of the canoe, Adrian found that the elemental seemed to have completely dissipated. Natural darkness had overtaken him. And from the feel of his environment, he was sure that he was no longer in the City. The stream and the canoe had carried him along some natural escape route, doubtless perilous, that had brought him clean away from immediate danger.

"Trilby," he groaned again. Wherever his partner had been when the disaster struck, when the trap had tried to close on them, he realized that they might now, for all he knew, be separated by hundreds of kilometers.

The paddle was still aboard, wedged under one end of a thwart. The boy couldn't really recall putting it there. Taking up the implement again, Adrian shakily directed the craft to shore at the nearest level place. Then he got out and stood with his feet sinking into warm mud, trying to see back in the direction from which he had come. Vague, dark masses indicated heavy vegetation along both banks.

The heir to the throne of Tasavalta could be sure only that the City was now completely behind him, and that he was now standing, completely naked and utterly alone, on the bank of a strange river.

SIX

AS soon as Wood had completed the first phase of his magical attack upon Prince Mark's son, a process that took only a few minutes, the blond and beautiful enchantress called Tigris leaped astride the griffin once again. She waited for her master to mount behind her, ready to snuggle herself provocatively against him. But this time the magician had elected to use a different means of transport. He remained at a little distance from the griffin, standing in an area shaded from the moonlight by the knotted branches of a dead tree; and by means of the flickering spots of silver light his assistant was able to observe swift changes in his physical shape. Among other alterations, Wood's body as a whole grew smaller, and his own dark pinions came sprouting from his shoulders.

Tigris, seeing how things were, whispered a command into the griffin's ear, and the great beast sprang upward, bearing her into the air. She saw her master's shadowy form rise after her.

Their flight was not a long one, and it was conducted entirely through darkness and whistling wind. Tigris was aware when, at about the halfway point, the first other powers joined them in midair. Before they landed, several airborne demons, accompanied by other powers less susceptible to ready classification, had already met her master to fawn upon him. These immaterial creatures manned the outermost line of protection of Wood's domain.

Now, as the two humans and their escort descended toward the earth again, the wind abated somewhat. Their landing was in a wild and lonely place, still well within the natural boundary of night. The griffin crouched meekly on the rocky soil, making it easy for Tigris to dismount.

She did so with a quick jump, then looked around her. By the time Wood had landed too and she had located her master on the ground, his appearance was once more that of a handsome and broad-shouldered young man.

Standing within an ancient circle of stones, evidently a place for which he felt some special preference, Wood was holding the naked Sword of Chance up in his right hand and gazing at the blade. Here, in this pool of relatively deep natural darkness, Coinspinner responded to his touch with sparks, some of which were momentarily dazzling in their brilliance.

Despite his triumph in obtaining the Sword of Chance, Wood's thoughts at this moment were troubled. Having completed—satisfactorily, he thought—the first phase of his magical attack on the young Prince, he found it necessary to reach a decision: whether or not to go immediately into the City himself, to take possession of the trapped prey.

Tigris, while her withdrawn master pondered, had perched herself seductively upon an enormous skull nearby—the unfleshed head looked like that of some mythological beast, higher than her own head when she stood before it. Only the head of a great worm, she supposed, could be so huge—but she was no expert in inhuman anatomy.

Despite the pertness of her attitude, her voice was humble in tone when next she spoke, daring to interrupt her Ancient Master's private deliberations to ask him what his next move was going to be. Somehow, during the brief interval of travel from the gaming table to this half-real wasteland, she had come to be wearing a short black skirt instead of trousers, and now there was a flash of pale thighs when she crossed her legs.

Wood, turning his head to peer out of the shadows of the tall stones, gazed at her blankly for a moment. As a rule the great wizard was not insensible of his assistant's physical attractiveness—far from it. But now other matters of greater importance had first claim on his attention.

His attack on Prince Adrian, launched with the help of Coinspinner, was only one of these, though one of the most pressing. And his decision was still not made as to whether he would go himself into the City of Wizards and collect his prey.

But now he decided that there was one other decision to be made first, one that Wood had to admit must take priority over all the rest.

Holding up the naked length of Coinspinner, he inspected the Sword more closely. Frowning at the Blade as if he could wring its secrets from it by sheer force of will, Wood twirled it, somewhat awkwardly, in his strong right hand. At the same time he was resting his left hand on the almost identical hilt of Shieldbreaker, which very rarely left his side by night or day. Touching two Swords at once, he could feel his own immersion in the godlike power of the Swords. It was like no other power he had ever encountered, either in the ancient world from which he came, or in this one. Perhaps not even Ardneh or Orcus, his enemies of thousands of years ago, would ever have been quite able to match this.

Tigris, shifting her weight restlessly on the great skull, her short skirt riding yet a little higher, persisted in her nervous questioning: "What will you do with it now, my lord?"

For a moment he blinked at her distractedly, as if he were not quite sure who this woman might be who questioned him.

But at last he answered her aloud. "With Coinspinner?"

The magician held the blade up, then paused, holding it very still. "Perhaps I will destroy it."

For once his clever assistant could only stare at him without comprehension. "My lord?"

The man on the ground, he who could grow reptilian wings, or dispose of them again, whenever he chose to do so, chuckled dryly. "Do I mystify you, Tigris? But I suppose that is inescapable."

Then he twirled the Sword of Chance again, and cast it down before him forcefully, so that the point stabbed deep into the rocky earth, and the weapon remained standing upright.

His right hand, having thus emptied itself, went promptly to the other scabbard hanging at his other side. From that sheath it drew out his second Blade, equally dazzling to look at.

Now the wizard said to the young-looking, innocent-looking woman who sat above him on the great skull: "Look, here's Shieldbreaker!"

"I see it, my lord."

"Do you? Do you see that I am now granted an opportunity that may never come again? Here in my hand I now hold the Sword that blocked Coinspinner's power in tonight's game, when that power would have been used against me; this same blade can shatter the other's metal forever. Believe me, it can. It has done the same for both Doomgiver and Townsaver, in times past."

"But . . . O master, to destroy Coinspinner! Why?" Tigris was openly aghast at the thought that Wood could even consider annihilating such a magnificent weapon, an almost matchless treasure, nullifying the great advantage that he had just managed to acquire.

Actually, though the woman appeared to be taking seriously his threat to destroy the Sword, in her heart she could not really do so. Her master, for his part, could almost read her thoughts: Was this talk of destruction only some regal jest? But no, hardly that. She would know that

Wood was too sober to play such games, not much of a jester at any time.

She would, he thought, probably be virtually convinced that his talk of shattering a Sword was only some kind of a test he had devised for his subordinate.

While on occasion he might arrange such tests, now he had no time or inclination for them. Nor had he much patience for giving explanations. Still, he saw that if he wanted any intelligent response from his assistant at all, something in the way of explanation was a necessity.

"I am perfectly serious, girl. Consider that this unpredictable Sword now lying at my feet will always pose an obstacle to me, or to anyone else, who seeks to attain perfect power."

"My lord?"

"But you really don't see that, do you?"

"My lord—"

He gestured impatiently. "Suppose that I managed to get into my possession every Sword, including this one, of the ten that still remain intact. Yet this one, with its cursed independence, might fly away from me at any time. It might leave me, and then it might create problems for me, only the gods know what problems, once it had arrived in the hands of someone else."

Tigris, having grasped the point as soon as it was stated plainly, was quick to be reassuring. "You'll find some clever way around that, my wise and powerful lord. Some way to bind Coinspinner's power forever to your service, and to that of no one else."

Wood answered slowly. "I might. Such magic would be a supreme challenge, but I might attempt to manage it—if ony I were not so busy just now with other matters. On the other hand, if I destroy the Sword of Chance now, now while I have the certain power to do so . . ." Again he brandished Shieldbreaker. There was no other known means to destroy any of the Swords. "Then I need fear Coinspinner's power never again."

Once more Tigris shifted her shapely weight on the great

skull, her pale thighs flashing as if she could not choose to be anything other than seductive. "And yet," she murmured. "And yet, my master hesitates."

The master, plunged deep in thought again, scarcely looked up at her. But he did reply. "I do. I hesitate, indeed. Whilst Coinspinner is in my grasp, I can use its power to achieve . . . great things. Yes, already it has given me advantage. Presently I'll have Prince Mark's princely whelp firmly in my grip. And then I think his father—aye, and his grandfather too—will cease to be such sharp thorns in my side."

The woman spoke cautiously. "I understand that your decision regarding this Sword must be a very difficult one, my lord."

He did look at her now, and carefully. "Do you understand, Tigris? Do you begin to grasp my problem? I wonder if you do."

And Wood closed his eyes briefly, casting abroad his inner vision, doing his best to follow the progress of the spells he had cast and the powers he had dispatched to snare young Adrian. The trouble was that the Tasavaltan whelp was guarded, better protected than Wood had ever realized . . . but yet, with Coinspinner's help, success now seemed imminent.

Oh, the overwhelming force of Chance, of Fortune, that came with this Sword was too great a power to give up!

And yet . . .

The wizard opened his eyes. He paced about, groaning intensely though almost inaudibly. Demons and spells were of no help to him now. His mind was in a frenzy, unable to come to a decision.

Then abruptly he stopped in his tracks. Suddenly he issued a sharp order. "Back to our headquarters! I will make my decision there. Wait, this time I will ride with you."

The griffin, which had dropped out of sight for a time, now appeared again as if from nowhere, spread its wings and lowered its body to make it easier for the people to get aboard. In another moment, the creature and its double human cargo had whirled into the air again.

This leg of their flight was considerably longer than the first had been, though still not long enough to bring them into daylight.

The aerial voyage terminated at Wood's headquarters. This edifice, when seen from the outside, appeared to be—and indeed was—a fortress of dark stone, sprawling along a mountain peak. It looked a forbidding place indeed, its lofty stone walls surrounding the sharp central crag that arose within them. The two arriving humans, on landing inside the high walls, entered an aspect of the place somewhat more civilized in appearance. They dismounted from the griffin at one end of a courtyard garden. This garden boasted fountains and statuary, though many of the plants that grew in it were not ordinary flowers. Blue flames, welling from some of the fountains, provided an eerie but serviceable illumination.

Nor would the statues have been of ordinary appearance, even in ordinary light. Two of the strangest among them, standing about a meter apart from each other at the lower end of the garden, were of stone carved into the shapes of squat and ugly men. This pair of grotesque carvings had been standing here before Wood built his fortress, and evidently represented a remnant of some ancient and evil shrine that had occupied these lonely heights long before he, or any other man now living, had ever seen them.

The night by now was far advanced, and overhead the sky was strange with shapes that were not ordinary clouds. An observer familiar with the City of Wizards might have been deceived into thinking that this garden and its immediate surroundings belonged to it—indeed, that this represented one of the City's more dangerous neighborhoods, remote from the much less perilous, relatively prosaic region that Trilby and Adrian had entered. But in fact this mountaintop formed no part of the City at all, though at times the magical intensity within this domain was equally great.

Wood had put down Shieldbreaker—he felt secure enough to do that here, in the middle of his own stronghold —and was now pacing about his garden with the Sword of Chance, swinging and twirling the blade in a physically inexpert way, occasionally hacking down some exotic plant. He cursed the weapon, almost steadily, because of the problem that it posed him. But yet he hesitated, not quite able to make up his mind to smite it into fragments with the overwhelming power of the Sword of Force.

At last the magician ceased to pace. Throwing back his head, he shouted at the sky: "No, I *must* use it once more!"

And once more, gripping the Sword of Chance in both hands, Wood hurled his trapping spells against the small and distant figure of Prince Adrian.

Tigris, who had followed her master on his rambling course across the garden, was perching now upon a comparatively new stone statue that bore the shape of some grotesque and probably imaginary beast. She shivered on the chill stone of her new seat, and felt a pang of anxiety as she listened to his voice call out the spells and sensed their potency. Skilled enchantress that she was, Wood's powers awed her. This man, the Ancient One, this Dark Master she now served, simply knew too much, and was more powerful than any human being ought to be. If for any reason he should ever tire of her, or decide that she was dangerous—

His new ordering of spells complete at last, Wood hastened to carry Coinspinner down to the far end of the garden where the light of the flaming fountains was dimmest, and the ugly twin statues stood. He had reason to believe those images might have a helpful influence in what he was about to do. Balancing the bare blade carefully, he set it in place with his own hands, so that Coinspinner, catching one spark of light, formed a straight and slender bridge of steel between the pair of stone grotesqueries, running from the left shoulder of one across the right shoulder of the other.

Silently, Tigris had followed her master. She was frowning worriedly, like a small girl, scuffing her bare feet in the damp, cold grass. She noted that the wind was rising. In the distance, but swiftly blowing closer, rainstorms threatened.

Having set the Sword of Chance very carefully in place, the wizard spun around, urgently commanding any of his servants who might hear him: "Now, quickly, put Shieldbreaker into my hands!"

Tigris, hopping down instantly from her latest perch, the statue of some bull-like beast, was about to run to obey. But invisible forces had heard the command also, and were ahead of her. Enslaved powers had already taken up the Sword of Force, and were now pressing the ultimate power into the hands of the magician.

Accepting the blade, Wood heard and felt the thud of energy in Shieldbreaker's black hilt. And then that energy cut off abruptly. Wood did not understand until he had turned back to the twin statues, with Sword uplifted to deliver a shattering blow.

The space between the stones, where he had placed the Sword of Chance, was empty.

The ugly, lifeless statues mocked him with their eyes, hollow sockets with stone depths illumined suddenly by distant lightning. Coinspinner had taken itself away. His luck was gone, and the gods alone, if any gods still lived, knew where.

Rain drenched him suddenly. As far as Wood could tell, the rain and lightning were completely natural.

SEVEN

SHORTLY after dawn, Talgai the Woodcutter, as was his daily custom, said good-bye to his small family, turned his back on their little riverside hut in its forest clearing, and with his loadbeast and his tools headed off into the deep woods to see what he could find there of value.

It was a fine morning. The woodcutter, a wiry, somewhat undersized man approaching middle age, hummed as he hiked along. Now and then he amused himself by whistling bird imitations, and sometimes he was pleased to hear an answer from the forest canopy.

For the first few hundred meters the trail he had chosen ran beside a stream, but at the first branching he turned away from the water, tugging at the little loadbeast's reins to lead it uphill.

Two hours and numerous trail branchings later, Talgai had ceased to whistle. For some time now he had been struggling along a small side trail, so little-traveled and overgrown that the intruder was forced to hack with his long brushknife at encroaching small limbs and under-growth to force a passage. Trees in uncountable numbers, live and dead, surrounded him now, and had done so since he left home, but he only glanced at their trunks in passing and then ignored them. To earn a reasonable livelihood with the small loads that his single beast could carry, he had to, sometimes at least, find wood that was good for more than burning; and today he was determined to do just that.

Having made half a kilometer's progress along the overgrown trail, he happened to glance upward through the canopy, trying to fix the sun's height in the sky. Just as he did so his eye was caught by the gleam of something mysteriously, piercingly bright amid the greenery.

Sidestepping carefully, squinting upward for a better look, Talgai soon discovered that the bright gleam emanated from the blade of a sword, which was stuck through a treetrunk. It was a miraculously beautiful sword, looking as out of place here as something in a dream.

To the woodcutter it seemed for a moment or two as if the spectacular weapon must have been planted here just for him to find. Who else was going to be coming through here, after all?

But that, of course, was nonsense.

Now Talgai had halted, standing almost directly below this metallic apparition and staring up at it. It was certainly a glorious weapon to say the least, quite out of the class of any kind of tool that Talgai had ever seen before. And as marvelous as the presence of the thing itself were the circumstances of its presence. The bright blade was embedded in the tall tree as if perhaps some giant's arm had forced it there, so deeply that half its length came out the other side.

Talgai had never been a fighter, and was basically uninterested in weapons. Nor was he, in the ordinary sense, a treasure hunter. But the finish of that steel, even seen at a distance of several meters, and the bright straightness of that blade were far too impressive for him to simply pass it by.

There was a problem, in that the sword was well above his reach as he stood on the trail, and the tree that it transfixed was somewhat too thorny for an easy climb. The woodcutter had to remove his bundle of tools from the back of his little loadbeast, and then stand precariously balanced on the animal's back himself, to bring his right hand within reach of the black hilt.

He thought he felt a faint vibration in the Sword when he first touched it, but in a moment the sensation vanished.

Getting the Sword out of the green, tough trunk took even more wrenching and tugging than the man had expected. But eventually, with Talgai's strong grip on the black hilt, the keen blade cut itself loose.

After hopping down from the loadbeast's back, the woodcutter inspected his find with wonder. The black hilt, he now discovered, was marked with a small white symbol, depicting two dice. Talgai, who seriously disapproved of gambling, frowned. And the symbol explained nothing to him. He thought of himself as a practical man, one who stayed close to home in mind as well as in body. He had barely heard of the gods, whose disappearance a few years ago had caused much excitement in the world's more sophisticated circles. And Talgai had never heard at all of the gods' twelve magic Swords.

Well, what ought he to do now? The woodcutter looked around him rather nervously. To him the presence of any sword, especially when unsheathed, suggested combat. And surely a weapon like this must belong to some wealthy owner, who, if he was not lying slaughtered in the bushes nearby, was bound to come looking for it eventually.

Talgai was too honest to even think of keeping the weapon if he could find its owner. But he could look forward hopefully to a substantial reward.

The fact that this precious length of steel had been stuck so forcefully in a tree created in Talgai's mind the vague suggestion that other violent events might have occurred nearby. But his widening search, peering and hacking his way among the trunks and undergrowth, discovered no evidence to support this idea. His calls, first soft, then loud, all went unanswered. And no sign anywhere of recent travelers. There was in fact no indication that anyone except himself had passed this way in a long time.

Presently the woodcutter gave up the fruitless search and
returned, Sword in hand, to his patient loadbeast. Standing
in one of the rare beams of sunlight that reached the
ground through the thick cover overhead, he fell to exam-
ining his find more closely.

The Sword's supernally keen edge did not appear to have
been damaged in the least by the rough treatment it had
received, and Talgai could not resist trying it out on some
nearby brush. The tough twigs fell off cleanly, mown as
neatly as if they had been tender grass. He whistled to
himself. This was a better tool than any brushknife or
machete he had ever owned!

He reloaded his other implements upon his beast and
began to move along the trail again in his original direction; he could usually think better when engaged in some
kind of physical action. As he walked, he slashed with his
new tool at obstructing twigs and branches. Long and
heavy as it was, the bright blade balanced very neatly in his
hand—

And then the handle seemed to twist. His foot slipped at
the same instant, and he dropped the blade.

Bending to pick it up, he thought himself lucky that he
had not gashed his leg or foot with it. While he was still
bent over, he happened to glance under some nearby
branches, through a gap in the greenery opened by his last
random slash.

Thirty meters or so away, leaves of a unique coppery
color shimmered, dancing lightly in a random breeze,
glowing in one of the slender, random beams of sunlight
that managed to find their way down through the high
green canopy above.

The woodcutter made a sound like a long sigh. He did
not straighten up, lest he lose sight of what he had
discovered. Instead, stooping and crawling under other
branches, he maneuvered his way closer to his find. It was,
as he had known from his first look, a rare tree, one of the
species Talgai was always looking for. Its heartwood, highly

prized as incense, made this tree worth more than any other Talgai could have found.

After making his way back to his loadbeast and his tools, Talgai needed only a brief time to hack a good path through to the tree, and a little longer to fell it with his axe and then despoil it of its central treasure.

With such a small though worthwhile cargo packed in his loadbeast's panniers, he needed work no more today—or indeed for several months. Not that he was really able to imagine such a period of inactivity, unless it should be enforced by illness or injury. But certainly he would range the forest no more today. Instead, he decided to set out at once for the nearest sizable village, where he would be able to convert his precious wood quickly to coins and food, and where he also might discover some indication of who might have lost such a valuable weapon.

Moving at an unhurried pace, Talgai did not reach the settlement until after midday. The small cluster of wooden buildings dozed as usual in the sun; a few of the inhabitants were at work in their gardens, while others rested in the shade of their verandas, or under the few ornamental trees that had survived the woodcutters' onslaughts within the town itself.

There was a river, small and generally somnolent, passing along the edge of this town, the same stream on which Talgai had his hut. The river made it easy to ship logs downstream from here to the city markets, where they were used for construction as well as fuel.

The proprietor of the local woodyard was an old acquaintance of Talgai, and greeted him in a friendly way. He was also glad to buy Talgai's cuttings of valuable heartwood for a small handful of coins, paying a price rather higher than the woodsman had expected. The townsman also marveled at the marvelous weapon Talgai was carrying with him, and at the story of how it had been found. But neither the proprietor of the woodyard nor any of the hangers-on who gathered to hear Talgai's story could offer any constructive suggestion as to who the true owner might be, or how the treasure had come to be embedded in a tree in the deep woods.

At last the businessman suggested: "If you can't find the owner, Talgai, maybe you'll be thinking of selling it?"

The woodcutter shook his head. "I'm a long way from that. I must try to find the owner first—and if I can't, this makes a marvelous brushknife. And such steel, such an edge, I believe I could even cut a tree down with it if I had to!"

"There's magic in it, then. Well, that's easy to believe."

"Yes, I suppose there is." Talgai frowned. Nothing in his small experience of magic had led him to think that it was ever quite safe or trustworthy.

Talgai was just passing out of the woodyard into the street when he turned for one more word. "You know, I think this tool has brought me good luck. I mean, it led me to find that cinnamon-wood." Then he walked on.

Not wanting to appear armed and threatening while he was in town, he had wrapped the sword in a piece of canvas, part of his usual equipment, and put it under his arm. Thus burdened, he now proceeded across the street to the single inn of the village.

The husband and wife who owned the inn were also old acquaintances of Talgai. They were glad to see him, simply as friends, and pleased to furnish him with a midday meal in return for one of the smaller of his newly acquired coins. As to the sword, they marveled at it even more than had the proprietor of the woodyard, but they could offer no more helpful comment.

A handful of other customers were at the inn, and a couple of these were travelers from afar. The first of these outlanders gazed at Talgai's prize blankly when it was unwrapped and displayed. Nor could he tell the woodcutter anything of any passing strangers, at least not of anyone who had lost a treasure and was offering a reward for it.

But the second traveler from distant places froze, a spoonful of soup halfway to his mouth, at his first glimpse of the sword. As soon as this man was ready to resume normal motion and speech, and had examined the blade more closely, he swore that he knew what it was—quickly he outlined the story of the Twelve Swords, and claimed that he had been privileged to see one of the others, twenty years ago.

"What you have there, woodcutter, is the great Sword Coinspinner—the Sword of Chance, it's also called, sometimes. By all the gods! And it was just stuck in a tree limb, in the forest? By all the gods, hard to believe, but there it is. I can believe it, though, of this one. They say Coinspinner is liable to just take itself away from anyone who has it, at any time, without rhyme or reason, and then show up where someone else can find it." The traveler shook his head. "No point in looking for the owner, I'd say. It's yours now." His tone seemed to imply that he was glad, just out of a general sense of wariness, that the Sword was not his own.

"It does seem to have brought me good luck." Talgai offered the idea cautiously.

His informant chuckled, shook his head, and chuckled again. "I should think it might do that," he said.

"May it bring you good luck forever, Talgai," the innkeeper's wife cried spontaneously.

"Talgai? Is that your name?" This came from the first far-traveler, the outsider who had been of no help in identifying the Sword. "And you say you are a woodcutter?"

"Talgai, yes sir, that's me."

"What a very remarkable coincidence! Would you believe that when I passed through Smim, two days ago, I overheard someone shouting that he wanted to get word to Talgai the Woodcutter?"

"But how can that be? Who in that town would have any message for me? I've never even been there."

"Well. It happened when I was in the town square. I heard a voice shouting, and looked up, and there was a man standing at one of the barred windows in the house of government—they have the jail cells up there, you know." Here the speaker paused, almost apologetically.

"Go on!"

"Well, there was a man up there, shouting, just calling out to anyone who'd listen to him—there were quite a few people in the square. He kept pleading for someone to take a message to his brother, who he said was Talgai the Woodcutter. It seemed—well—a somewhat mad way to attempt to send a message. But it certainly caught my attention, and I remembered. And then I suppose the poor fellow probably had no better means at his disposal."

"Did he say his name? Did he look anything like me? Was his hair the same color as mine?"

"I'm afraid I didn't notice about his hair, or what he looked like in general. Yes, he did say his name—Booglay, Barclay, what was it now?"

"Buvrai," said Talgai, in a small voice.

"That sounds like what he said. Yes, I'm sure that's it."

Everyone in the room was staring at Talgai now. He asked: "What was the message?"

"Only that he was imprisoned there—and under sentence of death."

There was a pause in which no one said anything. Then Talgai's informant went on: "In six days—I remember him calling that out into the square, over and over. In six days he was going to be hanged. There was a scaffold in the square . . ."

Talgai was standing utterly still, looking as if he had no trouble in believing any of this. He asked: "For what crime had this man been sentenced?"

The traveler, looking gloomy, said he didn't know for sure, but he thought it might have had something to do with an offense committed in a Red Temple. He did know that major offenders from a wide district around were often brought to Smim for trial and execution.

Talgai nodded sadly. "My brother was always the wild one. I haven't heard from him for many years, but . . ."

His informant, seeming embarrassed, muttered something about how those places, Red Temples, of course had a reputation for wild behavior among their customers, but still . . . anyway, the execution was going to take place in a very few days. There would just about be time for Talgai to get there before it happened.

His old friends and his several new acquaintances were all looking at the woodcutter awkwardly, and some of them at least offered condolences.

Talgai was still holding the marvelous Sword, and now he gazed at it with a peculiarly mournful expression.

The innkeeper offered: "Maybe, were it not for the lucky Sword, you wouldn't have known . . . I suppose that's good luck in a way."

Within a few minutes of having received the grim news, Talgai was moving briskly along the trail to home. Clucking to his loadbeast, he tapped its rump with a stick to make it hurry. The beast looked back at him once, in dignified and silent protest, then stepped up its pace just slightly.

Walking the trail with a good stride, Talgai brooded sadly about his brother's wasted life, and the all-too-credible news that he had just received. He would have to make good time if he was going to reach the town where his brother was imprisoned before it was too late to see him alive. But before starting on such a journey, of course, Talgai would have to go home and at least tell his wife and children what he was doing.

Some of the cash the woodcutter had obtained for the rare wood would go with him in his journey, for he knew that in large towns cash had a way of being essential. But he would leave half the money with his wife, to make life a little easier for her should Talgai be somehow delayed in his return.

Talgai had taken the tale of Coinspinner's powers with at least a grain of salt; he knew it was wise to take that attitude with travelers' tales in general, and especially with regard to tales of magical achievement. Still, considering what had happened to him, Talgai, since finding the Sword, he had to believe that it was bringing him good luck. Yes, even in the case of the bad news. If his brother was now going to die, it would be good to have at least a chance to see him first.

Talgai had already decided, without having to give the matter much thought, that he must take the Sword with him on his journey to town. What little Talgai had ever seen of prisons inclined him to fear that it might be difficult for him to see his brother even when he reached the prison. To do so he would probably have to deal with officials who were likely to want money—officials anywhere always seemed to do that—and even when given money they were likely to be difficult to deal with.

Yes, Talgai was going to need all the luck that this strange tool called Coinspinner could bring him. And as for his brother . . . well, luck probably had little to do with the predicament in which Buvrai found himself, though that scapegrace would doubtless blame everything on his bad fortune, as usual.

Coinspinner. Talgai muttered the name to himself over and over again, trying it out. He certainly couldn't say that he liked the sound of it, however lucky the Sword might be. A name like that certainly suggested gambling, and in gambling lay ruin for rich and poor alike.

An hour later, Talgai the Woodcutter had reached home, had conveyed the good news and the bad news to his wife as well as he was able, and was already saying farewell to his worried family and getting ready to start out again.

He might have chosen to travel to Smim by boat—that would have been easier than walking, and a little quicker—except that his wife might well have need of the boat while he was gone, and it was hard to say how long that was going to be.

The wizard Trimbak Rao in his studio had learned of the attempt to ensnare Adrian very shortly after it took place. Naturally the Teacher controlled powers of his own that were connected with the City. And these entities had been on the scene, in the Emperor's old park by the Red Temple, almost at once—Trimbak Rao never allowed his apprentices to enter the City entirely unwatched and unprotected.

Within an hour after the eruption of Adrian's elemental and its violent clash with the powers subservient to Wood, Trimbak Rao was on the scene himself—he had private means of getting there, much faster than any hiking apprentice. In fact, he had within his compound what amounted to a secret entrance to the City, though as part of his students' training he preferred to let them seek out their own.

As befitted his status as teacher, Trimbak Rao was suitably elderly in apperance, and in his demeanor there was often an air of mystery. Just now this air had been replaced by frantic eagerness. On his arrival in the park adjoining the Twisted Temple, the magician winced at what he saw, and stood for a moment with his eyes closed, looking like nothing more or less than a tired old man.

The land in the immediate vicinity of the park had been thoroughly devastated, though the Temple and many of the other nearby buildings remained essentially undamaged. Not so the dam, which Trimbak Rao remembered well. It no longer existed now. Much altered was the river's channel in the immediate area, particularly going downstream from this site, where a number of buildings had in fact toppled. Raw heaps of shattered rock, intermingled with soils of different colors, now covered most of the area that had been a park, and his precious square of paving tiles had been quite buried. An earth-elemental, and quite a strong one, had erupted here, no doubt of that. What else might have happened was going to take longer to determine.

Nodding to himself, the Teacher looked around. One thing at least was sure; the mighty adversary, Wood, had evidently determined not to come to the City himself just now. Or, if he had come, he was already gone again. Trimbak Rao, with a faint shudder of relief, relaxed his posture of defense, and dismissed certain powers he had brought with him. He had come ready, as ready as he could be, to fight for his apprentices, though knowing full well that such a direct encounter against Wood himself could hardly have been other than suicidal.

Exercising some more subtle powers of his own, Trimbak Rao soon managed to locate several items of great interest, including some of his apprentices' discarded clothing, packs, and weapons.

While he stood with an abandoned pack in his hands, considering, there came a minor landslide in one of the tall piles of raw earth nearby, and a sympathetic quivering of the ground beneath. One of the new mudholes was beginning to fill in. The fabric of the City was already starting to restore itself after the violent disruptions.

The Teacher persisted in his efforts to find Adrian and Trilby, but at first he was unable to find a trace of either one.

In the middle of a certain incantation, the wizard came to a pause. An idea had just struck him. Where, he thought to himself, is the canoe? He remembered full well that that vessel had been here on his last visit to the park. Well, it was hardly strange that it should be gone now, with the entire course of the river blasted. Whether it had gone with either of his apprentices was more than he could tell, but at least he could have hopes.

Two flying messengers had accompanied him from his studio, and now he dispatched them both to Tasavalta, by separate routes. It was his bitter but necessary duty to let Princess Kristin know that some kind of disaster had befallen, and the heir to the throne was missing.

With all the speed that could be managed, still more than a full day had passed before high-ranking aides of the Princess had reached the studio of Trimbak Rao, but now the Teacher and these representatives were holding an urgent conversation.

The eminent magician and teacher of magic Trimbak Rao did his best to explain to them just what had happened to Prince Adrian.

Kristin's counselors now assured Trimbak Rao that of course the Tasavaltan hunt for both Woundhealer and Coinspinner was going to be pressed firmly. Though right now it looked as if both Swords might be gone permanently out of reach.

Adrian, as all who knew him had come to agree, had the potential to someday become a true magician-king, the like of which had not been seen for a long time.

For the sake of the realm, as well as for the youngster himself, it was necessary that this potential be properly developed.

Trimbak Rao was still optimistic that Adrian was safe and could be found—though perhaps not really as optimistic as he sounded.

Trilby's fate was just as uncertain. Trimbak Rao still nursed hopes that the girl would make her own way back to her Teacher's headquarters in one piece, bringing news of what had happened.

"Your powers are still searching for her in the City?"

"Of course. Even as they search for Prince Adrian."

"And where do you place the responsibility for what has happened, wizard?"

The Teacher bowed his head. "Much of it is my own. I do not seek to evade that fact. I believe there is no doubt that the hand of Wood was behind the attack."

No one disputed that. But no one assured the magician that he himself was free of fault.

He tried to answer accusations that had not been voiced. "Apprentices who have reached the level of the Prince and this girl regularly accomplish what I was asking them to do. I saw no reason to think they would be unable to do so!"

EIGHT

ADRIAN, standing ankle-deep in mud on the bank of an unknown river, felt certain that in the course of his downstream passage in the canoe he must have passed out of the plane of existence containing the City of Wizards. But he had no idea where he was, only that the magical aura, the feel of the world around him, was blessedly familiar. He was back in the world in which he had grown up.

Trimbak Rao had warned his students of a great many of the complications involved in the several routes leading into the City and out of it, and of the danger of their getting lost if they should deviate from the course he had planned for them to the small park and back. But, thought Adrian, the Teacher had utterly failed to warn them of anything like what had actually happened.

But then he had to admit it probably wasn't the Teacher's fault. Adrian, in his new state of shocked alertness, now understood clearly that he and Trilby on entering the City must have fallen under the spell of some extremely subtle and most powerful enchantment. Whatever that enchantment's source, it had caused them to put aside all normal caution, and to forget or disregard all but one of their Teacher's warnings, the minor and routine admonition not to be too much in haste. And they had allowed themselves to be distracted from their goal by trivialities until it was almost too late for Adrian to escape the forces gathering against them there.

He wondered now whether awareness had come entirely too late for Trilby—or whether it had never come to her at all.

The naked Princeling shivered, though both the air and the mud in which he stood were quite warm. He found no reassurance in trying to take stock of his situation. Not only had he lost his clothing, but his pack and canteen and hunting knife as well.

Probing the darkness around him as best he could, with a mind now free—as far as he could tell—of enemy influences, Adrian decided that he was safe for the moment.

Of course he and Trilby had thought themselves safe in the park beside the Red Temple, too.

Once the conflict had openly erupted there, events had moved so fast that Adrian had had no opportunity to be much frightened. But fear was overtaking him now.

"Trilby? Trilby!" he called, softly at first, then louder. But he received no answer. And he had no sense, either magical or mundane, of where the girl might be.

The little river, mysterious and nameless, into whose muddy bank his feet were slowly sinking, revealed no secrets as it went murmuring on toward its unknown destination.

At least there was no sign that the threatening forces the Prince had just escaped were going to pursue him here outside the City. No immediate threats were apparent, though the magical portents for the future here were ominous, now that he looked at them carefully. He decided that he had better not stay where he was if he could help it. Certainly the physical environment afforded by this river-bank was not attractive—besides the treacherous footing, he stood confronted by a wall of growth, a great part of it thorny, dense to the point of impenetrability. Nor did anything the boy could make out upon the river's opposite shore suggest to him that conditions would be more congenial there.

The night air here, wherever he was, was really surprisingly warm, and when he had splashed ashore the water had felt warmer than he remembered it in the City. The sky was clear and looked normal, and the time here, as near as Adrian could judge it by the visible stars and planets, was an hour or two before dawn.

But he had fled the vicinity of the twisted Red Temple on near midafternoon of a sunny day, so either he had been unconscious for many hours—his own subjective feelings argued against that—or some major transformation in space or time had taken place.

The Prince's mundane senses of smell and hearing, as well as his perceptions specially attuned to the airs of magic, indicated to him the presence of some large and very likely dangerous beasts in the nearby jungle, on both banks of the river. When he tried to pick out other sounds from the murmur of the river and the noise of insects, there were occasional low growls to be heard disturbingly near at hand, and feral snufflings deep in the brush. There was also a passing odor that reminded the boy of giant cats.

His repeated calls for Trilby had slowed and faltered to a stop, but now he tried her name again. The only result was some increase in the animal noises nearby.

Fortunately he wasn't condemned to stand here until dawn; he still had his boat. Looking upstream, in the direction from which he had come, he could see nothing useful with his eyes, and in the world of magic could perceive practically nothing but a glow, distant but powerful, that could only represent the City. If he were to try going in that direction, he would have to run the risk of reentering the place from which he had just managed to escape. An ordinary person might be in no danger at all of entering the City, no matter which direction he chose to go; but Adrian, magically attuned as he was, might not be able to keep himself from entering its plane of existence once he came to the border.

Even gazing steadily in that direction was difficult for him now. When he did so he found that his senses were still half-dazzled by the power of the deadly confining magic that he had only just managed to escape, and of the elemental that had saved his life. Though at some point it had ceased to follow him downstream, that elemental was not yet dead; he could see its ongoing struggle with other, malignant, powers still mounting like a fire on the horizon.

And if he, Adrian, did reenter the City of Wizards, the next exit he managed to find—assuming that he could stay alive long enough to find one—might well deposit him in some environment very much worse than this one.

His only remaining course of action was to take his boat on downstream.

Just on the verge of pushing off again in the canoe, Adrian paused. His ears had just brought him a new sound, a somewhat distant doglike howling. There was nothing intrinsically magical or very strange about the sound, but in the lonely darkness it was ominous. Adrian heard the howl again; it was getting closer.

A moment later, wading in the shallows, he had pushed off the canoe and swung himself into it, his weight balanced between the gunwales, as it glided out into the stream. Fortunately he'd had years of experience in handling small boats, including canoes. Tasavalta abounded in mountain streams and lakes, besides bordering on the sea.

Taking up the carved paddle again, the young Prince probed the darkness alertly with all his senses, trying to hold a downstream course as close as possible to the center of the stream.

And now that he was on the water again, this time with his mind clear—as far as he could tell—and all his senses functioning, he found something strangely attractive, soothing, about the river itself.

The stars of a moonless sky shimmered in the water beneath him. The canoe swiftly answered his least touch with the paddle; who did this craft belong to, anyway, and why had it been so conveniently available for him just when he needed it? He was still unable to detect anything in the way of any magical aura left about the boat by its previous usage or users. Well, that was not strictly true, perhaps; there were a few traces, the psychic analogues of smears and smudges, but nothing meaningful.

The question and its corollaries worried him. Had the boat's availability, just when he needed it, been sheer accident? Or had it been purposefully arranged? If there had been no boat to carry him away, how might he have fared?

The howling came again, the distance at which it originated impossible to gauge. Still the Prince thought it might be following him, though he could not be sure on which bank of the narrow river it had its source.

Now Adrian remembered a brief mention by Trimbak Rao of certain carnivorous apes that infested a forest growing along one of the City's edges. Those apes were known to be dangerous to humans, and were claimed by some to be fully as intelligent as messenger birds. In darkness and loneliness it was all too easy for the boy to imagine such a creature producing just such a howling sound.

Now, as he steered and propelled the canoe downstream, Adrian tried his best to achieve some mental or magical contact with Trimbak Rao. But that proved to be impossible. The magical glow of the City behind him still dominated the air and sky, partially dazzling his extra senses. Also, he was beginning to suspect that another kind of blockage had been imposed, as if by the same deadly enemy who had tried to trap him in the City.

Trying now to reconstruct the disaster that had almost overtaken him there, Adrian found that the cause of those events was still unclear. The one thing of which he could be absolutely sure was that the near disaster had been no accident. Some enemy of enormous power and subtle, murderous cunning had set out to kill or capture him— and Trilby, possibly. And in Trilby's case the attempt might have succeeded.

Fighting down a brief renewed attack of panic, Adrian concentrated again on his progress downstream. The current was now bearing him swiftly through the darkness, and his occasional strokes of the paddle, meant to steer, added speed. But now, even as he began to take comfort in his rapid progress, the river broadened and the current accordingly slowed somewhat.

Probing the night as well as he was able, staring into a vague gap in a black shoreline, he decided that the river here was joined by some tributary stream almost as large as itself.

The psychic glare of the City at last began to fade noticeably behind him. Now Adrian, after a day's journeying and the great exertions of trying to escape from the City's dangers, found himself physically exhausted. The snug little boat, drifting in almost complete silence, provided the illusion at least of shelter and safety. Here the night air, still and damp, felt warmer than ever.

Deciding that he had better rest while he had the opportunity, he tied up his canoe to a snag, a half-sunken log protruding above the surface near midstream. Sleepily he murmured a minor spell he had found useful against marauding insects, and another intended to bring him wide awake at the approach of danger. Then he stretched himself out as comfortably as possible in the bottom of the boat and abandoned himself to slumber.

Stars and planets turned above his inert form, and gradually the sky in the east began to lighten. Once again before dawn the sound of howling came, still faint with distance, but possibly somewhat closer than before. The exhausted sleeper did not stir.

Full dawn with its bright light came at last, and with the light Adrian moved in the bottom of the boat. A moment later he sat up quickly, blinking at the day. *Now,* he thought, *at least I know which way is east.*

The morning sky, partly cloudy, looked reassuringly normal. The river here flowed chocolate brown in daylight, and was not quite as wide as he had judged it to be in darkness. The dark green jungle, shrouding each bank beyond a narrow strip of mud, still looked well-nigh impenetrable even in full daylight. Now, in the upstream direction, the extrasensory glow of the City was superimposed upon the sun in Adrian's perception. To him that glow still formed a threatening pulse of danger, tending to dominate both land and sky.

He scooped up river water in his hands and recited a short testing spell, while watching the tiny, soft mud particles beginning to settle out. There was no reaction to the spell, indicating that the water was safe to swallow.

After drinking of the river deeply—and returning to it in exchange some water of his own—Adrian untied his craft and resumed his downstream progress. He used the paddle as before, keeping the canoe away from either shore.

He was hungry now, and providing himself food by magic alone would be an undertaking somewhat more difficult and complicated than merely testing the water. He decided to try to feed himself by mundane methods alone, if that proved possible. If, without a knife, he could somehow sharpen a wooden spear, he could try some spearfishing. Or he might put a hand in the water and try magicking a fish to come within his reach.

Before he could quite decide on either effort, some recognizable wild fruit trees appeared, and he put in to shore to gather breakfast. Hunger dulled for the time being, he pushed on.

As the sun rose higher, Adrian began to feel its full heat. Digging into his memory, and applying a little thought and effort, he managed after a couple of false starts to create a spell that tanned his pale skin immediately, in such a way as to preserve him from the worst effects of the solar fire.

Hours passed. The river wound on, kilometer after kilometer, with no change in itself or in its banks. This jungle country, damp and hot, was vastly different from anything to which the boy had been accustomed, either near his home or in the vicinity of the workshop of Trimbak Rao.

Shortly after resuming his journey, Adrian thought that he heard last night's howling once again. Whether the source was closer or more distant now was hard to say.

Except for the occasional sites where fruit trees grew, he had yet to discover any place on either shore that tempted him to land. Some of the dangers were obvious, taking the shape of thorn trees and wasps' nests. Other perils were not so obvious, but Adrian had noted them. Here and there along both banks he observed the spoor of large animals, and in one tall tree he spotted a nest or crude sleeping platform such as he had heard was sometimes made by the carnivorous apes.

Still keeping the canoe near midstream most of the time, Adrian drifted, paddling as necessary. Once more he landed to pick some fruit.

About an hour after that, he came to a small island that appeared to be a safe place, supporting a few trees tall enough to cast some shade upon the water. There, Adrian tied up. With his craft all but completely concealed by the bulk of the island on one side and some overhanging branches on the other, Adrian sat cross-legged for a while in the bottom of the boat, eyes closed, first meditating to calm his mind and then trying to see into the psychic distance.

The heat of the day increased, but as he sat motionless, engaged in mental activity, he was hardly aware of it. In less than an hour he came back to himself with a start, finding his body drenched in sweat. He slipped out of the boat into the water, which was now considerably cooler than the air.

Now, even floating in the cooling water, it was impossible to relax. His vision had made Adrian more frightened than he had been since making his escape from the City.

His psychic probing had shown him that the Sword Coinspinner had somehow been used against him at the Red Temple by his enemy, to augment by good luck the power of the spells employed. No wonder he had almost been trapped and crushed, despite his own struggles and his mentor's precautions! It would be no surprise if Trilby had been caught. The real wonder was that he, Adrian, had somehow managed to escape.

After a brief active swim, during which he was careful never to get more than a few meters from the boat, he climbed back into the canoe again and sat on the middle seat, not meditating now but simply trying to think. He was determined not to panic, despite the forces he had glimpsed arrayed against him. On his side, he had his own considerable powers. He had strong friends, who would be trying to help him. And he had time now in which to think.

On Adrian's emergence from the water, the air at first felt cool around his body, but as his skin dried it warmed again.

. . . and with the heat, fear came back with a rush, like a worried friend.

It was time now to think about Coinspinner.

Meditation and psychic probing were all very well, sometimes extremely valuable. But intelligent, reasoning thought was still more important.

The Prince in his period of silent concentration had been able to determine, at least in a very rough way, the location of the Sword of Chance—at the moment it was somewhere vaguely ahead of him, in the general direction of flow of this still-nameless river. And this discovery Adrian found puzzling.

In fact, he had just perceived several things that puzzled him; one of them was that the person who now possessed the Sword seemed to have no magic of his or her own. This person was therefore almost certainly not the mighty magician who had so powerfully attacked him.

Adrian's education, intended to fit him to rule a nation someday, had included much information about the nature and history of the Swords. He was well aware that Coinspinner had the tendency to move itself about, and that it might well have taken itself away from his enemy soon after he or she had used it.

However his enemy had lost the Sword, that deprivation had not come a moment too soon for Adrian's survival.

Now the boy pondered intently for a short time, wondering if a really powerful and learned wizard in his position would be able to make the Sword come to him, by the power of his own magic; certainly such a feat would be very difficult for anyone, if not totally impossible.

Once again sitting in a semitrance, the boy tried to send his mind, his presence, to the proper place, the present location of the Sword.

It was a daring move, and he was not entirely sure that it was the proper one to make, but he attempted it nevertheless.

In any case, the effort failed.

At the moment it seemed that neither logical thought nor psychic probing was going to get him any further. The young Prince untied his boat and let it drift downstream again. From time to time he used the paddle, mechanically, to keep the craft from drifting too near either of the shores.

The howling that had engaged his attention still persisted at irregular intervals. The Prince was growing more inclined to classify it as one of the ordinary background noises of the jungle, even though it still seemed, when he took careful note of it, to be coming closer.

As the boat drifted, he repeated his efforts to establish by means of magic some contact with his parents, or, failing that, with some of his friends and other allies or potential allies—Trimbak Rao and Trilby were of course included in these attempts. But to Adrian's disgust he discovered that, for the time being at least, he still could not even sense the direction in which any of these important people might be found.

Whenever he looked behind him, upstream, the gradually receding City still burned in its unceasing glow of complex enchantment. To a vision as sharp as Adrian's the City continued to cast its garish radiance across the sky, dazzling and dimming the capabilities of his special senses.

Still, keeping track of the location of the Sword of Chance, now moving somewhere ahead of him, was no trouble at all. Once he had found it, like a fiery brand Coinspinner had seared its image and its presence into his perception. The only difficulty Adrian experienced was to keep the brightness of that Sword from interfering with other psychic perceptions. Yes, he felt absolutely sure that Coinspinner was there ahead of him somewhere, a good many kilometers distant but not moving very quickly; and if it stayed approximately where it was now, and if the river maintained its present direction, he was sure to be carried closer to the Sword.

And Coinspinner was being borne now in innocent hands. Perhaps, he thought again, that would increase his chances of being able to get his own hands on it.

Perhaps. Well, he would try. At the moment he could establish no other reasonable goal. He was traveling in a generally westerly direction—but where was he going? He could not even guess intelligently which way he ought to go to get home.

As the day wore on, and Adrian's slow progress downstream continued, some truly giant trees came into his sight on the northern bank of the river. These towered scores of meters above the ground, standing much taller than the highest buildings of the City.

Catching his first glimpse of this soaring grove, the boy at first interpreted it as a high hill, set back somewhat from the bank. Only on coming closer had he realized that the appearance of a steep hill was produced by the grove of trees, much taller than the other species of the forest, but growing on approximately the same level of ground.

Adrian had heard of such trees, but had never seen them before. Their appearance now suggested to him that he might be entering the country of the wood-dwelling and wood-crafting Treen people, who lived in close relationship with those giant trees.

Tying up his boat for the night at a snag near midstream,

and making another psychic effort, Adrian began for the first time to get a better look at the distant presence of his chief enemy. It was Wood, undoubtedly; and he was awesomely stronger than even Adrian had expected.

It was impossible for the Prince to tell exactly where Wood was; but at least Adrian could confirm that it was not his enemy who now held the Sword of Chance.

As a well-informed heir, the Prince knew perfectly well that this deadly dangerous man could be expected to be carrying Shieldbreaker.

In light of the fact that Wood was somewhere else, the Sword of Chance now began to appear to Adrian with ever-increasing probability as an objective that he might be able to reach and take.

There was of course the chance that Coinspinner would have moved itself again, to some considerable distance, before he was able to come up with it. Whether the Sword was going to remain in the hands of its present owner for another hour, another day, another year, or many years, was beyond the power of anyone to predict, by magic or other means. Well, he could only try.

Tying up for the night at a small island, Adrian managed some magic on a sizable fish, hypnotizing and lulling his prey into the shallows until he was able to hurl it out of the water with a fierce grab. Then, after painstakingly gathering some firewood, and a successful effort at pyrokinesis, he cooked his catch whole and attacked it with a sharp stick and his teeth. By now his hunger had reached the point where the results actually tasted good.

The night passed for Adrian without incident, and his solitary journey downriver continued in the same way for most of the succeeding day. No more of the gigantic trees appeared. The unbroken walls of jungle had followed the river for so long that he had almost begun to wonder whether they were the result of some enchantment—when unexpectedly there came a change.

The first sign of human presence occurred late in the

afternoon of that second day. It came in the form of a long-deceased and almost-fleshless head, dried by means of smoke or magic, and erected on a pole stuck in the mudbank just above the high-water mark. The thing was hardly more than a painted human skull, equipped with eyes of clay and shell.

If this sign was meant as a warning to intruders, one traveler at least was ready to take it to heart. Adrian put in to the opposite shore at once, and did what mental scouting he could manage of the terrain and the river just ahead. This time his extra faculties availed him little; but when he sniffed repeatedly and carefully he could detect a faint tang of woodsmoke in the damp air.

Pulling his canoe well up on the shore, he did his best to conceal the craft with some loose brush and some minor magic. Then he settled down to wait for dusk.

As soon as daylight had dimmed enough to offer good concealment, he put out and drifted once again. The small village, consisting of only a few huts, was just around the next bend.

Adrian, warned and with time to make preparations, was able to steer silently to the far side of the stream, and to use magic to keep himself from being noticed. True total invisibility would be very difficult to achieve, but in the circumstances it was not hard to make people think for a few moments that his canoe was only a drifting log.

As he passed the village, some six or eight of its inhabitants were visible around a central fire. The men and women, light bronze of skin, with straight brown hair, were wearing only loincloths, while their children ran among them naked. These head-collectors were a wiry, active, and handsome people. Adrian and his canoe went drifting by in utter silence; even had he employed no magic, it was quite likely that no one on shore would have been able to see him in the gathering night.

He was not mistaken in thinking that these were the people who had put up the warning. More prepared heads were on display within the village, mounted over doorways and on decorated poles. These effectively discouraged any faint hopes the passing traveler might have entertained of being able to land here after all.

Having thus begun traveling by night, the Prince decided that it had definite advantages. Besides, he wished to put as much distance as was feasible between himself and the skull-collectors' village. Darkness diminished physical vision, but had no effect upon Adrian's magical perceptions. He continued drifting and paddling until almost dawn, by which time he judged he might be safely out of the territory of the people who put up shriveled heads.

Hungrily prowling the deserted banks of the river for food at dawn, he found some turtle eggs and cracked and ate them raw. At this time he decided also that in future he would build fires only by day, and that he would do his best to keep them from smoking.

Having disposed of the eggs, the Prince recognized a couple of species of plants, and, using another stick, dug up an edible root or two. These, brought along in the boat, would keep him going for some time if he could also make an occasional find of fruit.

Starvation could be kept at bay indefinitely by such makeshift means as these, but still Adrian's craving was growing steadily for something like a normal diet. He considered trying to magic some food for himself out of whatever raw material he could find available, but again he decided that for the time being he had better conserve his energies for possible emergencies.

Gradually the recurrent howling had grown closer, and it was now near enought to become worrisome again; it sounded, after all, as if something were genuinely following him. But at the same time the sound had now been with him long enough to become familiar, and thus in a way it was no longer so alarming.

On the second day after passing the village, paddling at dawn, the Prince began to hear a roaring noise ahead.

Rapidly the volume of the sound increased. Its source could not be far distant.

Cautiously he paddled around a bend, staying near the right bank. Just ahead the river plunged into a waterfall, its steady thunder giving rise to a fine watery smoke. Adrian wasted no time in getting himself and his boat out of the water.

NINE

GENERAL Rostov and the wizard Karel, unable to decide on any entirely satisfactory way to immediately dispose of the high-ranking prisoner they had acquired in the high mountain pass, had decided to bring Crown Prince Murat with them, tied into his saddle, when they set out to follow the trail of the Culmian traitor Kebbi.

Rostov was not minded to explain any of his decisions to the treacherous thief he was compelled to drag along. But Karel, conversing with the Crown Prince at a rest stop, informed his royal captive that there had simply been no men to spare to escort the prisoner back to Sarykam. Most of the three cavalry squadrons were in hot pursuit of the Culmians who were fleeing toward their homeland with Woundhealer; only half a dozen troopers had come with the two Tasavaltan leaders on Coinspinner's track.

Their pursuit of Kebbi and the Sword of Chance had certainly begun without delay, and the pursuers kept up a brisk pace. Or rather they tried their best to do so. Hardly had the site of Murat's capture been left behind them when the first of many avalanches came down just ahead, wiping out a substantial section of the trail.

The fading thunders of this landslide could not quite drown out the voice of Rostov, as he profaned the names of many gods; when the tumult had subsided and the dust was beginning to settle, Karel, puffing, pointed out to the General with some satisfaction that this fresh obstacle represented a confirmation of his own magical divinations, a sign that they were certainly on the trail of Coinspinner.

Rostov's reply was not congratulatory.

Before the little party had worked its way around the slope rendered impassable by the first avalanche, another avalanche could be heard from the direction in which they were trying to advance. And, when that one too had been bypassed, yet another. Still they were able to make progress; both Tasavaltan leaders, and one or two of the cavalrymen among their escort, knew these mountains extremely well. And Coinspinner, perhaps, was not vitally concerned about them yet; they were still too distant from its current owner to pose him any serious threat. If and when they managed to close the gap substantially, doubtless the measures taken against them would be stronger.

Still, there was no thought of abandoning the pursuit that had just begun. Nor was it necessary, in the opinion of their most knowledgeable scout, to follow their quarry's trail very closely.

"I'll tell you how it is, sir," this trooper explained to Rostov. "A stranger here, looking to get out of the mountains in this direction, is pretty much going to have to go one way, the way we're going now. And whether he takes this branch of the trail here, or that one up there that looks like a different trail but really isn't, he's pretty certain to come out in the same place in the end. And I know where that place is. A sort of crossroads. A kind of inn stands there, or did a few years back, though it's not a place where I'd especially want to spend the night."

The General nodded grimly. "Then lead on, get us to that crossroads as best you can. Better that than try to track him along these mountainsides, with a Sword trying to bury us at every step."

Now progress became faster. Still the newly chosen route was longer, and it was necessary for the party to spend one night in a cold mountain camp before they reached the inn.

Karel did his best to defend their camp with spells before he went to sleep, and all through the night a guard was posted.

Murat, still tied by the hands and by one foot, was allowed to dismount and sleep under blankets.

In the morning, progress continued to be rapid. Rostov was now carrying Sightblinder packed away behind his saddle, where it was in easy reach should he decide to call upon its powers. Before many hours of daylight had passed the small party reached the inn, and a shabby place it was.

A few men, including one who must have been the innkeeper, emerged from its dingy doorway to squint at the visitors. In silence, and with an initial lack of enthusiasm, they studied the arriving party, which consisted of nine riders, most of them Tasavaltan troopers in blue and green, and included one prisoner in orange and blue, who was bound to his saddle and stirrups.

Under Rostov's determined glare the proprietor of the inn soon began to smile, and put on an air of hospitality. "Beg your pardon, sir, but I see you have a prisoner."

"And what of it?"

"Nothing, sir, nothing at all. Except that I know the whereabouts of one other man who wears a livery of orange and blue, the same as his."

Having received the promise of some kind of a reward if he cooperated, and the threat of a very different kind of treatment if he did not, the innkeeper hastened to lead his visitors to a shed, even more ramshackle than the main building and located somewhat behind it.

A riding-beast that looked too healthy and strong to be the property of any of these locals was revealed inside the shed when the door was opened.

"One of your cavalry mounts?" asked Rostov, turning to his prisoner.

"Unbind me," said Murat, "and I will try to make the identification for you."

The General glanced at the wizard, who nodded, almost absently. Then Rostov nodded too, and in a moment a

trooper had ridden up beside the Crown Prince and started
to loose his hands.

In another moment Murat was able to dismount freely.
Limping with cramped legs from his long confinement in
the saddle, he crossed the yard and entered the shed, where
he could study the riding-beast at close range.

"Yes, this is the mount Kebbi was riding when he left
us."

In another moment, when the door to the next room was
opened, the former lieutenant himself was discovered,
immured in a dark and cell-like hole. Kebbi looked up
from where he was lying on a broken cot. He was in his
undergarments, and for warmth he clutched around his
shoulders a coarse rag that looked as if it might have been
discarded somewhere around a stable. At the sight of
Murat, his face went through a whole series of expressions,
all quickly suppressed except the last, a look of bright
curiosity.

"Where is it, villain?" Murat demanded without pream-
ble.

Kebbi stood up. "Where is what, traitor?"

"You dare to call me that!" A Tasavaltan trooper restrained the Crown Prince from stepping forward to strike
his enemy with his fist.

Kebbi spread his hands in a gesture of innocence as he
looked around at the others. "I appeal to you, gentlemen.
Do I look to you like someone who has the Sword of Luck
in his possession?"

"Frankly, you do not," said Karel, frowning.

At this point the proprietor of the inn cleared his throat.
"Are you interested in my bondslave, here, gentlemen?" he
inquired of the Tasavaltan leaders, in what was meant to be
an ingratiating voice. "I can let you have him cheap."

Rostov shot one glance at the would-be salesman, who
immediately fell silent.

Murat noticed that one of the hangers-on was already
wearing Culmian boots that very likely had been Kebbi's.

"I suppose you tried to steal something here, too?" he demanded of his cousin. "And they repaid you in kind?"

Kebbi ignored the question. He was undertaking what sounded like an earnest and sincere explanation. "General Rostov, is it not? Sir, I wish that I could hand you the Sword that our people so treacherously stole from your Princess. But alas, I cannot, though that was my intention. I would not lightly disobey the orders of my superior officer." Here he glanced at Murat. "But what he did in Sarykam was unforgivable, and would not, I am sure, have been countenanced by our Queen. Traitor is, I think, not too strong a word."

Before Kebbi had finished, Murat was almost beside himself. Experienced diplomat that he was, he found himself for once speechless with rage and indignation.

Kebbi, with an air of confident innocence, was going on to explain that he had been trying to persuade these local people to send a messenger to Tasavalta, whose leaders would assuredly be glad to ransom him.

Rostov broke in bluntly. "I don't believe you. What has happened to Coinspinner?"

"Sir, General Rostov, I was trying to bring it back to you! But now it is gone, and through no connivance of mine. These men who have been detaining me can at least assure you of that."

The General rounded on the innkeeper. "Well?"

Briefly, as Murat listened in disbelief, the events of the dice game came out.

Kebbi put forward a story that Murat had to admit sounded almost plausible. The Culmian renegade claimed simply that he had been on his way to restore the Sword of Chance to Princess Kristin, and had thought to profit enough in a small wager to provide himself with coin for the journey.

"You bet the Sword itself? To win a few coins?"

"No, sir. In that case I stood to win a huge and dazzling jewel. Ask these men here, they'll tell you. A jewel, let me hasten to assure you, I would have given to Her Majesty Princess Kristin, as compensation for—"

"Never mind the jewel for now. You threw dice, while holding the Sword of Chance—and you lost?" This time it was Karel who asked the question.

"It happened that way, sir. I can't explain it, but it did. Ask these men."

The locals, even under threat, only confirmed the Culmian traitor's tale.

"And who was this man who won Coinspinner away from you?" Again it was Karel who asked, though by now he, and Rostov at least among the Tasavaltans, had come to realize who the successful gambler must have been.

"I have no idea, sir," said Kebbi helplessly.

The General and the wizard exchanged glances.

"And I repeat, sir, that I had no notion of any plot to steal the Sword if we were denied in our appeal to borrow it. I was shocked and horrified when I realized that my commanding officer contemplated such a theft, and at the first opportunity I did what I could to make amends. I could not get my hands on Woundhealer, but I thought that the Sword of Chance might provide the Princess decent compensation."

Murat saw with satisfaction that none of the Tasavaltans appeared inclined to accept the claim. As for himself, he began to denounce it violently.

"Shut up," Rostov told him.

Murat and his cousin glared at each other in silence.

The General, fists on his hips, faced the renegade lieutenant. "I ask you once again. *Where is Coinspinner?*"

"That stranger has it, sir. I repeat, I have told you the simple truth. I thought I would need money for my journey, to pay my bill here if nothing else, and to buy food. And so I gambled—and lost. These—gentlemen here can confirm my story."

Rostov kept hammering away. "You gambled with *that* Sword in hand, and lost it?"

"I say again, that is the truth."

The General nodded slowly. Suddenly, more than a little to Murat's amazement, the Tasavaltan leaders appeared ready to concede that the story might be true.

"Tell us more about this tall stranger and his companion. Tell us every detail you can remember."

The descriptions given by Kebbi and by the locals agreed in all essentials.

"How was he armed?" pressed Karel in his soft voice.

Kebbi blinked. "Why—with a sword. Not that he even had to draw it." Realization began to dawn on him. "I don't know if it was one of the Twelve—I don't know that much about the others. The hilt at least looked like Coinspinner's or Woundhealer's."

Karel nodded to his compeer. "Shieldbreaker—and that means Wood was here. And that he has Coinspinner now."

"And the woman with him," Rostov muttered. "She'll have been that hellcat Tigris."

Kebbi, speaking up boldly, did his best to find out whether the Tasavaltans had managed to retake Wound-healer. He soon heard enough to convince him that they had not.

"Where shall we begin to look for it, sir?"

"What do you mean 'we'?"

Kebbi at first pretended to be quietly crushed at the suggestion that he was going to be taken away by the Tasavaltans in the status of a prisoner, like Murat.

Murat, since he had been unbound, had been silently considering what his chances might be of escape, and had concluded that for the time being they were not worth considering.

Argument between the two Culmians, flaring up again, was interrupted by the arrival of a winged messenger, its wings spanning about the reach of a man's arms. This creature arrived in the sky above the arguing men, uttered cries of greeting, and came spiraling right down, to perch upon the neck of Rostov's riding-beast.

With quick but steady fingers the General untied the small white packet from the bird's leg, and ripped the enclosure open. The wizard looked over Rostov's shoulder as he read, and Murat watching carefully could see both men's faces cloud. Then they raised their eyes together to look at him, in a way that gave no comfort.

"What is it?" he demanded.

"Prince Adrian," the wizard responded slowly. "An attempt had been made to kidnap the young Prince or kill him. They don't know yet in Sarykam if he has survived or not."

Kebbi, very quiet now, was watching and listening, calculating as best he could.

In his mind's eye Murat saw again the lovely Princess; in his imagination he felt the grief and shock that would be hers. "Villainous," he muttered.

"Is that what you think, then?" The General's tone was sharp.

"Of course. An attack upon a child . . ." His voice trailed off as he saw the suspicion in his captors' eyes. "You can't think that *I*—"

"Or that I, either—" Kebbi burst in.

"We have been given some understanding of your honor. Both of you." Old Karel glared at them for a moment. Then his head moved in a brisk nod, telling the cavalry escort to get ready to move on.

Murat for a moment hung his head in shame, feeling the justice of that last rebuke. But only for a moment. Then he began to ask urgent questions, wanting to know more details of the attempt on Adrian.

The Tasavaltan leaders ignored him, though they did not try to prevent his hearing the few details that were known, when they passed this information on to the concerned soldiers.

In the leaders' minds, trying to go to the aid of the Prince was of course going to take precedence even over trying to recover Coinspinner—that would be pretty much a lost cause anyway, if Wood still had it.

Rostov told his sergeant to make sure that the men were ready to ride. There was some suspicion, exchanged in whispers between Karel and Rostov, that the theft of Coinspinner and the assault on Adrian were somehow connected.

"We have no evidence of that as yet. Rostov, my friend, if we are to try to help Prince Adrian we must go into the City of Wizards to look for him."

"If you can get us there, my men and I are ready."

Karel informed the General that he knew a way to reach the City fairly quickly from this place—or, indeed, from almost anyplace.

"What of these two Culmian birds? I want to bring them back to Sarykam alive, eventually, if that's at all possible. But I don't want to spare the men to escort them back there now. Not if the Prince is—"

"Then I think we must bring them with us, General. Physical bonds will no longer be necessary," said the wizard. Karel waited until Kebbi's boots had been retrieved for him, and some suitable outer clothing provided. Then, when the two Culmians were already in the saddle, he proceeded, with gestures and swift words, to treat each of them to his own satisfaction. The process was completed in the space of a few breaths.

Murat felt nothing from the wizard's work. Meeting Kebbi's cold glare with his own, he wondered whether they were now really bound at all. Well, he'd test that later.

Karel and Rostov, with their two half-willing prisoners, and the determined help of their six soldiers, set out to do their best at finding Adrian.

TEN

THE range of mountains in which the magician Wood had chosen to establish his headquarters arose near the center of a remote wasteland, many kilometers from any permanent human habitation. Wood's fortress, constructed more by means of magic than by physical labor, was indeed forbidding.

There were moments in Wood's life in which he felt the urge to surround himself with luxury, to taste some of the softer enjoyments that he was still capable of sharing with the great mass of mankind. For this reason the gardens, and some of the interior rooms, had come into existence. But today the great wizard was much too busy to pause for such pleasures. Attended by demons, familiars, and other nonmaterial powers, he and a very few close human associates were industriously practicing their black arts.

The main thrust of today's magical effort was the continued gathering of intelligence. And so far the results had not been pleasing. Prince Adrian, the spawn of Wood's old enemy Prince Mark, had so far succeeded in completely eluding the trapping spells and powers with which Wood had sought to bind him and crush him inside the City of Wizards.

There had been several reasons, all of them seeming quite valid at the time, why Wood had chosen not to visit the site of the failure personally. For one thing, the powers that had brought him word of the failure had also assured him that Adrian was no longer in the City.

Not only had the whelp escaped, but in fact the best evidence seemed to indicate that he was still alive and free. Moreover, the elemental he had raised to break him out of the trap had, in the process, destroyed one or two of Wood's more valuable nonhuman allies.

On receipt of this disconcerting news, Wood had promptly dispatched several demons that he considered relatively trustworthy, along with certain other powers, in an attempt to locate the missing Prince. Through these and other sources he had received conflicting indications as to Adrian's probable location. But when the most likely of these several locations were checked out, the boy could be found at none of them.

The chief difficulty in pressing the search successfully was that a fugitive from the City might easily re-enter the mundane world in almost any portion of a large continent.

There was a further complication. Another victim, this one a female apprentice of Trimbak Rao, had almost been ensnared within the trap. But somehow she too was still at large.

Not that the girl Trilby had any particular importance in herself. But the wizard considered that it would be interesting as well as amusing to examine her, and gather clues as to the strength of her mentor, Trimbak Rao, who someday was almost certainly going to confront Wood in open combat.

But Trilby was only an interesting detail. Wood's attention continued to be obstinately centered on Prince Adrian. The wizard was forced to admit that he himself had underestimated the youth's own abilities, which were truly incredible for one so young and necessarily so inexperienced. Well, in retrospect Wood could see that he ought to have expected something of the kind from one whose mother's family had produced the wizard Karel and a number of other adepts. And whose father's father was the Emperor.

About five years ago Wood had lost a valued human assistant, under somewhat mysterious circumstances, in the course of an abortive attempt to kidnap this same child. That episode was suddenly becoming somewhat easier to understand.

Evidently the precocious whelp had formidable defenders and allies as well as strong powers of his own. That there had been resistance really came as no surprise; but still, that Wood's best trapping spells, their effectiveness augmented by the power of Coinspinner, should have failed to snare this child was astounding.

Or else—

There was one point, however unlikely it might seem, that had to be considered. Was it remotely possible that the whelp's escape would ultimately rebound to Wood's advantage? Was it conceivable that the Sword of Chance, during the period when it was conscripted in Wood's cause, had calculated his advantage more accurately than he could do himself, and manipulated events accordingly?

Wood found that subtlety hard to believe, but he could not say that it was impossible.

An alternative explanation—and this was now beginning to seem to Wood the most probable one—was that the Sword of Chance had removed itself from his possession just as his entrapment spells were reaching the most critical point in their development.

Standing now in full daylight in his walled garden, among the variously grotesque statues, he muttered to himself: "It might have happened that way, yes. But even so, the whelp must be protected by some substantial powers of his own—or someone else's. Well, we'll see. In any case he's certainly not in the City now. And sooner or later I'll find him, and I'll have him."

It was at this point that Tigris joined her master in the garden. Today she was once more garbed in businesslike clothing, and like the other inhabitants of the stronghold she had been working hard.

"Which of our problems do you intend to confront next, my lord? And is this escaping boy truly of such great importance?"

"He is of importance, or will be, as a means of getting at his father. And at his grandfather too, I expect . . . in addition, I am growing very curious to find out just how his escape was managed. What kind of help he may have had. No, we are certainly not going to give up on him."

Here Wood turned to decisive action. Summoning another aide, he ordered the sending out of some twenty leather-winged messengers, carrying messages to certain allies of his in a number of places across the continent. The recipient of each message was near one of Adrian's possible exits from the City, and Wood's auxiliaries were bidden to seek hard for the young Prince and catch him if they could.

Then Wood and Tigris held a discussion on their best method of trying to recapture Coinspinner—and what they knew about who had it now. It was not yet possible to see this clearly; Wood thought the difficulty might be a corollary of the Sword's having recently moved itself away from him.

At about the same time that Wood and Tigris were holding their conversation in the statue garden, Karel and Rostov, along with their escort, their self-proclaimed ally Kebbi, and their original prisoner Murat, having left the vicinity of the mountain inn, were well along on their way into the City. Karel was leading them along a strange and illogical-seeming path, along which, as he commented several times, no other wizard, not even Trimbak Rao, would have been capable of guiding them.

"What about the famous Emperor?" Rostov prodded, just to see what kind of a reaction he might get. "Is he involved in this?"

Karel only grunted.

Both of the Culmian prisoners—though Kebbi claimed a higher status by right, he had not been able to achieve it—were still free from physical bondage. Entering the City, and moving about in it, would have been virtually impossible for them otherwise. But Kebbi and Murat found themselves quite effectively restricted by the brief treatment Karel had accorded them. Kebbi had said nothing about it. But Murat, whenever he turned his mount away from the wizard's, or turned his back on the old man while afoot, suddenly developed a strange leaden feeling in his soles and ankles. The sensation began to deepen into pain whenever he strayed more than a dozen paces or so from the leaders of the party. Very well, then, he was truly still bound. Later, he promised himself, he would experiment to see what the real limits were.

Rostov, his troopers, and the more-or-less willing Culmians, all under the guidance of the elderly wizard, had suddenly entered territory that was strange to them all except perhaps to Karel. Here they traversed several wildly divers kinds of landscape in rapid succession. Most members of the party found themselves seriously bewildered by sudden changes in weather, environment, and even alterations in the time of day.

The General grumbled whenever he felt like it. "Wizard, we're all convinced by now that our destination is somewhere exceedingly strange. What I want to know is, when do we arrive?"

Karel explained that they were entering the City by stages, and that although it might seem they were spending a great deal of time, even days, on the road, he planned that they should reach their goal on the same day they had left the inn.

And it was, in fact, by the best reckoning, that very same day when they arrived in the vicinity of the Twisted Temple.

"This is the place, then?" asked Rostov, staring at the peculiar streets, and the strange buildings, some of them near the little river tottering, looking about to fall. The sergeant and his five men had all, as if unconsciously, pulled their mounts somewhat closer to that of the old magician.

Murat had done the same. Meanwhile the Crown Prince of Culm had begun to wonder privately if, back in Culm, the traitor Kebbi was even now being mourned as one of the heroes who had managed to steal Woundhealer for the Royal Consort, giving up his own life in the process.

Something sly Kebbi had told him had suggested this possibility. "We are probably both being mourned there, cousin. You more strenuously than I, of course, as befitting your higher station."

Murat, though he had said nothing on the subject, was also wondering if, indeed, the Sword of Healing would ever get to Culm. By now he had been thoroughly convinced that the military and magical forces of Tasavalta were indeed capable; and the small Culmian force trying to get away no longer possessed any Sword of their own to give them an advantage.

The Crown Prince was even beginning to feel somehow responsible for the lovely Princess's missing son, though he told himself repeatedly that there was no logical reason for him to do so.

By now he thought, or at least hoped, that he had pretty well convinced Rostov and Karel of his innocence in that regard. Indeed, he had eagerly and repeatedly volunteered to assist them in the search for the Prince, if only they would let him.

Kebbi, on hearing this, to keep up appearances at least, had hastened to volunteer also.

Murat wished very strongly that he could do something to make amends to Kristin.

ELEVEN

HAVING driven his canoe solidly into shore, on the right bank of the river at a safe distance above the falls, Adrian tied up the craft and stowed the paddle. Then he made his way forward cautiously along the muddy bank, until he had come close enough to the falls to get a good look at the obstacle he now faced.

This was going to mark the end of his boating. Gazing down through a continuous mist of rising spray, the boy estimated that the drop was twenty meters in all. Not quite direct and straight, rather a complex of falls and rapids; but still more than deadly enough to eliminate any thought of riding or sending the canoe over it. But there might still be a chance—

Moving forward carefully along the bank, the Prince discovered that the rudiments of a path did make the descent beside the falls. Someone or something came up and down here with fair regularity. Patches of soil between the rocks composing the steep slope had been worn free of vegetation, but the bare spots were packed too hard to reveal any distinct tracks.

Again there was no sign of human habitation. Shading his eyes as he stood on the brink, Adrian gazed out into the distance. As far as he could follow its course toward the hazy horizon, the river below the falls was but little different from the river above. The same flat meanders resumed down there, the brown stream curving between the same dense walls of jungle, and the jungle extended away from both banks of the river, into the misty distance. No doubt about it, he was going to need the canoe if he could get it down there in one piece.

About to turn back to retrieve his canoe, he paused, taking one more look.

Kilometers away, some threads of smoke were rising, suggesting human presence.

Keep going downstream, certain Tasavaltan folk who were wise in the ways of the wilderness had taught him, *and sooner or later you'll come to a place where someone lives.*

Lugging the canoe up on shore, he dragged it to a place beside the brink, on the upper end of the descending riparian path. From here, getting down without a burden would be simple enough for an agile youth, but carrying his boat with him was going to pose a problem. Dragging the thin hull over the rough rocks was not going to do, of course; he would have to carry it cleanly.

After some meditation, and an earnest struggle with his memory, the Prince managed to recall a weight-subtracting spell he had learned for fun from a book he had discovered in his Teacher's library. Now the canoe, which had been barely liftable for a wiry twelve-year-old, became something like a manageable burden.

Once he'd got the canoe bottomside up, and himself beneath it in the proper balancing position, the job wasn't too bad. But using the lifting spell was tiring in itself, and Adrian had to stop, put down his burden, and rest several times before he was halfway down the rough descending stairs formed by uneven rocks.

When he was halfway down, he realized that someone or something was watching him. Eyes, inhuman eyes as he now realized, were focused on him from the jungle that clung to the steep slope only a few meters away.

Even as Adrian stood poised on a rock, uncertain how to react, several of the creatures came out of the greenery far enough for him to get a good look at them. From the first glimpse he had no doubt that these were the carnivorous apes he'd heard about. They were only about half the size of adult humans, lanky and almost humanoid, though moving easily on all fours in places where the footing was difficult. Their faces were not far from human, though their foreheads sloped back sharply, and their heads looked too small to contain truly intelligent brains.

Adrian set down the canoe, as carefully as he could, and pulled out the wooden paddle, the best semblance of a weapon he had available, from where it had been wedged under a seat. If worst came to worst, he'd edge his way backward, and risk a plunge into the falls. And it seemed likely that the worst was coming—club in hand, he thought he might have succeeded in standing off one of the beasts, but now there were six or eight of them confronting him.

The creatures showed their fangs and chittered at him threateningly. Surrounded on three sides by apes, and with his back to the waterfall, Adrian was on the verge of a near-suicidal plunge. The beasts closed in on him slowly, making noises that sounded like demented speech, waving their forelimbs and baring small, sharp carnivorous teeth. Their pale skins were half naked, half covered in patches of coarse fur, spotted green and brown, in a pattern that gave the beasts good camouflage against the background of the jungle.

The Prince, his mind working now in some territory beyond fear, wondered if they were accustomed to ambushing unwary travelers at this place, which seemed made to order for the tactic.

His instincts reached for magic. But there was very little in the way of magic that Adrian could perform to protect himself against animals. His most successful trick of raising an elemental was going to be no help to him now; for one thing, his energy had been temporarily depleted by the lifting spell, and for another, he sensed that the potential for raising an elemental in this particular spot was quite low.

The apes were closing in, and the boy was on the point of hurling himself desperately into the water, when something came crashing through the jungle.

Rescue, or at least a powerful distraction, had arrived in the shape of a bulky, shaggy, gigantic dog, now bounding out into the open. At first glance Adrian was almost ready to take the creature for a small bear; it looked as heavy as a big man.

Snarling and growling, the hulking, gray-furred dog charged the enemy and broke their semicircle. One of the simians, shrieking almost like a human, was killed outright by the dog's first rush, and another was caught by one leg and mangled a moment later.

This second victim, in its struggle to pull free, caught and tore one of the dog's ears with its teeth.

The remaining apes, who had not been prepared for this kind of opposition, were routed, at least for the time being.

Stooping, Adrian picked up several small rocks, which he hurled in rapid succession after the creatures as they retreated. He thought that he hit one of them at least.

Meanwhile the dog, giving its heavy gray fur a great shake, trotted growling through one last circle of the narrow and sharply sloping field of combat, as if formally establishing its dominion. Then the enormous male creature turned, sat down facing Adrian, and once more gave voice to the howl that the Prince had grown so accustomed to hearing during the days since he had left the City.

Adrian, his hands trembling and his knees now shaking in a delayed reaction to the danger, sat down also. "Here," he called, almost automatically. "Come here, boy."

Joyfully, in clumsy-looking bounds, the beast came to him with its tail wagging.

Probably, the Prince thought as he hugged and petted the shaggy bulk, there were a few other dogs in the world as big as this one or even bigger. But he could not recall ever having seen one quite this size. The massive neck bore no collar, nor any sign that it had ever worn one. There was no other mark, mundane or magical, of ownership.

Taking the torn ear gently in his fingers, he murmured a spell or two, doing what he could to stop the bleeding and promote healing; he was no great healer, but fortunately the wound appeared less serious than he had thought it would be.

"Wish I had something to feed you, dog—but at least you don't look like you're starving." Rather the opposite, in fact.

Now Adrian noticed that the beast's forepaws had a curious appearance, almost as if the forepart of each paw was incompletely divided into fingers. Or, he thought, as if the digits had once been truly divided in that way, and had now almost entirely reverted to the true canine form. The division in its present state was not complete enough to be at all useful; there was no way these paws were ever going to be used as hands.

The creature's teeth, when Adrian dared turn back a dark lip to obtain a good look at them, were truly formidable. And the eyes, large and brown, were somehow suggestive of intelligence.

Once or twice during this intrusive examination the animal again raised its head and howled. The sound was softer now, but still undoubtedly the same howl that Adrian had been hearing all the way from the City's border.

Having completed this preliminary inspection, Adrian sat down again on the edge of a rock. The dog, tail wagging, came closer, to rest its huge head and massive forepaws on the boy's leg. It crouched there looking up at him as if it hoped to be able to communicate.

He suddenly felt much less alone than he had at any time since his separation from Trilby.

"Why have you followed me all this distance, fellow? And what am I supposed to call you? No collar, no name. But you don't act wild. So, I think that you must have a name." And Adrian scratched the beast gently behind the ears.

It raised its great head slightly, obviously enjoying the

treatment. It panted, dog-fashion, tongue lolling out. More than ever it seemed to want to talk to Adrian.

The first requirement was to get the canoe down the remainder of the hill, so that it could be launched in a moment if the apes returned. When Adrian had accomplished that, he seated himself to rest on another stone, as comfortably as possible, and called the dog to him again. Then he summoned up such probing powers as he could manage on short notice, and as seemed to him appropriate. Taking his new companion's head between his hands, he set himself to looking into those very canine eyes, trying to see what might be behind them.

A few moments later, the apprentice magician was forced to blink and look away. Strange memories indeed were crashing and reverberating inside this animal's skull —of that much he was already sure. Undoglike memories, that seemed to have to do with power, among other things . . . Adrian could not be sure what kind of power was indicated, but certainly something more than mere physical ability. The vague perception had vanished almost as soon as he had tried to pin it down.

Then the boy momentarily held his breath, as he was struck by a new idea. Could this creature before him conceivably be a human being, one who had been trapped in some great shape-changing enchantment? He had heard of such things, but only as dim possibilities. He had never come close to encountering a case before.

But after thinking the idea over, and applying certain magical tests, Adrian felt sure that such was not the explanation. This being now crouching before him with lolling tongue and watchful eyes had never been human in the past, and certainly was not human now.

The Prince stroked the animal's head again. Its generous tail wagged slowly.

"Then were you once the pet or the tool of some great wizard or enchantress? That would explain much that is strange about you, dog. Though I don't see how it would explain how you come to be here now."

The animal only panted, gazing at Adrian steadily. It seemed that any further effort to find an explanation was going to have to wait.

"We'd better get moving again, downstream. You're coming with me, aren't you? Of course you are. There's no way I can force you, but I sure hope you're willing."

As soon as Adrian stood up, the dog got to its feet too, as if anxious not to be left behind. He spoke to it words of soft encouragement, still slightly worried that it might change its mind.

"I'll get the canoe in the water first, then we'll move downstream a little, away from these falls. I saw smoke, which means a village down there, and it stands to reason this whole river can't be deserted. So I'm going to need some clothes, a minimum anyway—I think I can fix that. And nothing like the clothes I was wearing when I left school—someone might be looking for those." Grasping his own hair, he pulled some of the longer strands in front of his eyes and studied them thoughtfully. Accumulated dirt, along with some side-effect of his tanning magic, had caused a definite darkening. He could probably pass as belonging to one of the riverside villages, for example that of the head-collectors.

And maybe, Adrian thought suddenly, he and his new companion would be able to work out some kind of cooperative hunting agreement. He wasn't exactly starving, but for some days now he'd been looking forward keenly to his next full meal.

When he had the canoe in the water again, at a cautious distance downstream from the tumult at the foot of the falls, the dog appeared to understand at once what he wanted it to do next. It jumped into the small craft first, landing as lightly as possible and balancing neatly amidships, while Adrian standing thigh-deep in the water held the vessel steady. Then the dog lay quietly, with its considerable weight distributed along the centerline, while he got in.

Adrian picked up the paddle and shoved off.

"You know what a Sword is, boy? No, how could you. But they're very important, and there's one of them not far ahead—I can smell it there even if you can't—and we're going to try to get our hands on it. Our paws, maybe?

"Now that I've got someone who'll listen to me, and I can tell you're listening by the way you move your—"

The Prince leaned forward, reaching out with gentle fingers. Hadn't it been the dog's right ear that was torn by the ape's teeth? No? the left one, then . . .

Neither ear showed the slightest trace of ever having been injured.

TWELVE

AT dawn of the day following the one on which he'd found the Sword, Talgai the Woodcutter was once more traveling a forest trail on foot, though this time without the company of his faithful loadbeast. He was making his way sadly and steadily toward the large town of Smim, where, as he had been told, his only brother was being held in jail, awaiting execution.

Talgai's newly acquired lucky Sword, still wrapped in its piece of ragged canvas and at the moment carried balanced on his left shoulder, was coming with him. On his back the woodcutter bore a small pack, containing a few items of spare clothing and some food. Talgai's wife, always sympathetic when she heard any tale of woe, had included several of her famous oatcakes, in an effort to do what little she could for the condemned man.

The journey might have been accomplished more swiftly and easily by water, since Talgai's hut and the town of Smim were both on the same river. But he had decided to leave his boat at home, in case his wife should need it; and anyway the road to town was reasonably safe. Particularly so, he thought, for a man carrying such a lucky Sword. With Coinspinner in hand, Talgai doubted not that he would be able to reach the town on foot, in plenty of time.

Should he fail to make good time, he could always travel by night as well as by day; but Talgai doubted that matters would come to that. As he hiked, he reflected on the bad and unhappy life led by his brother Buvrai—as far as Talgai knew, Buvrai had been in trouble almost continually since he was a boy. Not that Talgai knew much about the details of his brother's life, particularly in recent years. Nor did he wish to know more of the sad story than he did. It seemed too late to do anything about it now.

Talgai judged that he was making good time throughout the day, and as darkness approached, he found a convenient spot and stopped to rest. He dined frugally on a portion of the food he had brought with him, not forgetting to save the oatcakes for the prisoner, and augmenting his own dinner with some roadside berries. Then he wrapped himself in the cloak that his wife had insisted he bring along, and slept in the grass not far from the side of the road. This was nothing particularly unusual in the woodcutter's life, and he slept well.

Next morning he was up at dawn and off again.

During his first day's hike he had encountered several people along the way, the numbers very gradually increasing as the road broadened and the town grew nearer. But on this second day, having started on his way so early, he again had the road to himself for a time.

For a long time now he had been out of sight of the river, but now both river and road were curving in such a way as to make them run close together. Talgai took the first good chance to wash his hands and face, and get a drink. Just as he was straightening up from the water, someone nearby made a slight, throat-clearing noise.

He turned to see a wiry, long-haired boy of about twelve, and a huge gray dog, sitting together on the grass along the bank. Beside them a well-made canoe, hewed out of a single log, had been pulled ashore.

"Good morning, sir," the lad said brightly. He was wearing only a twist of bark cloth around his loins, like one of the river people, but his speech sounded very odd for one of them.

But certainly well mannered.

Talgai nodded. "Good morning to you, young sir. That's a nice canoe you have there."

"Ah—thank you." The boy was staring at Talgai's canvas bundle. "Sir, are you by any chance headed down the river? If so, I'd be glad to offer you a ride."

"Well, as a matter of fact, I am. My name is Talgai."

"And mine is Cham." All magicians adopted different names at times, and this was one that Adrian had sometimes used. Meanwhile the dog was doing his loutish best to demonstrate that he, too, approved of Talgai. The woodcutter could only marvel at the huge and impressive beast, while trying to fend off its more energetic advances.

For several hours before he encountered the woodcutter, Adrian had known that the Sword of Chance was very near.

He had put ashore in darkness, and then, with the great dog whining softly at his side, had walked slowly past the sleeping Talgai in the hour before dawn. The Prince had looked at Talgai and at his bundle—and then he had made preparations for this meeting.

Adrian had considered attempting to seize the Sword from the sleeping man—and he thought he might have succeeded, for the man was not actually in contact with Coinspinner as he slept. But the boy had hesitated, uncertain whether such a theft under these conditions would be either justifiable or wise.

The truth was that the apprentice magician, having now caught up with the Sword he had been pursuing, was having trouble trying to decide what to do next.

It was already plain to him that the man now carrying the Sword was no magician, and no warrior either. The way he casually set down the Sword of Chance in its rude canvas bundle, and turned his back on it—anyone who wanted to seize the weapon could grab it away from this incompetent, or so it seemed.

Still, Coinspinner was presumably now acting on this unsuspecting man's behalf—and it had not turned him away from this encounter with Adrian, a feat that, Adrian supposed, would have been well within the Sword's powers to accomplish. What was the meaning of this, for Adrian himself?

There were times, his father had often and solemnly told him, when it was necessary for one who bore a high responsibility to be ruthless. Still, Prince Mark was not often ruthless himself, and Prince Adrian had been raised with the ideals of simple fairness and honesty before him. He himself was in no immediate danger, as far as he could tell. How then could he justify stealing the property of this innocent and trusting man?

Another thought occurred, to confuse the Princeling further. Suppose his powerful enemy, Wood, who had almost succeeded in killing Adrian in the City, was coming after him again. Wood was known to possess Shieldbreaker, and Shieldbreaker would destroy any other Sword, indeed any weapon of any kind, that was brought into physical opposition to it. But suppose that Wood was coming after Coinspinner too—?

Adrian was no closer to solving his problem as he got into the canoe, leaving the heavier Talgai to shove off and step aboard. The new passenger, obviously skilled with boats, insisted on paddling for a while. With man, boy, and dog aboard, the canoe was now fully loaded, and riding low in the water.

A few hours later, when boy and man had agreed that the time had come for a rest stop, they beached the canoe in a likely-looking place and stepped ashore.

The dog quickly disappeared into some nearby woods, and Adrian could only hope that the beast was hunting.

Meanwhile Talgai, unpacking his own modest store of

food, took the oatcakes out of his pack in the process. He was on the point of stowing them away again, and offering to share some of his plainer provisions, when he took note of the hungry look on Adrian's face.

After what looked like a brief struggle with himself, the man offered: "Here, lad, these are very good cakes. Would you like one?"

Adrian certainly would.

Before the first oatcake was completely gone, the dog had come back from the woods with a fresh-killed rabbit, which he dropped at Adrian's feet. The beast tarried to receive a pat and a word of praise, then bounded back into the trees again.

"Your dog is trained as a hunter, then! Remarkable!"

"Yes, sir, he's really a remarkable dog. I feel quite safe with him around."

Meat having now been provided, a fire was the next requirement, and to that end Adrian was already gathering some dry twigs.

Talgai had come equipped with flint and steel, so there was no need for Adrian to display, or try to hide, his fire-raising powers.

By that time a second slaughtered rabbit had been delivered, in the same way as the first; once again the dog had paused to gaze steadily at Adrian for a moment, before plunging back into the woods. Adrian got the idea that now the beast would be hunting for himself.

While the meat was starting to cook, filling the air with unbearably delicious aromas, Talgai shared more of his oatcakes.

He broke off a piece of one for himself and nibbled it, but then handed the rest over to Adrian. "I have no taste for these today. But you are too thin, your ribs are showing. Eat!"

Then, while the boy ate, the man sat back, chewing some dried fish he'd brought with him. And suddenly he began to pour out his troubles, the fact that his brother was doomed to die in a very few days. And that there seemed to be nothing that could be done about it.

"Tell me, young sir, is it really good luck to be warned of a brother's impending death? What good is a warning when there's nothing that you can do about it anyway?"

"Good luck?" Adrian, feeling that he sounded stupid, but not knowing what else to say, echoed the question.

And suddenly the woodcutter was unwrapping Coinspinner, and telling the Prince a different story, that of his lucky Sword.

The telling faltered; Talgai appeared to be somehow impressed with what must have been the strange expression on the boy's face, as Adrian stared at the Sword.

"Here, would you like to hold it? Do you think that you would be happier if you were lucky too? But be careful, the blade is very sharp indeed." And the woodcutter slid Coinspinner forward, hilt first, beside the fire.

Very cautiously indeed the Prince reached forward and took the black hilt into his own hands. Reached for it, took it into his hands, and felt the power . . .

This was not the first time that Adrian had been entrusted with a Sword to handle. Possibly—he couldn't remember with any certainty, because he had been very small—possibly his father had once even let him touch this very hilt, years ago in the royal armory at Sarykam, The Prince had no need now to try the edges of this blade with his finger to know that the simple man across from him was telling him the simple truth about their sharpness.

Good fortune, great fortune, had come, here and now, into his hands. It was evident that if a possessor of the Sword of Chance decided to give his luck away, the Sword's own powers were not going to act on his behalf to prevent his doing so.

"I could use some good luck," the Prince muttered, raising the stark beauty of the blade beside the fire, gazing at it. But even as he spoke, he knew that he was going to have to give Coinspinner back.

It didn't help to tell himself that this poor simple fellow, now smiling at him from across the fire, would actually be better off without such powerful magic. That a Sword, any Sword, would only complicate poor Talgai's life, expose him to unexpected danger, attract the attention of powerful enemies. It didn't even help to consider the possibility that Wood might even now be coming after the Sword and its possessor, whoever that might currently be.

Adrian, reluctantly, but feeling that he could do nothing else, handed back the Sword. He passed it carefully, hilt first, and Talgai took it carefully and rewrapped it in his piece of canvas and laid it by his side. Soon the rabbits were cooked, and soon after that they were eaten. By that time the great dog, with fresh blood on his muzzle and looking satisfied, had rejoined the two humans beside the fire.

Adrian listened sympathetically, and the dog appeared to do so, as Talgai repeated and elaborated upon the sad facts concerning his brother.

"He was always getting into trouble," said the woodcutter, shaking his head sadly. "Yes, even from the time when he was as young as you are. Maybe even before that. I remember well, our mother always used to say that if Buvrai kept on as he was going, he would come to something like this, sooner or later. It's just a good thing that she's not around to see it."

Adrian put in a few words now and then, expressing his sympathy as best he could. Twice he was on the point of saying something else, and twice he forbore.

It seemed that his suggestion might have been unnecessary in any case. Talgai seemed to be working his way toward the same idea on his own. Without prompting the woodcutter had fallen into a study, frowning at his canvas package.

"Of course," he said at last, thinking aloud, "of course I might try to buy his freedom. A treasure like this—it is a real treasure, even I can see that. How would I go about it, though?" He raised his eyes as if appealing to this village boy for a suggestion.

For all his schooling to be heir to a kingdom, Adrian couldn't think of what to say, or think, or do. At the moment all he could think of was that he'd had the Sword, yes, the real Sword, right in his own hands a moment ago. And then, like the damned fool idiot that he must be, he'd handed it right back again. Given it right away.

The woodcutter brightened. "Of course, the Sword itself is so lucky, maybe it would keep me from going about things in the wrong way. Until I actually handed it over to someone else. To the prison warden, or whoever. But . . . I wonder . . ."

And now it seemed to Adrian that yet another idea, this one the real step forward, had dawned at last on Talgai.

They spent one night on the journey, Adrian sleeping in the canoe, at Talgai's insistence, because it was probably a little safer there, while man and dog and lucky Sword lay all close together on the grass nearby.

The travelers were all up early and on their way, and now it was obvious, from the rapidly increasing human presence on the banks and in the river, that they were getting very close to Smim.

When Coinspinner acted next, it was a subtle move, and Adrian did not at first recognize the small event for what it was.

Talgai was taking another turn at paddling. In the midst of another lament about his brother, he turned his head, broke off in midsentence, and pointed toward something on the shore.

"What is it?" Adrian asked.

"A friend of mine. Old Konbaung, he used to be my neighbor. There he goes. But now I remember, he had a relative who worked in the court! I must catch up with him, maybe he can do something for Buvrai."

Driving hard with the paddle, Talgai turned the canoe

abruptly toward the place where he was certain he had seen his old friend. There was a footpath there, following the riverbank, and one branch of it turned and angled inland, doubtless heading to town.

Running the canoe ashore, the woodcutter leaped out impetuously into the shallows. "Thank you for giving me a ride, lad. All the good gods be with you. I hope you find your parents."

Adrian stuttered something, but he was too late. The man with his back turned was already up the bank and striding rapidly inland, the Sword of Chance a nondescript bundle on his shoulder.

The dog, after bounding around irresolutely on the muddy bank for a time, whining and yapping, suddenly decided to accompany Talgai, and went running inland in pursuit. The Princeling yelled after the nameless beast, but it ignored him this time.

Now the Sword was gone, and for a moment Adrian hesitated, on the brink of running after it. That would, of course, have meant abandoning the canoe, and he felt reluctant to do that after the many difficulties the craft had borne him through.

While yet he wavered, his mind was made up for him by the appearance of two men. These were both armed and unsavory-looking, and one was strolling upstream along the bank while the other moved downstream to join him. They were going to meet at the place where Adrian was hesitating.

"Hey, kid! Nice boat you've got there. Where'd you get it?"

He might have tried some magic on them, but it had become almost instinctive to conserve energy, to use enchantment only as a last resort. Instead, Adrian pushed off the canoe again and paddled out toward midstream. The river was wide enough here for him to—

Only when he was twenty-five meters or so from shore did he become aware of the two sizable boats, big enough to hold half a dozen men each and both crowded, that were closing in on him, one from upstream and one from down.

There were several other craft on the river also, but all of those were distant, and none were concerned with what was happening here.

The two ominous boats had got within fifty meters or so of Adrian, perhaps, before he could be sure that he was the object of their interest.

At the same time, the two men on shore, of similar appearance to those in the boats, were walking along the bank, staying opposite Adrian's canoe, ready for him if he should try to land again. And the men on the bank exchanged brisk arm signals, obviously prearranged, with those in the boats.

"Let's see what you're hiding in the bottom of your boat there, lad," a voice loaded with false heartiness called out to him. It belonged to a man standing in the prow of one of the two craft closing in. On this man's shoulder there perched a winged, half reptilian-looking messenger.

Wood and his people used such creatures. Adrian felt his heart sink. "I've got nothing hidden!"

"Let's just take a look." The man grinned.

They think I've got Coinspinner with me. If only I did.

Now a middle-aged woman, something of an enchantress from the look of her, was calling out from the other boat to the male leader, telling him something about the magical aura she was able to see around Adrian. She could quite definitely confirm his identification as the missing Prince.

"Good, we've got him, then. And where's the Sword we were to look for? Has he got it there?"

"I doubt that very much," the woman called back. "If he ever had it, I think it's gone now, and no telling where."

The two boats were moving steadily closer. With many oars apiece, they could easily overtake him on the water if he tried to flee.

"That's the canoe we were told to look for, no doubt of that. And he's the right age."

The leader, smiling, spoke softly to the creature on his shoulder, whose beady eyes inspected Adrian. In a minute, the Prince thought, he's going to send it back to Wood, with word that I've been taken.

There was no way to escape—diving, trying to swim away underwater would be simply foolish.

Adrian's reaction to being trapped was the same near-instinctive reflex that had served him well before. Just as the two other boats were closing in on him, he reached with his mind into the depths of the earth, and fought for his life in the only effective way he could manage.

Call upon heat, call up pressure, evoke great density and mass and elemental toughness. The layers of rock beneath the muddy riverbed shifted, vibrated, pounded with the sudden stress of their own energies, being manipulated in a new way. Relief came with concussive force. Suddenly the materials upon which Adrian's mind was working split; a river-elemental was born almost accidentally, becoming separately objectified from the earth-elemental stirring at a deeper level.

Great pseudopods of water burst up into the air, overwhelming both large boats. Fortunately no innocent craft were near enough to be drastically affected. Gigantic geysers of rock and mud and water, flung higher than trees or houses, struck up into the air, projecting fragments high and hard enough to sting and wound the flying reptile, throwing it into a panic. It had sprung into the air from its master's shoulder at the first eruption, even as the man himself was hurled out of his boat.

One shoulder of the nearest erupting wave caught Adrian's canoe, lifted it above the river's surface, and dandled it like an infant for a moment. But the creator of the creature was able to soothe his creation successfully, and just in time; his return to the river was no worse than a splashing fall.

Unfortunately for the men and the woman in the two large boats, they were unable to take wing. Their craft were capsized, spun and hurled in midair, and men who were weighted with weapons, some of them with armor, did not fare well upon being suddenly plunged into deep water. Clinging to his own canoe as it pitched and tossed, the Prince saw with horrified fascination, how the mud and water surged and raced and spun around their bodies, turning them over again and again, sucking them under when they might have fought back to the surface.

Rock and earth hurled toward the sky splashed back into the river. Unlike the eruption in the City, this one left few visible effects a few moments after it had occurred. The great waves raised locally were quickly dying as they spread. The mud spewed up fell into muddy water. Only the drifting shapes of the two capsized boats, and the bodies of the drowned or drowning, could be seen as its results. The two men who had been standing on shore were engulfed in a huge wave, and Adrian could see one of them, covered with mud, running in panic for some nearby trees.

Adrian's canoe had not been damaged, though nearly swamped by water pouring in. Bailing frantically and not too effectively with his hands, he could not spare much attention for what was going on around him. He was aware of the flying reptile, still cawing in anguish, as it went laboring away on damaged wings.

The reaction of exhaustion came over the Prince, and he slumped in the canoe, on the point of losing consciousness. The body of a drowned man, bumping lightly against the side of the canoe, roused him to horrified new efforts.

At last, with most of the water bailed out of his craft, he was once more paddling downstream. Vaguely he had decided to go toward the docks of the town. As he paddled, he could still sense the aftershocks caused by the elemental's violence rippling through the layers of rock deep beneath the river. He could hope that what he had done wasn't going to set off a real earthquake—he continued to exert his best efforts to damp things down again.

Half dazed, the Prince found himself thinking of the

great dog, and wondering what had happened to him. Well, he wasn't going to hang around to look for him.

If I had taken Coinspinner when I had the chance, and held on to it, that couldn't have happened.

Right now Adrian was obsessed with one thought only. He was grimly determined to regain his contact with the Sword.

THIRTEEN

TALGAI, as he trudged into the town of Smim with his lucky Sword still wrapped in canvas and still riding on his shoulder, reflected on the strange and frequently puzzling things that had happened to him in the course of his journey—and for most of which, he was sure, the Sword he carried was somehow responsible.

High on the list of oddities was the lucky meeting with the hungry lad who had happened to be paddling his canoe downstream, and who had offered him a ride. And there was the peculiar dog—peculiar to say the least—that even now was still following the woodcutter at a distance. Whenever he glanced back he could see it, coming along the path behind him, thirty or forty meters back. He didn't want to call the dog to come to him, although he would have enjoyed its company, because it belonged to the boy, after all.

And then there was the incident, less than an hour ago, that had caused Talgai to leave his benefactor and proceed on foot, trying to catch up with a man he thought he knew.

While paddling the canoe, Talgai, glancing inland, had been convinced he'd spotted an old friend. But of course the fellow, when the woodcutter had finally overtaken him, had proved to be a total stranger, though the resemblance to his old friend was indeed remarkable. By the time Talgai had discovered his mistake, however, he could see the town quite close ahead of him and there was no point in turning back to the canoe. Gripping his bundled Sword now, he made a wish that young Cham should have a safe trip and meet his parents successfully—somehow Talgai had got the notion that that was what the boy was trying to do.

A moment later, Talgai's mind was once more filled with his brother and his brother's predicament. He hastened on.

At some point since he'd last left home, the woodcutter wasn't sure just when, the idea had begun to grow in his mind that Coinspinner's magic might even be able to rescue his brother from execution. Provided, of course, that he, Talgai, could somehow contrive to get the Sword into Buvrai's possession.

Certainly Talgai could not ignore the possibility, if it offered any hope at all.

The path he had followed from the riverbank had soon joined with another, larger, one, and that in turn with a road that was considerably larger still. Traffic of all kinds came in to being and steadily increased. Presently Talgai found himself entering the busy city on the high road from the east, along with an assortment of carts, wagons, occasional mounted folk of the upper class, and other humble pedestrians like himself.

The town of Smim was busy though not particularly large, being otherwise unremarkable of its kind. But its size was great enough to be confusing to the woodsman, who tended to feel ill at ease in any settlement larger than a dozen houses.

Still he experienced no difficulty in locating the prison. Very near the center of town, this facility occupied the two upper levels of one of the largest and tallest buildings in sight. The windows of the building's two lower levels displayed rooms full of clerks puttering about, doing incomprehensible things at desks and tables.

Fearful that he might, after all, have arrived too late to help his brother, Talgai began stopping people in the street and asking whether any execution had taken place in the past several days. The answers he obtained were mainly reassuring in that regard, though one man chose to try to plunge him into despair with a tale of horrible dismemberment on the scaffold, for no reason at all that Talgai could see. But the woodcutter did manage to learn, from several sources, that a public hanging was indeed scheduled for tomorrow at dawn.

Evidently he had not arrived too late—thank the Sword for that. But certainly there was no time to waste.

After quenching his thirst at a public watering trough— for some reason several well-dressed passersby favored him with amused glances as he did this—the woodcutter walked completely around the prison and the attached administrative complex, looking things over from every angle. It was of stone construction, and it was certainly a large building, he remarked to himself unnecessarily when he had observed all sides of it. Perhaps the largest he had ever seen. The trouble was that having inspected this large building thoroughly Talgai really had no better idea of how to proceed than he had had before.

Returning to the square in front of the prison, he rather timidly observed the grim-faced guards, armed and uniformed, who were stationed at the building's doors and in its one visible courtyard. An even more disconcerting sight was the ominous-looking scaffold that had been erected twenty meters or so from the front of the prison, right in the public square. The scaffold was of logs, and it had a well-used look.

Despite their bright uniforms, the guards all looked as grim and sullen as the walls they guarded. As Talgai stared at them, and thought of the authority that they must represent, it seemed to him that any appeal for mercy was doomed to failure at the start. He might, of course, attempt to bribe someone, using the marvelous Sword he carried— he had no doubt that at least some of these people could be bribed. If only he knew better how to go about such things, or if he had more time in which to learn the proper ways—but in fact he had hardly any time at all.

Likely, the woodcutter thought, if he tried bribery he'd only approach the wrong person, or make some other mistake that he couldn't foresee, and get himself arrested. He'd hand over the Sword, and that would be that. The Sword would protect him only as long as he actually had it with him, close enough to touch. He understood that now. And once he'd handed over his lucky tool to someone else—well, there'd be no protection for himself or his brother either against these scoundrels. Whatever his brother's faults, he felt sure just from looking at the men who were about to hang him that they were scoundrels too.

Getting himself arrested wouldn't be a good idea. It wouldn't do his brother any good. And he, Talgai, had a wife and small children dependent on him.

But he was going to have to do something. He was sure of that when he stood gazing at the gallows. Just thinking of watching any execution, let alone his own brother's, made Talgai shiver. No, he wasn't going to be able to stand here and watch anything like that happen to Buvrai.

So be it. Therefore he must try to get the Sword into his brother's hands. The only question was, how to go about it?

One method of course would be to make his attempt at the last moment, when Buvrai was actually being led out to his death. But Buvrai's hands might well be bound then, Talgai supposed. And if the condemned man was unable to reach for the Sword and grasp it, make it his own, how could it do him any good?

Deep in gloomy thought, Talgai strolled aimlessly about the square before the prison. He was bothered by growing worries about the impending fate of his wife and children. Suppose he got himself into trouble that would keep him from ever seeing them again.

Standing under the gallows, he resolutely put such fears behind him. His brother's predicament was immediate and real, and therefore it had to come first.

Now, once Talgai had firmly made up his mind as to what he wanted to do, his good fortune took effect again and things began to fall his way at once.

Only moments after his decision at the scaffold, as Talgai stood looking up at the front of the prison again, he was able to identify the window of his brother's cell without any trouble. This was possible only because, fortunately, his brother came to the window and looked out while Talgai happened to be watching.

The cell window—it was heavily barred, like all the windows near it, so Talgai assumed that it opened into a cell—directly overlooked the square, providing a good view of the gallows, which at the moment was claiming Buvrai's thoughtful attention. Most of the windows in the wall were heavily barred with ironwork. Those on the ground floor opened into offices of some kind, shadowy tiled and paneled rooms where clerks and administrators sometimes appeared.

"Buvrai! It's me! Down here!"

The prisoner saw and recognized his brother gazing up at him from the street below. He shouted something back, and the two exchanged waves.

Glancing at the guards, Talgai saw that they were watching with bored expressions and a minimum of interest.

The two brothers conversed some more. Buvrai, starting to rave now, shouted that he had been imprisoned unfairly, because he had incurred the enmity of the Red Temple, who had falsely accused him of cheating in a game of chance.

"Is that all?"

"They say I killed a man. But it's all lies."

"How can I help you?"

"If you want to help me, get me out!"

The building containing the prison was no more than four stories high, and the condemned man's cell was not at the top. Still, Buvrai's window was much too far above the ground for Talgai to be able to simply walk up to it and push the Sword in between the bars. Nor did there appear to be any feasible way to climb the wall and get within reach.

"You've got to do something to get me out of here. See

the governor or something. They mean to hang me tomorrow!" Buvrai went on, shouting renewed complaints
against the Red Temple.

Whatever the truth of Buvrai's claims, his situation
sounded bad. It sounded so bad that Talgai was beginning
to have doubts again. How could good luck help against
impossibility? What kind of a miracle could even
Coinspinner possibly work in such a desperate case?

"Tomorrow, Talgai! Will you do something?"

"Yes, yes, I'll try!" he shouted back.

The guards were still watching and listening impassively.
Probably they heard similar shouted conversations all the
time.

The woodcutter couldn't imagine what good a lucky
Sword was going to be in this case. But he tried as best he
could to suppress his doubts. He clung as hard as possible
to a simple faith that the weapon he had been carrying was
going to do something effective.

Now Buvrai was shouting down more instructions for
him, something about Talgai's trying to see someone who
was being held in the women's cells on the ground floor.
Maybe she could think of something, some way to get them
both out. The woman's name sounded like Amelia.

Presently, because his brother's yelling, his concocting of
desperate, half-witted schemes, was only confusing him
now, and nothing was getting done, Talgai waved once
more and hurried off to think, out of sight of the prisoner's
window.

At last, after some agonizing minutes of indecision,
trusting in Coinspinner's power but seeing no other way to
harness it properly, Talgai decided that the only thing to do
was to simply stand back and throw the Sword up at his
brother's window.

He wondered urgently whether he ought to yell up a
warning to his brother just before he threw the Sword, so
that his brother would come to the window and reach out
between the bars and catch it.

If anyone could catch a blade like this one, spinning in midair, without cutting off his fingers.

Well, Talgai supposed, it might be just at that point, the Sword's first contact with a new owner, where the miraculous good luck might be expected to come in. And if luck failed there—well, Buvrai, at least, had nothing to lose.

The woodcutter considered whether he ought to leave the Sword wrapped, but bind his canvas bundle tightly before he heaved it up, so it would be able to fit in between the bars when Buvrai caught it. Yes, Talgai supposed, that would be the way.

At last, with his bundle ready, and himself as ready as he could get for whatever might be going to happen, Talgai came out into the open square again, and walked steadily closer to the prison.

Buvrai was watching for him. "Well?" the prisoner shouted impatiently.

"Well," Talgai called back. "Here's all that I can do for you, brother. The best that I can do."

"Here? Where?"

"Right here. Coming up."

Talgai considered that he had a good eye for distances, and a good arm for throwing. When he threw the Sword up, with even a little luck it ought to go just about where he wanted to send it. It would almost certainly come within his brother's reach, provided that his brother was standing at the window. Maybe it would even fly right in between the bars. So, if he acted now, while his brother was at the window and presumably ready to react . . .

But Buvrai, instead of paying heed when his brother, who had evidently taken leave of his senses, appeared to be ready to throw some kind of awkward bundle up to him, just turned away from the window at the crucial moment, expressing his disgust.

Muttering the closest thing to a prayer that he had mouthed in a long time, directed indiscriminately at any god who might be willing to listen, Talgai ran forward two long steps, and with both hands, using an awkward, almost unplanned sidearm motion, heaved the Sword.

Gazing upward, holding his breath, Talgai saw the canvas-bundled Sword of Chance, spinning in midair, align itself so precisely with the configuration of the barred window that when it reached those bars it went flying neatly in between them, the bundle lacking even a centimeter to spare on either side. In a year of trying he could never, without magic, have made the cast so neatly.

In the momentary quiet that held before the watchful guards began to shout at him, he could even hear the dull clang of the muffled steel as it landed on the cell floor.

After that there was another moment, there were even several moments, in which Talgai might have tried to run away, with some chance of success. But he could not move, because he was waiting to see what was going to happen next.

Before he had thrown away the Sword he had realized that in doing so he would divest himself of its protection. Still, it came as something of a shock when rough voices shouted accusations at him, and rough hands seized him by the arm and collar.

Talgai was surrounded by outraged prison guards, who were arguing over what to do with him. One of the guards struck him on the side of the head, and others, seizing him by the arms, started to drag him into the prison building.

Meanwhile the condemned man, who had just turned away from the window following a sharp verbal exchange with his brother, looked up sharply as there was a whisper of sound from that direction, a small sound caused by the dull cloth wrapping of a flying object grazing one or more of the window bars. There was a dark shape flying in the air within the cell, followed by a dull metallic thump on his stone floor.

Gaping stupidly at the bundle that lay there now, wondering how in the world it had ever managed to get in through the bars, Buvrai was able to recognize his brother's voice, once more yelling at him from outside. But he was not able to make out the words.

Days ago, long before Talgai's appearance, the prisoner had given up the idea of ever being rescued by anything other than some superb stroke of luck. In fact he had never had any real hope of other kinds of rescue; certainly he belonged to no gang, he had no friends—except Amy, who was jailed herself—interested enough in his survival to organize a jailbreak plot. In fact it was quite possible, or at least the prisoner sometimes thought it was, that some of his own supposed friends, certain people who had once been his partners, had connived to get him into this trouble.

But luck was different. The prisoner was always ready to count upon his luck to save him somehow. And so, when Talgai had appeared, Buvrai had allowed himself to begin to hope again. Until, of course, he remembered that his brother was a fool, had always been an unlucky fool, and in the nature of things always would be.

After staring uncomprehendingly for a moment at the object now lying on the floor of his cell, the prisoner realized that this must be luck, if it was anything. In another moment he had moved to seize and unwrap the bundle. In his hands, which were now suddenly trembling and uncoordinated, the object inside the canvas felt like a weapon; it felt like a wrapped-up sword.

Talgai was not only an unlucky fool, he was absolutely crazy to think that a sword, any kind of sword, would help him fight his way out of an iron-barred stone cell. But even as Buvrai's mind acknowledged this, his fingers kept busy undoing the simple knots that held the canvas closed. There was, after all, nothing else for him to do.

Buvrai knew something of the Twelve Swords, but nothing had been further from his thoughts; and the true nature of this weapon failed utterly to dawn on him at first.

The small white symbol happened to be turned away when he first looked at the black hilt.

With some flickering hope, grasping for any faint indication that Talgai must have had more in mind than just arming him with a sword, Buvrai looked eagerly for some written message stuffed inside the canvas. But there was nothing of the kind.

Could Talgai even read and write? His brother wasn't sure. It didn't seem to matter.

Trembling between weeping and laughing hysterically at his brother's folly, Buvrai clutched the black hilt in both hands and held the weapon up. In spite of everything, the sheer quality of the blade impressed him. He even had the feeling that he ought to recognize it, recognize it as something more than—

There came now a fresh outbreak of shouting outside in the square. The prisoner, Sword clutched hard in his right fist, hurried back to his window, grabbing a bar in his left hand to pull himself up so he could see better what was happening in the square. He was just in time to see his faithful brother being dragged away toward the guardhouse in the ground level of the prison building.

Muttering profanities against a host of gods and goddesses, he turned from the window again. Talgai had sent him no message, no help, beyond the bright steel itself.

Except that now Talgai's brother was beginning to feel the sensation of magic in his hand. He was not a magician, but like many other folk he knew the feeling. Buvrai stared at the weapon in bewilderment.

Moments later, the prisoner was jarred out of his near trance by a noise at his cell door. Sword in hand, he turned to face it. Once more he wondered in a confused way, hoping against hope, whether some desperate attempt at rescue might after all be in progress, whether whoever was in charge of it had sent his brother to see to it that he was armed.

The key was being turned in his lock, and now his cell door was yanked open from outside. No rescuers stood there. Rather three guards, with their own weapons drawn, burst into the cell to confront the prisoner.

The faces of the three uniformed men were angry, but not in the least worried. They remained confident even when they saw the Sword Buvrai was holding. They no more recognized one of the Twelve than he had. Still, it was obviously a formidable weapon, on purely physical terms, and they stopped their advance at a respectful distance.

One of the guards tentatively reached out with his free hand toward the condemned man. "Come on, hand it over now!" he commanded in a threatening voice. Then he pulled his empty hand back quickly when Coinspinner's keen point shifted in his direction.

The prisoner, who did know something of the art of swordsmanship, caused the bright point to trace a slow circle in the dim prison air. "Why should I?" he demanded.

"Huh?"

"I said, why should I? What'll you do if I don't hand it over? Kill me?"

Even as Buvrai spoke, the realization was finally dawning on him that this gift that had come flying so strangely in at his window was, must be, a thing of powerful magic. How else could it have passed through the bars in such a way? And that magic, of course, was the reason Talgai, perhaps not so totally foolish after all, had given it to him.

And now at last the thought, the memory of the existence of the Twelve Swords of the gods, rose above Buvrai's mental horizon. Not that Buvrai had ever seen one of those fabulous weapons before; but what else could this be?

What he had to worry about now, the prisoner thought, was the nature of this particular blade's magic. Just what in all the hells was he supposed to do with it? He recalled that the Twelve Swords were very powerful, but what were their individual properties? Yes, he remembered now that they all bore little symbols on their hilts; but just now he was not in a good position to pause for a look at this one.

Desperately he brandished this blade of unknown potency at the three jailers, who were now advancing once more,

a few centimeters at a time, scowling at him as they moved.
He waited for the Sword's power, whatever that might be,
to take effect. Or for the rush of some unknown friends and
allies down the corridor, to take his enemies in the rear. Or
for—

What actually happened next was that his three enemies
charged him simultaneously.

Their charge was not coordinated, and it would not have
been a well-considered move, even had the weapon in the
prisoner's hand been no more than ordinary steel. The
little cell lacked the latitude necessary for the attackers to
bring their greater numbers into play effectively. As matters befell, at least one of the jailers handled his weapon
very clumsily in the confined space, jabbing the man next
to him, whose own arms involuntarily jerked sideways.
Within the next moment all three of Buvrai's enemies were
wounded, one of them severely; the attack collapsed without the prisoner needing to strike a blow.

In another moment his attackers were retreating in
confusion from the cell, the two who were less badly hurt
dragging their more seriously injured comrade with them.

Despite the jailers' confusion they did not forget to slam
shut the door behind them, and the prisoner could hear the
key being turned in the lock, confining him as securely as
before.

What next? Bewildered as much as ever, his pulses
pounding in his ears, the prisoner turned back to his
window and once more looked out. At the moment,
everything outside appeared discouragingly calm. In his
state of dazed excitement, he forgot to examine his Sword's
hilt for symbols while he had the chance.

Standing close inside the locked door, he could hear the
excited voices of his adversaries out in the corridor:

"Bring pikes!"

"No, someone fetch a crossbow!" And feet went scurry-
ing away.

Magic throbbed in the prisoner's hand. He could feel it,
he had had enough experience with magic to do that. But

he had no idea what, if anything, this power might be able to accomplish for him.

As Buvrai waited, feeling newly helpless, he gradually became aware of a sound like distant thunder. Where was it coming from? Somewhere far away. Or was it?

Outside the window, the sun shone; out there, out in the world, it was a fine day. But inside his cell things were different. Now the rumbling came again, and the prisoner thought that he could not only hear it but feel it faintly, coming up through the floor beneath his feet . . .

Now—and there was no doubt at all about this—he could hear his enemies in the corridor quietly approaching the door again, mumbling their plans to one another. It was hopeless to try to understand what they were saying through the barrier. Quickly the prisoner slid away from the door, pressing his body into the one corner of the room where they'd have trouble hitting him if they shot through the little observation hole.

. . . and now, no possible mistake about it this time, the prisoner *could* feel the building shiver faintly, and see a fine trail of dust come trickling down from a new crack in the cell's ceiling. Whatever was going on . . .

And now the jailers were unlocking the door again, undoubtedly ready with some new way to kill him.

The door burst open once more, and with the crash the prisoner, Sword raised, leaped back into the center of the room again. His only thought now was that at least he was going to cheat the hangman.

Even as the crossbowman, crouching centered in the doorway and flanked by swords on both sides, leveled his powerful weapon, the prisoner could feel the stone floor begin to sway beneath his feet. No mere rumbling this time. Things had gone beyond that.

The stone floor lurched violently just as the guard's finger touched the trigger. The bolt, released with a harsh twang, shrieked past the prisoner's right ear to shatter itself against the quivering stone wall beside the window.

The prisoner had lost his balance with the lurching of the

floor, and he fell in the opposite direction from the bowman. Buvrai in falling managed to retain his grip on the Sword, and was lucky enough not to cut himself on the keen blade. Now he started to get to his feet again. The bowman in the doorway, crazily oblivious to everything but his duty, was reloading with mechanically moving hands. The prisoner was going to have to rush him, despite the leveled blades of the other guards—

And now the earth was thundering continuously beneath them all. Around them in the building wooden beams were breaking like trees in a windstorm, although there was no wind. A large stone crashed from the ceiling, narrowly missing the sergeant of the guard. More stones came after it.

That broke the spell. With hoarse cries the three jailers abandoned their duty and turned in unison to flee for their lives, leaving the cell door open. Up and down the corridor the screams of other prisoners resounded.

My luck has changed too late, too late, thought the prisoner with a condemned man's detachment. More stones tumbled from above, driving him back away from the open door, one impact after another in front of him urging him back against the window where he could only grip the bars one-handed, for still he clutched his Sword. *Too late to do me the least damned bit of good. I'm going to die in an earthquake instead of on the—*

He had not quite time to complete that thought before, with a tremendous roar, most of his cell's floor disappeared into a sudden cloud of dust and mortar. At the same time, greater masses than ever came down from above, hurtling and crashing past his head.

Still gripping the black hilt convulsively in his right hand, the prisoner locked both arms through the window bars. He clung to their support, felt the thick iron vibrating. When one of his feet was suddenly left unsustained, this grip preserved him from a fall.

He was still alive, even unhurt, at least for the moment.

And then for another moment, and another after that. With his eyes shut, he waited to be killed.

When several more moments passed and nothing violent happened to him, Buvrai opened his eyes again. Now the dust was thicker, making him cough and choke. Through its gray clouds the cries of the injured and the dying rose up as if to emphasize his luck.

Something stranger even than an earthquake was happening now. The space that had once formed the dank and shadowy interior of his cell had somehow become illuminated by the sun. In a few moments a breeze had cleared the dust a little. The prisoner could now see that he was standing on a short and narrow shelf of stone, all that remained of his cell's floor. This shelf projected from a fragment of wall, the highest part of the building that was still standing.

Now the wind, moving with unaccustomed freedom across these newly exposed stones, blew still more of the dust away. The tall, jagged remnant of intact stonework was suddenly bathed in the full sunlight.

And now the man who had been a prisoner could see, in the middle distance, other buildings that had partially or completely collapsed as well. The entire center of town was changed, and drastically. To Buvrai's ears drifted the sounds of a hundred or a thousand human voices crying out in shock, in pain and horror, uttering pleas for help.

Presently his own shock eased enough to let him move again. Carefully bending almost double, the man who had been condemned to die forced the sharpness of the Sword's blade into a small crevice in the wall, just above the tiny ledge on which he stood. Now the black hilt served as a firm handgrip, on which he could lower his weight and swing himself down. The strong blade bent a little, but he could feel, in its springy strength, that it was not going to break. And now Buvrai's extended toes, groping downward, found another foothold, in just the place where one was absolutely needed.

Slowly, moving one limb after another with numbed care, no longer really aware of any danger, he continued to clamber down the skeletal wall. Always he found the minimal handholds and footholds that were required. Always the Sword came with him, and twice again he dug it into crevices to provide himself with one more grip.

Presently Buvrai, Sword still in hand, was able to drop onto the top of a massive pile of rubble whose bulk had once represented most of the structure of the prison.

Once the former prisoner had reached that level, the rest was easy. In relative safety he scrambled down the rest of the way to the ground. Meanwhile the cries of the dying, the shocked, the injured, continued to go up all around him.

Dazedly ignoring these horrible sights and sounds, the once-condemned man began to walk away to freedom. Then he turned back, remembering something. The women's wing of the jail, a one-story wing at the eastern end of the structure, had suffered comparatively little damage. He moved unsteadily in that direction.

He had not yet got clear of the wreckage of the main body of the prison before he heard the agonized howling of a great dog. In another moment Buvrai could see the huge gray beast, digging frantically into a pile of rubble, as if it were compelled to try to rescue whoever was trapped there.

Something about the sight caused it to remain etched into Buvrai's memory. But he did not stop. Mechanically, stumbling over stones and broken timbers, he moved on toward the women's wing.

The outer door of that low structure, unguarded now, was jammed almost shut. But when Buvrai pried at it with the Sword the door sprang open. Inside was weeping and wailing chaos, but little in the way of real injury. Luckily for the women, the upper stories of the main building had not collapsed in this direction.

Taking down a ring of keys from where they hung on a handy hook, Buvrai began to open inner doors. At first he hardly recognized Amelia among the little crowd of haggard females, garbed as she was in some remnant of an unfamiliar dress, and with her hair all matted and her face devoid of makeup. When he did spot her, the other women gave his Sword plenty of room in letting him reach her. Her eyes were shocked and blank, and she said nothing. The other prisoners flowed past, and most of them were already outside by the time he got Amelia to the door.

Once outside again, he turned away across the square, tugging Amy with him. Nothing was going to stop him now. But something did, before he'd gone six steps. It was the sound of his name, called in a low, distorted voice. The voice was unrecognizable at first, sounding like that of a dying man.

But it had called his name.

Still tugging the befuddled Amelia with him by her wrist, Buvrai looked for whoever had called him. Presently he almost tripped over the head of his brother. With only his head protruding from the mass of collapsed stones and timber, Talgai appeared to be hopelessly trapped, and Buvrai thought he must be on the brink of death.

The former prisoner crouched beside his rescuer, who had now become a helpless victim. One look and Buvrai decided that there was nothing he could do.

Talgai's face and hair were gray and featureless with settled dust, his countenance was twisted in pain.

And now, after being able to exchange a few words with his brother, the woodcutter slumped into unconsciousness. His brother couldn't tell if he was alive or not.

The man who had been rescued began trying to use the Sword to pry away part of the wreckage. Luckily he inserted it into the pile of debris at a key point, and the beam pinning his brother swung and toppled away.

The great gray dog, come running up from somewhere, capered.

But the man Buvrai had managed to release still lay unconscious, and perhaps dead.

Thinking vaguely that there was nothing more that he could do for him, Buvrai stood up.

Gripping his Sword firmly, he took his woman by the arm, and started walking. Sooner or later the survivors here were going to recover from their shock, enough to remember that they still had a killing scheduled for tomorrow.

FOURTEEN

ADRIAN, recovering from his faintness, had left the scene of his last skirmish well behind him, and had the town docks of Smim in sight ahead. He was paddling strongly toward them when a sudden thunderous rumbling and a slowly rising column of dust turned his attention toward the center of town, which was somewhere inland, invisible behind buildings and trees. Listening as the distant screams began to arise, the Prince could only conclude that Smim was being devastated by an earthquake, or something very like one.

Waterborne as he was, Adrian could feel no vibration physically. Nor could he detect any magical disturbance. That the renewed violence in the earth might be an indirect result of his raising an elemental was a distinct possibility, but if it was so, there was nothing he could do about it.

Only somewhat later, when he had heard eyewitness reports of events in the center of Smim, did he begin to appreciate how intense, though narrowly confined, the earthquake's destruction there had been. At the time, watching from the river, Adrian saw only the light shaking of trees and buildings close to the river, a faint indication of the rolling and staggering of the ground farther inland. He could hear, mingled with the cries of humans, a number of dogs, near the town and in it, howling wildly and painfully, and he wondered for a moment if one of those howling was the great gray beast for which he had never been able to find a name.

Within the next few moments the boy became aware, even with his mundane senses, of a great tremor that came running through the river bottom, kicking up brief, strangely shaped waves. And at the same time a renewed burst of human screams, frightening though faint with distance, yells of shock and terror and pain, came carrying to Adrian across the water.

Then, almost as abruptly as it had begun, the rolling and the shaking of the earth was over. From out near the middle of the river everything on shore looked just about as before, except that now Adrian could see the plume of smoke or dust, or perhaps a mixture of the two, rising bigger than ever from some unseen source a couple of hundred meters inland. He supposed that it must be coming from somewhere near the middle of town. He hoped that the kindly woodcutter had not been hurt.

Suddenly Adrian suspected that Wood might be responsible for what was now taking on the dimensions of a real disaster. He had no real evidence, but who was more likely to initiate something that did this kind of damage?

But in the next moment the young Prince forgot almost entirely about Wood. For now the Sword of Chance, whose image had never entirely left Adrian's perception, was once more looming larger and larger in his field of mental vision.

Someone—a man—he could not tell if it was Talgai or not—was now carrying Coinspinner steadily from the interior of the town toward the waterfront. The bearer was not yet physically visible from Adrian's position, but the boy was sure that he was approaching at the pace of a swift walk.

And would the great dog be coming back with Talgai? Adrian couldn't tell. Driving hard with the paddle, he steered his small craft nearer to the docks, which were now practically deserted. Everyone at this end of town must have run to see what was happening just inland . . .

Wanting to get a better look, Adrian wished that he dared to stand up in his canoe . . . but no, there was no need. The Sword was now coming into view.

And here it came. The bright gleam of the long blade was unmistakable, borne in the right hand of a middle-sized man of about thirty years of age, who was headed toward the riverfront at a brisk walking pace. With his left hand this man clasped the arm of a young woman, and he was towing her along. She made no resistance.

From behind the couple, well inland, smoke and screams continued to go up. Adrian paddled closer.

As the couple grew nearer, the Prince could see that both of them were pale. The man, with shaggy brown hair, was roughly bearded. The woman, somewhat lighter in coloring, barefoot and wearing a cheap-looking dress, looked somewhat dazed.

The naked Sword and the figure who carried it would undoubtedly have drawn some attention in the street at any ordinary time. But just now, the one or two other folk who were visible near the docks were paying them no heed. All their attention was focused inland.

As the pale-skinned pair, still moving at a steady pace, drew still closer to the docks, Adrian could see that the woman was a few years younger than the man, and moderately attractive, though certainly no great beauty. The man's clothing hung loosely on him, as if perhaps he had recently lost weight.

Having now come right down the waterfront, the man began to pull his passive companion along the modest row of docks. He was looking for something, all right, and what he sought could hardly be anything but some quick and convenient means of getting out onto the water. There were a few clumsy-looking rowboats available, and a couple of slightly bigger craft, all of them securely tied up but unwatched at the moment.

"Going downstream, sir?" Adrian called loudly, at the same time driving his canoe right up against the dock. "Quick transportation here!"

The man looked at him without surprise, as if he had been expecting Adrian's offer, or some equivalent. He said shortly: "Don't fear the Sword, lad—I'm just carrying it for good luck. All right, here we come!"

And it was fortunate that luck came with the two passengers, for they proved to be totally ignorant of the proper ways of getting into a canoe, or riding in one; and the man at least was in too much of a hurry to even try to be careful.

"Just sit down, sir, right in the middle! Keep low, ma'am, hold as still as you can. That's it, that's it, sit toward the middle."

Then they were in, the woman forward, the man amidships. He put his heavy Sword down in the bottom of the canoe as soon as he was in—more to hide it, Adrian was sure, than to help achieve balance.

Once the load had been more or less stabilized, by means of luck and his shouted orders, the Prince, now seated in the stern, plied his paddle energetically. In silence, they headed steadily downstream. Adrian was already watching for a chance to grab the Sword, but he was determined to wait for a good chance, and so far there had been none at all.

And vaguely he continued to wonder what might have happened to Talgai, and to the great gray dog; and about what sort of disaster might have overtaken the center of the town of Smim.

Presently Adrian cleared his throat. "Something going on back there in town?" he asked at last.

A meter in front of Adrian, the man's head turned a few centimeters. "Couple of buildings fell down. Am I going to tip this damned log over if I look back?"

"No, sir, you can turn your head. Just keep your weight in the middle as much as you can. And move slow."

Shifting his body gingerly, the man turned partway around, showing Adrian his pallid face. A certain looseness of the skin around the jowls, visible through a scraggly beard, gave the impression that his face had once been plump.

The man's eyes, full now of a towering relief, and perhaps other satisfactions, settled somewhere over Adrian's shoulder, in the direction of the town they had just left. The sound of yells had faded. The Prince took a quick look back himself. Already some trees on the river bank were beginning to block the view effectively, with only the top of the drifting dust-or-smoke column visible above their crowns. Again Adrian wondered what might have happened to Talgai; of course the simple man was quite capable of handing the Sword over to someone else, to almost anyone, and getting into trouble that way.

Of course the man the woodcutter would have really wanted to give the Sword to was his brother.

Studying the pallid face in front of him, the Prince thought that perhaps he could detect a faint resemblance. And the hair of this man was practically the same color as Talgai's.

Turning forward again, the man spoke to his companion, and Adrian heard him call her Amy. Then he turned back, grinning at the Prince.

"Lad, my name's—Marland. What's yours? Never mind, I think I'll call you Mudrat."

"Whatever you like, sir," agreed Adrian, still paddling. After so many days in an open boat, days of mud and sun and magic, the description was probably not far wrong.

"I'm Amelia," said the young woman suddenly, from her place in the prow, leaning slightly sideways to look past the man at Adrian. Once more the canoe came close to tipping over. But Adrian did his best to counterbalance, Coinspinner doubtless helped, and they kept gliding along.

Evidently Amelia was starting to come out of her fog. Now she lowered her eyes to something in the bottom of the boat, the Sword no doubt. It was as if she was becoming aware of it for the first time.

"Where'd you get *that*?" she demanded of the man,

lowering her voice, as if she imagined that might keep Adrian from hearing.

"My brother gave it to me," he answered shortly, not bothering to lower his.

Talgai had named his brother in Adrian's hearing, but the name certainly hadn't been Marland. Buvrai, that was it. Well, that hardly mattered. This man could only be the escaped convict—Talgai hadn't said what his brother had been convicted of.

There was a good current, making downstream progress swift and steady. Already the town of Smim had disappeared, along with almost all of the dark aerial plume that rose above its rooftops. And now even the outlying portions of Smim were gone. An occasional shack or other building still appeared near the river, but the forest had come close to reasserting its monopoly over both banks.

Now the man who had called himself Marland turned his head to Adrian again. "How far downstream you going to take us, Mudrat?" The man didn't sound threatening, or even as if he wanted to be nasty; the Prince told himself that the newly bestowed name was probably just Talgai's brother's idea of a little joke.

It seemed a safe assumption that the escapees would want to go as far as possible. "I'm going a long way, and I don't much care if I go a little farther."

"Aha. Running away?" The man could understand that, and smiled his approval. "That's the idea—see something of the world.

"Kid, do you know anything about a big city called Bihari? This river runs into it eventually, a couple hundred kilometers from here."

Anyone who knew geography at all had heard of Bihari, and certainly Adrian was familiar with the name, though he had never been anywhere near the place before. And if the man was right, the Prince now had, for the first time, a pretty good idea of where on the continent his emergence from the City of Wizards had brought him out.

"How'd you like to get a look at a real big city, kid? Yes, I can see you would. Don't worry, you'll love it. Much better than living in the jungle. Say, have we got anything to eat aboard?"

"Afraid not, sir."

The woman murmured something in a querulous tone, as if she might be ready to give up now and go back to where she might be fed. Or maybe she was only wondering what was going to happen next.

"That's all right, Amy, first things first. We're out of the jug now, and we're not going to starve. Are we, Mudrat?"

"No, sir."

"Damn right we're not. Not with"—and the man faced front again, and bent over what lay in the bottom of the canoe—"not with my little good-luck charm here."

Throughout most of the day the weather had been fair. But by late afternoon, when the canoe had made two hours of steady progress downstream from the town of Smim, the sky had clouded over heavily. Shortly thereafter it began to rain. And shortly after that the rain began to turn to hail.

Adrian drove the canoe around a sharp bend, and there, just ahead, looming gray through the rain's curtain, was a large ruin—a fragmentary bridge. An intricate stone abutment remained standing on each shore, and four evenly spaced stone piers made a staggering progress across the river's width, but nothing remained of any of the spans between.

On the right shore, which was somewhat nearer, the broken abutment offered a sort of cavernous shelter under its thick arches.

Under a bombardment of hailstones suddenly grown painfully, dangerously large, Adrian turned the canoe's prow sharply in to shore. The three people scrambled onto the muddy bank, and with the help of Marland, whom the larger hailstones were consistently avoiding, Adrian carried the canoe and paddle up into shelter with them.

Once having reached a refuge, they paused, gasping, surveying the overhanging mass of old masonry above them.

The air had turned chilly. The rain had begun abruptly, a cold, sudden drenching that would have been commonplace in summer in the high country, but was surprising here.

"Wish we could get a fire started," muttered the man, swinging his Sword and glaring at the world.

"Maybe I can," said Adrian shortly. He was growing tired of offering politeness, undeserved and unappreciated. "Help me find some wood."

Both of his companions fell to eagerly enough, scrounging for dry chips and scraps under the arches of old stone. Neither of the adults seemed to find it surprising that their young guide thought he would be able to start a fire. Maybe they just assumed he had some ordinary means at hand. Perhaps, before they were imprisoned, they had been accustomed to having servants start fires for them. They were both certainly very impractical about boats.

Not about Swords, though. At least not the man. Of course he had no sheath for Coinspinner, no way to carry it except in his hand. But it was staying with him like an extension of his arm. Adrian, who had begun to hope that his chance to seize the Sword would come at any moment now, was forced to be patient once again. He built some of the gathered chips and twigs into a little pile.

And the man, looking in a pleased way at the freshly melted mud outside their refuge, murmured something about how any tracks they might have made were going to be washed out.

Adrian, sitting back on his heels after puffing a spark of wizard's fire up into a hungry little flame, caught Amelia looking at him with a strange expression on her face. He wondered if she'd noticed how that spark had been born, without benefit of flint and steel, or any other common means of fire-starting.

But a moment later she resumed her task of gathering,

calling the man to come back and help. Actually the dry earth floor of their refuge concealed a good supply of wood fragments; over the years a great many fires must have been kindled in this shelter.

Adrian continued to build and nurse his little flame. Until Marland, in the course of his search for wood, while prying up a suspicious lump with the indestructible sharp tip of the Sword of Chance, came upon something that he found considerably more interesting.

From under a thin layer of hardened earth, he pulled up a copper scabbard. To judge by its length, it must once have been used to hold a great two-handed sword, some weapon considerably longer than Coinspinner.

Marland promptly tried the fit of his bright Sword in the old scabbard, which proved to be broad enough and considerably more than long enough for its new burden. The Sword of Chance slid in with room to spare. He frowned at this thoughtfully, smiled, and set the scabbard carefully aside. Then unhurriedly he resumed his chores, chopping up some of the larger pieces of firewood with his Sword's keen edge.

Taking note that Adrian was watching him, he misinterpreted the boy's interest.

"Well, sprout, what d'ya think? Quite a big knife, hey?"

"Yessir, it's very impressive."

"Yeah. Well, you be sure to keep your hands off it, hear me? There's a magic spell on this Sword, a curse that'll do terrible things to anyone who even touches it, except me. Unless I tell them to touch it, of course."

"Yes, sir." The warning had been spoken with impressive conviction, and the young Prince, knowing what he knew, found it not at all difficult to look suitably impressed.

A little later, when a suitable reserve of wood had been established, the man went back to pick up the scabbard again. The ancient copper was still intact, and looked quite serviceable. Of course the leather straps that had once supported it had long since deteriorated, and had crumbled away when Marland pried the thing up out of the dirt.

Originally this sheath, holding a weapon too long to be carried at a man's belt, must have been worn high on the back. The great length of a two-handed sword would have made it difficult to draw, so the scabbard was open partway down one edge, allowing for the angle required by the normal human length of arm.

The man was thoughtfully studying Coinspinner's fit in this container. "Good enough. Yes, good enough. I'll need some straps, or cords, to tie it on. Shouldn't be too hard to find. Not with a little luck." He smiled privately.

"It does look like a good fit," Adrian offered cautiously.

"I'll tell you what it really looks like. It looks like I'm carrying another sort of weapon altogether, doesn't it?" And the man who called himself Marland, sounding more and more pleased with himself, suddenly laughed.

But Amelia wasn't looking especially pleased. By now she had found the softest place in the dry dust under the ruined abutment, and now she was attempting to find a comfortable position in which to settle herself there. Adrian thought that she looked utterly weary. She lay down in the dust without flinching, like one of the very poor, or like an animal. Or, perhaps, like someone who had grown accustomed to being in prison.

Marland, turning to her to say something about his Sword, instead fell silent and stood for a moment contemplating her, rubbing his jaw. Then he shifted his gaze suddenly to Adrian. "Hey, Mudrat? Now you've got the fire going, how about you taking a little walk, and see if you can scare up something to cook?"

Adrian glanced at the world beyond the open archway. "All right." The rain still poured down, but the hail seemed to have stopped. He saw what looked like an opportunity. "Would it be all right if I borrowed your Sword? I don't have a knife or—"

"No."

"I just thought it would be a handy tool if I—"

"Forget the damned Sword. Just remember what I said about it before. Now take a walk."

Well, it had been worth a try. "All right. Maybe I can scare up some food."

"That's great, kid." Marland relaxed again. "Take your time, there's no hurry." And he turned his attention back to the woman.

The Prince walked past the upside-down canoe, and out into the rain. Now that the hail had stopped, neither rain nor air felt cold, and in his near nakedness he was indifferent to getting wet. Hailstones still lay here and there, making chilly little piles under his feet, and melting drifts of ice.

He was still standing only a few meters outside the artificial cave, wondering whether to explore upstream or down, or inland, when he heard a murmur of voices from the shelter he had just left. The voices were followed by a soft laugh from the woman, and that in turn by silence. Adrian felt a faint rush of blood to his face as he realized the most likely reason for the man's wanting to get rid of him for a time.

The Prince wasn't worried about his two passengers running off while he was gone; they did need food, and they couldn't handle the canoe. Of course with the help of Coinspinner the man could probably handle any boat he wanted to; but maybe he didn't realize that yet.

The man and woman weren't the only hungry ones. The Prince turned his steps downstream along the riverbank. He was wondering whether with a little carefully chosen dowsing magic he might uncover some turtle eggs, or maybe even catch a turtle. In one of the upland rivers with which he was familiar, this kind of mudbank would be an ideal place to look for turtles, but of course things could be different here.

There were snakes and lizards also to be considered— and there indeed was a king-sized snake, coiled upon a log just at the water's edge. Adrian had no idea whether that unfamiliar serpent might be poisonous; if so, of course it could still be good to eat. Magic might help him capture it, but he felt reluctant to use magic if it could be avoided.

Magic cost energy, and it left traces in the world. And if Wood was still looking for him, the more traces of his art he left around, the easier that seeker's task would be.

Deciding to come back for the snake if nothing easier showed up, the boy moved on downstream. He had not gone far when a whiff of woodsmoke in the rainy air caught his attention. It might be smoke from his own fire, but— yes, this was another fire, cooking something.

The sun was beginning to break out now, the rainfall spattering slowly to a halt. Adrian turned inland, climbing quietly. Lances of sunlight striking at the little piles of hailstones made them steam.

On top of the first small hill, in a clearing surrounded by a little grove of trees, sat a middle-sized, middle-aged man wearing traveler's, perhaps pilgrim's, gray. He looked as dry as if no rain had ever fallen on him at all, and he was cooking something, pale-looking meat, on a spit over a small fire. Whatever it was smelled very good.

And lying comfortably near the man's feet was a familiar bulk of gray fur. The huge dog raised its head now, looking in Adrian's direction, and emitted a soft whine.

Adrian paused just beyond the ring of trees, looking things over cautiously. The little pile of offal discarded near the fire contained what looked like snakeskin, and yes, there on the ground was the serpent's neatly severed and bloody head, jaws gaping, fangs sunk helplessly into a stick of wood.

Then the man looked up at Adrian, and the Prince forgot all about the snake, and even, for the moment, about the dog.

"Hello," said the gray-eyed man, quite unsurprised. His sleeves had been rolled up somewhat for the work of butchery and cooking, revealing powerful and hairy fore-arms.

"Hello," said Adrian. The dog got to its feet and came to meet him, and he scratched it abstractedly behind the ears.

"You may," said the man, "have caught a glimpse of me once or twice before in the course of your brief existence.

But I don't suppose you've ever had a really good look.
I'm—"

And at this moment the boy felt quite certain of what
two words were coming next. He was not exactly right.

"—your grandfather. I'm sure you've heard something
about the circumstances of your father's birth?"

"Yes, sir, I have." Then Adrian hesitated. "But you
don't . . . you don't look . . ."

"I don't look quite old enough to be your grandfather?"
Adrian nodded.

"No, I suppose I don't. Are you frightened of me?"

The Prince wanted to deny it. But under the gaze of
those gray eyes he found it hard to say anything that was
not true. "A little bit," he admitted at last.

"Good! Good, that's about the right attitude. You're not
so frightened that you couldn't come to like me, I hope?"

Surprisingly those last words had sounded almost wist-
ful. There was another pause, during which Adrian found
himself moving, as if unconsciously, a little closer to the
man. "I don't think so, sir," he said at last. "But I don't
know you yet."

"I know you pretty well, though. So that's all right. All in
good time." By now the boy was standing quite close to the
man, and Adrian's grandfather, the Emperor, put out a
strong but gentle hand and took him firmly by the chin and
cheek, and turned his head a little back and forth, looking
him over carefully. The inspection took only a moment,
and then Adrian was released.

"When you see your father again," the Emperor said,
"tell him that I am well pleased by what I see in you. So far.
By the way, I'm very pleased that you didn't try to steal the
Sword from the woodcutter."

"Yes, sir, thank you. It didn't seem right. Uh, Grandfather?"

"Yes."

"This dog. Did you know that he was . . ." The Prince
gestured vaguely.

"With you for a time? Yes, I knew that." The Emperor

reached out to thump the beast's ribs, and got a tail wag in return. "I even know his name."

"He's your dog, then? What is his name?"

"In a manner of speaking I suppose he's mine. More mine than anyone else's, perhaps. His name is Draffut."

"Sir? Oh, you mean he's named after—the god."

"No, I don't mean that at all." The grandfatherly eyes looked stern for a moment. "I mean that he once walked six meters tall on his hind legs, and had two hands, and spoke as clearly as you or I. People called him 'god,' but I think he never claimed that title for himself."

Adrian was goggling, gazing speechlessly from man to beast and back again.

"And then," the Emperor went on, "Draffut ran into a problem. He killed a man, and in his case that was especially damaging . . . but in time I think his problem can be solved." Once more he thumped the ribs, and the shaggy tail waved somewhat faster. The Emperor looked at his grandson, smiling. Subject closed, for the time being at least.

"Oh," said Adrian, at last.

"You had some other question?" his grandfather asked unhurriedly.

"Yes. Yessir, I do. What am I going to do about—?" With head and shoulder the Prince gestured toward the ruined abutment, where his canoe and his passengers waited, one of them keeping a tight grip on a Sword.

The Emperor said: "That's going to be up to you."

"Oh."

"Don't sound so disappointed. You're doing all right so far. In fact you're doing very well. And you're not as much alone as you may think. I had the canoe there for you when it was needed, didn't I?"

"Oh. Oh!" The second monosyllable was a little brighter. "The man has a Sword, Coinspinner. I expect you know that. I'm going to try to get it away from him."

"I'd be very wary about trying that. But, Adrian, son, I

expect you can handle the situation, and I'm not going to take it over for you. Believe me, I have my reasons."

"Yes, sir. If you say so."

"I do say so. Now, I take it that gathering food was one of the reasons that brought you out for a walk in the rain. Have some snake, it's quite good." The point of a small dagger, whose handle had suddenly appeared in the Emperor's hand, came out to probe at the roasting meat, and with swift delicacy separated a sizable chunk from the remainder hanging on the spit.

Adrian accepted the hot gift in callused fingers, and a moment later he was chewing. "This's good. Mmm. Thanks."

"You're quite welcome. Here, have some more. I'd send you back to your—can I call them companions?—with some more of this, but I fear they might be overly curious as to where you got it. But let me show you a little trick, and you can catch another snake. All you need is a forked stick, and it's easy to avoid the fangs."

Less than half an hour later, Adrian returned to the shelter. He noticed that his small fire had been allowed to go out, but a good supply of wood remained, and with a little fakery it ought to be easy to pretend to be rekindling a surviving spark.

At Adrian's entrance, carrying a live snake, Amelia recoiled. Still lying in the dust, she stirred and pulled her dress straight, checking to see that all the fastenings were in place. But Marland, who had been squatting near her, jumped up and came forward rubbing his hands together, his eyes alight, when he saw the fat snake coiled around Adrian's arm, the fanged jaws rendered helpless by the boy's grip just below the head.

Marland got the idea at once. "Hey, Mudrat, you're a great provider!"

Coinspinner was produced, and in Marland's jealous grip did excellent mundane work in severing the serpent's head, then quickly skinning and cleaning what remained. By that time Adrian had a spit ready, and the fire going again.

Before dark their downstream journey was resumed. Marland said he wanted to travel as far as possible before camping for the night.

FIFTEEN

IN an effort to save time, and feeling confident in his own skills, Karel had elected to guide this small party into the City through one of its more dangerous entrances. Several times in the course of the journey, serious-looking obstacles had loomed, physical barriers or virtual walls of magic. But so far the old wizard had led them through the difficulties safely.

Karel and Rostov, their semiparoled prisoners Murat and Kebbi, and the half-dozen Tasavaltan troopers with them had now reached the area within the City of Wizards that was their goal. All of them were now contemplating their strange surroundings, made all the stranger by the devastation wrought by an earth-elemental. That at least was the agency assigned by Karel.

Whatever the cause of it might have been, Murat observed privately, it was obvious at first glance that some violence on a large scale had occurred here, not long ago. Some mighty force had smitten the surface of the earth at this point, whether from above or below he could not say, and the land was still scarred with radii of cracks that looked as if they might be healing. The land was still upthrust slightly here and there. Walls had fallen down, and trees. Many of the latter had been uprooted and their foliage was dead or dying now.

The little river that followed a crooked trench through the middle of this scene of devastation was now running calmly enough, but it was easy to see that its previous course had been somewhat disrupted. A low place, that might once have formed an extensive pond, was now a small sea of mud, drying and cracking around the edges under the pressure of the City's peculiar and sometimes multiple sun.

As the Tasavaltan wizard had several times assured his companions, time flow in the City was apt to be different from outside, so it was very difficult to judge how long they had been here already, or how long their mission was going to take. In any case, their efforts in getting here had already used up more time than the wizard had hoped they were going to have to spend.

Again, now that they were in the City, Murat and Kebbi each had a trooper assigned to him as guard. It was not, Rostov assured Karel, that the General did not trust the strength of the wizard's guardian spells. Rather it was that the Tasavaltan cavalrymen had little else to do anyway.

As for the two Culmians themselves, so far they were coexisting in an uneasy truce. They eyed each other with suspicion and spoke to each other only when absolutely necessary.

"Are we to set up a camp, then?" Rostov demanded of Karel, who sat his mount beside him. "Or can you tell at once which way we ought to go from here?"

The old wizard appeared to ignore the question. "The Emperor's Park," he muttered, as if to himself, as he looked out over the bit of pleasant greenery adjoining the distorted Red Temple.

"Why do you call it that?" asked Murat, riding a little closer. He found his question ignored, as he had more than half expected.

Rostov could doubtless have found out if he had asked, but he was not that much interested in names. "Are you sure this is the place where the Prince dropped from sight?"

"Quite sure. The remnants of Wood's magic are very strong. And there are some of Adrian's as well."

Karel now turned his attention from the tortured land-scape, and focused on what looked like a most peculiar Red Temple, standing just next door. This structure was still in one piece following the recent upheaval. But still its shape was so distorted that Murat assumed it had been seriously affected.

"I have been here before," the apple-cheeked wizard was now muttering to himself. He nodded. "Yes. Several times, though my last visit was many years ago. Much has changed."

"I should think it has," said Rostov practically. "Now how do you propose that we begin our search for the Prince? Or do you wish to leave that detail to me?"

The wizard was not really ready for that question yet. Shaking his head vaguely to indicate this, he dismounted and strolled about a bit on foot. Then he paused, turning away from the Temple again to point in the general direction of the muddy depression. "There used to be a pond here. A dam, a small dock, and pleasure boats—there's what's left of the dock, at least." He indicated some planks and timbers lying forlornly in the mud.

"And this bit of land belongs to the Emperor, you say?" Murat persisted.

This time he got an answer. "Yes. Or it used to, when it occupied some portion of the mundane world. I don't know how it got to be here in the City. None of his doing, I suppose. More likely some spiteful prank by one of his enemies."

"I suppose he has many of those," offered the Crown Prince, who was not at all sure that any such being as the Emperor really existed.

Once again he got no answer. Karel, getting down to business now, called for such help as some of the others could give him, in holding certain charms and mumbling words. He was soon able to ascertain that some very powerful trapping spells had recently been used at this location—and he was pretty sure that Wood was their author.

"Trapping spells?"

"Yes. Charms to keep a person or people in one place, usually by annulling their desire to leave, or indeed to do anything but kill time. Making them forgetful of their own affairs. Such spells can be very effective when done properly—as these would certainly have been."

Rostov looked around in all directions. "No demons."

Karel agreed. "I think not. Wood may have learned not to send such creatures against the royal house of Tasavalta. But it would seem that he's adopted other methods that may work."

Returning to his survey of the site, he soon began to provide some details concerning the elemental—or, possibly, more than one—that had recently been raised here.

"That, I'm almost sure, was the lad's own work. And as soon as the elemental or elementals were raised, they came into violent conflict with the powers embodying the spells, or representing them . . . with the result that you see around you."

"And the young Prince?" asked Rostov, sticking to the point. "What happened to him?"

"As I read matters, the result of the fight was that Wood's spells were shattered, and therefore Adrian probably managed to escape with his life, somehow—we know that Trimbak Rao was here, shortly after the clash, looking the place over. I don't know if he came back later, and managed to find out something new."

"How can we be sure," Kebbi put in, "that the Prince wasn't caught after all, or killed?"

"We can't be absolutely sure."

"If he survived, if he escaped, where is he?"

"I believe he went downstream."

"Then we can follow." The renegade pointed with a brisk gesture. "That's straightforward enough."

"Not quite." Karel went on to explain that only a little way downstream the little river before them approached an exit from the City, where it split into several little rivers, each of them with as much water in it as the original, and each assuming a different course across the mundane countryside. It would be difficult for any magician, even himself or Wood, to be sure which one of those branchings Adrian had taken, assuming the boy did go downstream.

"But what gives me the most hope is, that if he had been caught, his captors would be gloating now, and I suppose demanding ransom of one kind or another." Karel paused. "Of course, as I said before, I cannot be absolutely sure that the Prince is still alive."

"Well, given all that you say, sir, how do we conduct our search?" Kebbi kept trying to promote himself out of the status of prisoner.

Before the wizard could reply, a brief disturbance interrupted the searchers' conversation. Two of the troopers were shouting for help, trying to get one of their fellows out of the hedge bordering the grounds of the Red Temple. The man refused to move, they reported, he wouldn't speak, and he looked strange.

Karel, on the spot in a moment, soon had the victim free. Some remnant, it appeared, of Wood's trapping magic was still effective, but by his art the Tasavaltan wizard had been able to push the obstacle away.

Another trooper spoke a warning: "Sir, someone's coming." The hooves of two riding-beasts were crunching through the ruins of a nearby building.

Trimbak Rao now made his appearance, a young girl riding at his side. The Tasavaltans, and Murat at least, rejoiced to hear from him that this was Trilby. Quickly Trimbak Rao reported that he had managed to locate the girl only yesterday, quite near here. She was essentially unharmed, though she had been lost for several days, wandering and hiding in the City in a state of shock and terror. She had agreed to come back to this place today, under escort, to tell Adrian's great-uncle and his loyal friends whatever she could about his disappearance and her own difficult escape.

When the girl had been introduced to everyone, she looked around, and said in a low voice: "It was—it was just very bad. I thought I was starting to know something about magic, but then—this was happening to us, and I never knew it."

Karel was grandfatherly, and very soothing. "Stronger magicians than you would have fallen under those spells in the same way, daughter. Be calm, now, and tell us what you can."

Trilby did her best.

"Once the Prince and I got this far," she said, indicating the place where they were standing, "it was like we just—stopped. We did everything but finish our business and get out. We talked about how strange things were here. We sat around talking about nothing.

"We even swam in the pool—or at least I swam, while Adrian went out exploring on his own. And then he came back, and I started out to have a look around—but I can't remember any more." She bowed her head helplessly.

"Try again, daughter. Maybe I can help you." And Karel took the girl's hands in his. He was probably capable of giving real help in this matter when even the powerful Trimbak Rao had not yet had much success.

A few moments later, the girl said: "Yes . . . wait. It's starting to come back to me now."

And now Trilby was able to remember the presence of a single canoe, drifting in the small pool above the dam, or rather tied up at the end of the little pier.

Karel appeared to find this very interesting. "What kind of a canoe was it?"

"A dugout. I remember thinking that was strange . . . and then . . . I remember thinking how odd it was, there was no magical aura about that canoe at all."

Again the old wizard nodded, as if he found this of significance.

Then Trilby went on to describe where she'd gone on her solo scouting trip. At first with Adrian, when they'd just arrived here, and later on her own, she'd examined some of the strange architectural and decorative features of the Red Temple yonder. She talked a little about those strange things now.

But right now the most important thing in her own mind was that she, who had been in command of the expedition, had failed to see it through. Trilby felt very guilty about her failure. Especially about leaving Adrian alone at poolside—

"Not your fault, daughter, not your fault. No one had any reason to suspect the kind of attack you both endured. Come now, tell us all you can remember about what happened."

The discussion continued. Meanwhile four troopers had been posted as sentries nearby, while two waited in reserve. And some of Karel's and Trimbak Rao's powers were serving in the same capacity.

Haltingly, still struggling with her emotions, the girl told the listening men how things had gone for her on that terrible day, what she'd experienced when overtaken by Wood's overwhelming assault.

"And then—then while all this foulness still held me in, it seemed like the earth was buckling up under my feet— that was Adrian's elemental, I know now—and all the while, even then, the crazy voices kept soothing me, telling me I needn't worry about any of it.

"I wanted to get away, and I couldn't. I wanted to yell, to scream for help, and then I realized that I couldn't even do that . . ."

Trilby, having finished telling the essentials, began to cry.

Karel kept after her, gently. "And you have no idea, no clue, what happened to Adrian?"

"No, no idea at all. I'm sorry."

"It's not your fault." He patted her gently. Karel could be very convincing, and his assurance seemed to be at least partially accepted.

And shortly thereafter, Trimbak Rao departed with the girl. He was taking her back to his headquarters, where some of her relatives were waiting. He and Karel had made a tentative arrangement to confer later on what magical measures ought to be taken to locate Adrian.

Murat and Kebbi had been listening to all this with Rostov and some of the troopers. Murat, having given his word of honor, was not seriously considering an escape attempt at this time.

Kebbi was a different case.

Rostov spoke, "Well, wizard? I have effectively yielded command to you, but I must persist, it seems, in prodding you to action. Where and how do we commence our search?"

"No satisfactory answer has presented itself so far. I will do my best to find out; stronger measures are going to be required."

The wizard brought out some of the impedimenta of his craft, and got down to business.

He appeared to be surprised at the first results of his divinations. "I had thought we would be directed downstream," he muttered.

"And we are not?"

"No."

"Then where?"

Karel turned his face back toward the Red Temple whose twisted bulk loomed over the little parklike area.

"There?"

"There." Karel sounded rather surprised himself.

Murat had a definite impression that the Twisted Temple, as seen from the perspective of the Emperor's Park, was growing larger and more ominous as time went by. No one else commented on any change, so he supposed that it was only in his imagination.

"I wonder if there's anyone in it now?"

"Alas, that question lacks a simple answer."

Karel, who had heard a thing or two about this particular facility, explained some of its peculiarities to his frowning listeners. This was a very special Red Temple, containing within itself access to the City from the outside. By this means certain preferred customers were brought here (at a premium price, of course) from certain of the Temple's sister establishments around the world.

Here, in a Red Temple enclave within the City of Wizards, the forces of magic could be employed in a certain, relatively economical, way, to augment the effects of pleasures available elsewhere; and, perhaps more importantly, to provide certain pleasures that were nowhere else available at any price. Or so some of the discreet advertising claimed.

Inside those misshapen walls, magic was used, almost routinely, to augment the effects of alcoholic drink and other drugs. To heighten the delights of the gourmet, and the glutton.

"And, naturally, to increase the pleasures of sex as well," Karel said. "In there, inhuman powers are capable of assuming for a time the human form, incubi and succubi more beautiful than any natural human flesh can be."

"It sounds an interesting place," the General commented dryly. "Shall we begin, then?"

SIXTEEN

DAYLIGHT was fading rapidly when Adrian and the two people with him finally came ashore for the night on the first day of their trip downriver from Smim. Sometime before they landed, Marland had begun to complain earnestly to his two companions about how grossly he had been maltreated by the Red Temple. Adrian at least was ready to listen, and to him the man recited many details about how the priests and guards of the pleasure palace had cheated him, and accused him falsely of cheating and of murder.

Adrian thought that Amelia probably had at least equal cause for complaint, but she was not complaining. Her resigned expression indicated that she thought complaining would be useless anyway. She seemed less disposed to seek revenge than to find some peace and quiet for herself. Adrian got the feeling that she really did not care much for Marland, but was putting up with him because he had got her out of prison, and because for the time being no one better was available.

On that first night, the three found shelter—you could hardly call what they did making camp—under a half-fallen and almost completely hollowed log, a snug and really comfortable place to which Adrian felt sure they had been led by the powers of the Sword of Chance. Marland, poking about on shore at dusk, his Sword in hand, had stumbled on the place without surprise. Already he was accepting miraculous good luck as no more than his due, and he had evidently come to trust in the Sword's powers without thinking much about them. Stretched out on the deepest drift of dead leaves available, with the black hilt clutched in one hand and the stained copper scabbard in the other, he was soon snoring.

Amelia, now evidently feeling a need to talk, stayed awake conversing with the weary Adrian for some time.

She asked the boy about his background, and he felt somewhat guilty for making up a fictitious family, a collection of cruel and demented people from whom he hoped to remain separated.

Amelia listened with half an ear. What she was really interested in was the chance to pour out some of her own troubles, which never got a very sympathetic hearing from Marland.

During this conversation the young woman revealed that she'd spent some time in the pay of the Red Temple—she didn't say specifically what her job had been, and Adrian had tact enough to refrain from asking.

It was while she had been working there that Marland—"He didn't call himself that, then"—had got to know her, and she him.

Two meters away, Marland, the copper-scabbarded Sword securely tucked under him, was snoring, dead to the world. Adrian, curious, asked Amelia: "Did he really try to swindle the Temple?"

"Hush!" hushed Amy automatically, with a glance in the direction of her sleeping man. Then, looking cynical and worn, she went on in a whisper: "What does it matter? In this world everyone tries to cheat everyone else anyway. And you know what? We're all sentenced to death already. So why not?"

Perhaps something in Adrian's face as he listened to this philosophy persuaded her not to elaborate on it. "Never mind, kid. Try to get some sleep."

And the truth was that the Prince was beginning to have great difficulty in keeping his eyes open. Remembering his grandfather's praise and encouragement gave him confidence enough to go to sleep.

He passed a comfortable and almost dreamless night. Awakening early in the morning, Adrian, lying still and doing mental calculations, decided that eight days had now passed since he and Trilby had so optimistically entered the City of Wizards. Where was she now?

The Prince's two companions were awake shortly after him. Marland was in a good mood, and allowed his guide to touch Coinspinner's hilt before beginning a hunt for food—although the man, ever cautious in matters concerning his good luck, kept gripping it at the same time. Doubtless the brief touch had some good effect, for Adrian quickly located a large clutch of birds' eggs, which were soon frying on a flat rock set next to the fire. While waiting for the eggs to cook, the three munched on some delicious fruit, just turning ripe, that happened to be growing nearby.

Again Amelia took note of Adrian's fire-starting methods. Taking advantage of a moment when Marland was absent in the woods nearby, she asked the boy straight out: "How'd you make that fire?"

The Prince had been expecting her to get around to direct questioning sooner or later, and had his answer ready. "I have a trick," he admitted openly. "It comes in handy lots of times." A fair number of people in the world had one bit of magic that they could do, some trick they had managed to perfect to the point of real usefulness.

"I bet it does." And Amelia looked thoughtful. Adrian watched to see whether she would pass this information quickly on to Marland. He couldn't be sure; but if she did, the man, to judge by his reaction, was not much interested.

Shortly after breakfast the three resumed their voyage downstream, with Adrian paddling as before. They had been under way for several hours when the Sword once more engineered the extraordinary.

The travelers were in the process of passing the junction of their river with another, slightly smaller, that came in from the direction of some hills. The onrushing tributary was fast and turbulent, even foaming from its rough plunging trip.

It was Amelia who saw the thing first, half buried in the mud, and called out to the others, and pointed. There on shore, in a minor promontory just where the rivers joined, was a squarish object of beautifully carved wood. Adrian paddled closer, beached the canoe, got out into the mud and began to dig in it with his hands.

What came to light was a tightly constructed wooden chest that must have fallen in from some bridge or boat upstream along the tributary.

"Don't open it yet." Sword still in hand, Marland took off his broken prison shoes and waded, grimacing at the mire, to join Adrian. "First let's get it solidly up on shore somewhere."

Between them that was soon accomplished, though the chest was encouragingly weighty. The next task was to get it open. The finely crafted lid was tightly closed, but secured only by a light clasp and lock that soon yielded to Coinspinner's flawless edge and steely weight.

Amelia let out a little cry in the moment after the lid went up. At first glance the chest appeared to be full of clothing, and on the top were women's dresses, all dry and unstained. As the upper contents were removed—Amelia seized them very carefully and spread them out on mud-free gravel—the receptacle proved to contain both men's and women's garments. The former fit Marland well enough for him to wear them, and most of the latter fit Amelia almost perfectly.

Her plaintive cry was for a mirror. And sure enough, that was the next item Marland, now rummaging toward the bottom of the box, managed to turn up.

Now Amelia, carrying an armload of clothes from the

chest, dodged quickly into the brush out of sight of the others. There she discarded her hated prison garb, putting on a new yellow dress.

By the time she emerged, carrying a new pair of shoes—she had decided to save them for later—Marland too had changed his clothes. He had also discovered a flask of brandy, and was ready for a minor celebration.

"Well, Mudrat—looks like there's nothing here for you. That's all right, you can walk around bare-assed and nobody minds. For dear Amy and myself here, though, things are different. We're going to have to upgrade our appearance considerably, and this's a good start." Wiping his chin, he offered her a drink, which she accepted, giggling.

When the flask came back to Marland, he generously extended it to Adrian. The boy accepted, but scarcely wet his lips with the fiery stuff. Suddenly a new hope had been born. The man might now drink himself insensible, or at least into a mood where he might let his guide and servant borrow the Sword for some good reason.

But that was not to be.

Marland doubtless had his obsessions and his weaknesses, but drink did not appear to be among them. After taking a second nip himself he put the flask casually away under a thwart. When, a moment later, Amy wanted more, he watched her drink, and sternly ordered her not to take enough to make her balance in the canoe uncertain.

The ransacking of the chest went on, and Adrian was not, after all, denied all benefit from its discovery. The chest also contained some candy, some cakes—not quite as good, the Prince thought while he sampled, as those given him by Talgai—and other useful preserved food. There was even a packet of tea, and a few small pots and dishes. A small amount of money would be less immediately useful.

Marland decreed a small feast of celebration.

At the bottom of the chest they found a large cloth bag,

tightly folded, in which most of the useful stuff could be carried aboard the canoe.

As for the chest itself, it was too large and awkward to come along. In the process of converting it to kindling for a fire, Coinspinner ripped open a hitherto unsuspected secret compartment, from which a couple of modestly valuable jewels came tumbling out into the light of day.

Marland grabbed them up, demonstrating more satisfaction than surprise. Now money would be available, at the next sizable town to which they came.

There was one more discovery, either in the secret compartment or a small but unhidden drawer nearby—a pair of dice. They came complete with a little cup of horn, decorated with carvings of a couple of Red Temple deities, in which to shake them before casting.

The bottom of the chest, still intact, was flat and fairly sizable. Marland set it on a flat place on the ground, and sat down suddenly in front of it, with his new dice cup in hand. The sheathed Sword was in his left hand, but the expression on his face was such that Adrian wondered suddenly whether even Coinspinner might have been temporarily forgotten.

That was not the case just yet—the man was careful to keep the Sword and scabbard in contact with his body as he sat.

"Hey," Amelia prodded. "You were in such a hurry to get on downstream?"

"Never mind. We can camp here tonight."

"Camp? In what?" She looked up at the open, partly cloudy sky.

She got no answer. Not the jewels, not the drink, not even his woman in her new dress had aroused quite the same interest in Marland's eyes as was evoked by the two little ivory cubes. While Amelia quietly retrieved the flask from the canoe and helped herself to another swig of brandy, he picked up the two dice and nursed them tenderly for a while in his fist. Then with a minor flourish he cast them out on his improvised tabletop. He scooped them up and threw them again and again, sometimes using the cup and sometimes not. His whole attention was concentrated on the results.

The Sword was now lying at Marland's feet, just barely out of contact with his body. Adrian watched both Sword and man with an almost equally concentrated attention.

He jumped when the man said suddenly: "C'mere, Mudrat. Forget about whatever it is you're doing. I want to teach you something about shooting dice."

Amelia, vaguely disapproving, and at the same time somewhat amused and interested, had settled herself on a nearby log, and was nibbling candy and looking on.

Digging into his newly acquired small hoard of petty cash, carried in one of his new pockets, the man dealt out ten small coins in front of Adrian, and set out an equal number before himself.

"Here's ten for you, boy, ten for me. Whoever loses all his coins first has to clean up the camp. Ever play dice?"

"No, sir." That wasn't exactly true, but true enough; certainly the Prince had never played in the way that this man seemed to mean.

Marland proceeded to teach the boy the rules. Actually the Prince already knew, in a hazy fashion, the game or a very similar version; but he allowed himself to be taught.

"Wait. Before we start, let me fix something." Among the men's clothes in the bountiful chest had been a couple of thin leather belts. Doing a little crude leatherwork with Coinspinner, Marland soon had these worked into a kind of harness. Presently Coinspinner's hilt, with the symbolic white dice barely visible, was peeking over the man's shoulder. Adrian glanced at it in private despair as he picked up the dice for his first turn.

It was going to be hopelessly difficult for anyone but the wearer to grab at the Sword while it rode in that position.

The Princeling threw the dice. Then Marland picked them up and threw them. Naturally enough, Adrian lost.

During the first few turns of the entirely one-sided game,

the man's eyes gleamed, as if with the commencement of fever, each time he won a coin. But long before ten turns had passed, well before Adrian's row of coins was entirely gone, Marland's expression had changed. He was beginning to frown.

Adrian still had three coins in front of him when the man broke off the game in a surly fashion, and swept up all the money indiscriminately to stuff it back into his pocket.

Noting Marland's expression—anger, though fortunately not directed at him—Adrian got up without comment and busied himself with some makework tasks around the fire.

Amelia meanwhile went to her man, putting her hands on his shoulders, studying his face, trying to discover what his problem was.

She hadn't long to wait. Standing now, he smiled ruefully and reached back over his left shoulder to pat the black hilt. "As long as I wear this, I win. I can feel it now, I'm sure of it. As long as I have this with me, I'm going to win. On every turn."

"Is that so bad?"

He gave her a look that said she didn't understand. "Bad? It's—" But at that point he broke off, frowning, as if unable to explain his own feelings or even understand them. At last he said: "It isn't gambling anymore. It's like—picking up money in the street. It's good to have, but there's no kick. You ought to know what I mean."

Amelia said nothing. Watching her face, Adrian thought she was tired of listening to this man, but she kept at it.

"Of course, if I were to take this thing into a real casino . . . one of the big ones . . ." Marland brightened as this thought occurred to him, but again fell silent.

"What are you thinking of doing, Buve?" Amelia sounded worried.

If he noticed the name by which she'd called him, he disregarded it. "What am I thinking? I'm thinking that this Sword is big magic. Really big. If it could get me out of that jail the way it did . . . I'm thinking that it's bigger than anything the Red Temple can put up against it. Any Red Temple."

Now his lady friend was really growing alarmed. "Buve, what are you planning now? What are you going to get us mixed up in? Remember what happened the last time."

"That's what I remember. I remember it all too well. I want to see that those bastards remember it too." He showed his teeth in a kind of smile, and patted her arm. "Last time we didn't have the gods on our side."

But the plan, whatever it was, was put aside for the time being, withdrawn from discussion, while Marland apparently tried to perfect it in his own mind.

For sheer compulsive amusement, to have some simple fun gambling with Adrian, the man now disarmed himself temporarily. He trusted Amelia to sit close beside him, her weight on the sheathed Sword, while he and Adrian played at dice.

This time, after fickle fortune had reversed herself several times, Adrian eventually won all the small coins. The boy had not tried to cheat with magic. Used fairly, the dice had finally favored the Prince, while Marland went through several stages of emotion.

Whatever force drove Marland into this game was not satisfied until he'd lost his whole allotment of ten coins, and was tempted to dig into his pocket for more.

He drew on his capital for ten more, and ten more after those. At that point his luck finally turned and he won all of the coins back. Before that happened, Adrian was beginning to consider magical manipulation of the dice to force a win for Marland and restore him to a good temper.

The evening around the fire was drawing to a close when there came a snuffling and a rustling in the undergrowth nearby. Two greenish eyes set wide apart reflected flame, and Marland grabbed for his Sword.

After one or two preliminary howls issued out of the encircling darkness, causing Marland to jump up, a huge gray beast came bounding into the firelight to greet Adrian extravagantly. It was the great dog the Emperor had called Draffut.

Adrian, trying to fend off the creature's demonstrations, and shield it from the Sword at the same time, at last managed to explain.

Marland sheathed his Sword again. "That beast isn't going to ride in the canoe with us!"

"No, sir, he sure wouldn't fit there. He can run along on shore, and keep up."

"Well, as long as he keeps his distance most of the time." The man considered. "Actually a beast like that might help me play the part."

"What part?" asked Amelia, plainly mystified.

"That of a man who's wealthy enough to keep a giant pet. Among other extravagances."

"Then he can come with us? I promise he won't be any trouble."

"We'll see." Marland frowned. "Has he got a name?"

Adrian, with some thought in mind for the Emperor's predilection for the truth, blurted out what he had been told: "Draffut."

Marland, appreciative of irreverence, got a good laugh out of that.

"From here on, kid," said Marland, next day, as they were pulling up to the docks of another town, "we're not going to need the canoe any longer. Don't worry, I'll pay you for it." It was never really money that concerned this man. "You're still coming with us, though. I'm going to have a job for you."

Draffut had disappeared, somewhere on shore. He had a tendency to do this, and Adrian felt reasonably confident that he was going to come back.

And he wasn't really worried about losing the canoe, either, though it was his grandfather's. Adrian expected that Grandfather could get it back if and when he really wanted it. With some vague idea, perhaps, of making such a recovery easier, the boy neglected to tie up the craft when they had got everything out of it. And there it went, riding the current on its own, turning freely with the breeze.

Having entered a sizable town, the three now began the process of rejoining civilization.

Looking for the best place to change his modest find of jewels to ready cash, Marland paced along the main street. Trivial incidents—a woman passing with a basket of laundry on her head, a baby crawling away from its mother—occurred to block him from the doorways of the first two stores he would have entered, but when he paused near the entrance of a third, a burdened loadbeast crowded him from behind, effectively nudging him inside.

Amelia and Adrian waited in the street. In what seemed like only a short time the man came out, smiling at them and jiggling a stack of coins in his fingers. "Just what the jeweler was looking for," he informed them. "It seems he's trying to construct a fancy brooch, and those little pebbles will just fit. How about something to eat?"

Having purchased sausages and pancakes from a street vendor, they stood on a corner munching.

"The more good things happen to us," said Marland, looking at Amelia, "the more afraid you look."

"I am afraid."

He snorted something, and took another bite of sausage. "You afraid, Mudrat?"

Adrian wasn't required to answer. Amelia was trying her best to argue with her man. "Look, Buve, we've got a good thing going now. A great thing. We've got some money, and—"

"*Some* money. Yeah. Hah!"

"You want more? We can get more, without—sticking our necks out again. We can go anywhere we want—"

"It's not enough. Not after what those bastards did to me—and to you—and what they almost did. I can go anywhere I want, all right, and I know where I want to go. I'm going to take it out on them."

Adrian watched as Amelia turned away. She was muttering something and he thought it might be prayers. Or maybe it was curses, or most likely some of each. She probably realized, thought the Prince, that her chances of talking Marland out of a scheme, once he'd made up his mind to it, were practically zero.

When they had finished their lunch, Marland walked ahead, strolling the street, doubtless trying to plan just what he ought to do next. Amelia and Adrian followed. They had the opportunity for another private talk, in which Amelia spelled out her fears in greater detail.

"Cham," she suggested suddenly, "your canoe's gone— he didn't pay you for that yet, did he?"

"No, ma'am."

"He will—he's not a tightwad. Where's your dog?"

"Around somewhere. He'll show up."

"Good. When he does, you might take your money and your dog and get on out of town. There's safer people than us for you to hang around with."

Adrian, wondering what to say, said nothing.

In a moment the woman continued: "Marland thinks you're lucky for him, and no gambler ever has enough luck. But whatever happens is not going to be lucky for you, kid. Or for me either. I can feel it."

"You're not running away."

"Me? No. He'd come after me, and with that lucky charm of his he'd find me. Besides, I—I had my chance a long time ago, and I didn't take it then." She seemed to feel trapped, compelled, in a way that young Adrian couldn't understand. It was foreign to his whole way of thinking.

"But you can go, sonny. He won't care about losing you that much. It'll be easy for him to recruit another helper if he thinks he needs one."

The Prince could not help feeling tempted. The overall geography was now definite enough in his mind that he felt fairly confident of being able to find his way home from here; he would have a little money, and of course his skills. But he interpreted what his grandfather had said to him as encouragement in his course of pursuing Coinspinner,

though it had included a warning to be careful while he did
so. And the Emperor trusted him, believed that he would
be able to get the Sword, or at least do a good job of trying.

So the Prince was not going to turn his back on the
Sword. Not now. "I guess I'll stick around for a while yet."

Amelia stared at him. The way she looked made him
believe that she could be really nasty if she wanted to.
"What do you think you're going to get out of it? Do you
think he's really going to make you rich? He doesn't care
about that, not really. He's going to get all three of us
killed, most likely."

"I'm staying. Marland's got a lot of luck on his side."

Amelia looked at him now as if she wondered who he
really was. "All right, all right. Don't say I didn't warn
you."

Adrian certainly would never be able to say that. And
despite his brave words and his decision he was worried.
Sometimes he had definite magical indications that Wood
was coming after him again.

On their first night under a roof, in the first cheap
suburban inn they came to, Adrian saw Marland sleeping
with the sheathed Sword pinned beneath his head and
body, making a hard pillow, no doubt, but the only one
that could give this man rest.

Once more the Prince, for a moment at least, contemplated trying to grab the Sword away. Grab for the black
hilt, tug it from the sheath. The trick seemed safe, and
almost easy. But always, knowing the Sword's power,
Adrian held back. And in fact, when he looked closer, he
saw that Marland had tied the hilt to the sheath with a
thread or thong.

No, Adrian thought, the only way to get Coinspinner
away from its owner was to have him give it freely. Of
course in this case the chance of that happening was just no
chance at all. Then why was he, Adrian, hanging around?
Because, he supposed, he was too stubborn to give up.

As they hiked between towns next day, the gambler was

ready to take his two confederates into his confidence regarding his plan to gain revenge on the Red Temple. Marland was going to have to tell both of them the plan in some detail, because he was going to need the help of both in carrying the plan out.

"The trouble is," said Marland, "that Coinspinner here is never going to let me lose. Not ever. Not even once."

"A lot of people," said Amy, "would like to have that kind of trouble."

"Shut up for a minute and let me finish. You see, the problem, my friends, is that the people who run the big casino are not idiots. They're—"

"The big casino." Amy stopped for a moment in the middle of the road. *"Did you say the big casino?"*

"Yes, my lady. Yes, my dearest. That's just what I said."

"O gods, I was afraid that's what you had in mind. What are they going to do when they see you come back?"

He put an arm around her shoulders and pulled her forward, set her walking down the road again. "They're not going to see me come back, my love. Because I don't want them to see me, and I'm very lucky now—haven't you noticed? Or if they do see me, they won't know me. I've lost weight since they've seen me last—a lot of weight. Plus, I have this new beard." He stroked it. Adrian thought it was looking somehow thicker and healthier in just the few days since Marland had started to become prosperous.

"They won't let you carry a weapon up to the gaming tables—will they?"

"You know something, Amy? I'm not going to ask their permission—now will you let me finish? They're not idiots, as I was starting to say, and if they find themselves up against a gambler who never loses, they're just going to close down the game, if necessary, until they find out what's wrong. And they're going to do that long before their bank is broken."

Amelia looked helpless. It was Adrian who had to ask the question: "So what are we going to do?"

The man flashed him a keen look, welcoming his eagerness. "I," said Marland, "am going to stay in the background, with the Sword. In the gaming room I'm thinking of—it's a very big room—there are little balconies, like box seats in a fancy theater, with curtains and all. I'm going to be holed up in one of those. You"—he pointed at Amelia—"are going to be bellied up to the table, a wealthy, bored lady, placing bets. And you, Mudrat"—the finger swung to Adrian—"are going to carry numbers from me to Amy. Carry them quickly and remember them carefully, without any mistakes. The numbers that I want her to bet on."

Marland paused, frowning at Adrian as they walked side by side. "We're going to have to find you a new name, Mudrat." He scowled at the boy critically, as if Adrian should have known better than to adopt a stupid name like that, or should at least stop clinging to it so stubbornly now that times were better.

"Yes, sir," said Adrian. "My name is really Cham. I think I mentioned that once before."

"All right, that'll do. Cham. Obviously we're going to have to get you some clothes, even fancy clothes, because you're going to be a page. Know what a page does? Never mind, you learn fast. We're going into the big time, kid. Maybe you'll need more than one outfit, because I don't know if we're going to be able to do all this winning in one session at the table . . . it would be better if we could."

"How much," asked Adrian, newly emboldened by being made a formal member of the enterprise, "are we going to gamble?"

Again Marland looked at him, welcoming an eager conspirator. "As much as it takes. We're going to beat them, gambling. Walk out of that place with a ton of their money—and make it look like the fairest and most honest game you ever saw. Cheating? Not us. No way. We're just lucky today." He dropped his voice, now sounding almost reverent. "It could happen that way, you know. It could happen that way, for someone, without any magic at all. All it would take would be a run of luck."

Amelia challenged him. "A run of luck like the world has never seen before!"

Marland turned to regard her, assessing the point judiciously. "No, not quite. Maybe once every hundred years, or every thousand, in the course of nature, a run of luck like this will come along. And we're going to make our run look as natural as can be."

Adrian, listening carefully, was becoming ever more intrigued with the challenge of doing such a thing and getting away with it.

The gambler was now explaining eagerly. "But we won't need a straight run. See, Amy, I'm only going to call about half the bets. The rest will be your choices, made at the table. Some will be good and some bad, just the way it works for every other player. Some of your own bets you'll win, and some you'll lose. But *all* the numbers that I pick, with the Sword, are going to be winners. Overall, our winnings are going to build up and up—and then fall back, sometimes, when you pick a loser. Sometimes we'll even lose huge amounts. So it's going to look like nothing but pure dumb, honest luck. We'll lead the house on and on, into a final wager—I don't know yet how much that'll be, I'll have to do some calculating. Think that out some more before we start. But it'll be enough to break their bank."

There was a pause of several heartbeats before Amy's voice asked, on a rising intonation: "Break the bank at the big casino?" The idea was finally getting through to her.

"That's what I'm saying."

"Won't they have their own magicians working?" Adrian, for the sake of credibility, thought he had better voice more skepticism than he felt; he had more acquaintance with the power of the Swords than Marland did.

Marland said: "Oh, they have wizards on their payroll, all right. They have some of the best in the world in their own specialty, which is anything to do with cheating at a game. But the Sword will handle them. I'll bet my life on it. Coinspinner'll slice them up like so much paper, and leave 'em standing there with their pockets empty."

Amelia, struck by a sudden thought, was fingering her new dress. It was certainly a long step up from prison garb, but still—

She demanded: "They're going to let me stand there in the big casino, at this high-powered table, and play, looking like this?"

Marland laughed. "You're not going to be looking like that, baby. Not at all. Not by the time we get to the big casino."

SEVENTEEN

THE Crown Prince Murat, physically unbound but still manacled by leaden magic in both feet, was following Karel, as the old Tasavaltan wizard led the entire party in a lengthy inspection of the exterior of the twisted Red Temple. By reason of sortilege Karel was convinced that the most likely way to finding Prince Adrian lay here. At one point the wizard paused in his examination, to point out to the General some ceramic tiles on the side of the building, tiles Karel said were similar to those the apprentices had been sent here to obtain.

Murat was willing enough to follow the two Tasavaltan leaders, meanwhile exchanging a few desultory snarls with Cousin Kebbi. Both Culmians could not help being distracted from their feud by the sight of a multiplex sunrise/sunset. This, as Karel informed them, and Murat could well believe, was a phenomenon that could be seen only in the City of Wizards. Perhaps a dozen sun images were visible at the same time. About half of these, red and only mildly warm, were arcing slowly down toward the rim of the sky, even as the other half threatened to rise above it. All finally blended into one red glow that spread its way entirely around the horizon.

There was a mutter of satisfaction at last from Karel. But it was not caused by the celestial phenomenon, to which he had been paying little attention. "This is the way we must go in," he announced decisively, indicating one of the many dark entrances to the Red Temple.

Rostov accepted the decision, and issued the necessary orders to his handful of armed men. The General was now wearing Sightblinder once again, its hilt coming frequently in contact with his hand or arm, and his identity tended to shimmer in the eyes of his companions.

The wizard led the way. Two troopers were left outside to hold the animals. Soon all other members of the party had filed inside the Temple, and the sky and its wonders had been shut out.

But hardly had they got themselves out of sight of the entrance when the wizard called a halt.

Beside him he beheld the General's figure, going through the kaleidoscope of changes customary for one who held Sightblinder. Karel, for all his own powers, was as much subject as anyone else to the spell of images cast by the Sword of Stealth. The figures now appearing in his perception, one after another, included some from his far-distant childhood, as well as the eidolons of Ardneh and of Draffut. The latter appeared crawling through the dark passage, under a ceiling much too low for the god's full six-meter height, displaying Draffut's unmistakable mighty fangs, great manlike hands, and look of serene intelligence.

In addition to these figures, the cycle seen by the old magician sometimes included the dread image of Wood, appearing now as a blond, handsome demigod, armed with Shieldbreaker.

I had not realized, thought Karel, *that I feared my great enemy as much as that, for the Sword of Stealth to limn him for me* . . . But he had not stopped to admire the images created by Sightblinder. He suddenly did not feel well. That was why he had come to a halt, leaning back against a wall, knowing that he must look uncharacteristically weary.

And now he understood why.

"Rostov," he said. "Get those two other men in here. The animals also."

The General gestured quickly to his sergeant before he asked the question. "What's wrong?"

"Plenty." Karel's breath was wheezing loudly now. "There's demon-smell and demon-sickness in the air. You'll be able to feel it in a minute. Wood is striking at us."

Murat and Kebbi exchanged uncertain glances.

"I mean the man," said Karel, looking at the renegade lieutenant, "who took your Sword from you. He goes armed with a greater weapon, Shieldbreaker. And he comes now escorted by a flight of his great pets. It will be all we can do to escape him with our lives."

The soldiers who had been left outside came into the Temple now, leading the riding-beasts.

Rostov, cursing, threw Sightblinder from him, in that instant resuming his own shape in the others' eyes. "If he has Shieldbreaker, this blade of mine is not going to avail us anything. But we know how to fight against the Sword of Force. What do you say, Karel? I'll tackle him barehanded, magician, if you can undertake to keep his bodyguard from killing me as I do so."

Karel shook his head. "I fear his bodyguard, as you call it, is much too strong. He is coming after us in force, with such an escort as would make any pledge of that kind on my part foolish. If worst comes to worst we may have to adopt some such plan, but before we settle for suicide let's try to get away. I hope we can make our escape in a direction that will allow us to continue our search for the Prince."

Murat was beginning to feel the demon-sickness now, deep in his guts. He'd heard of such but not experienced it before. He could tell from the faces of Kebbi and the soldiers that they were afflicted too.

"I think we can escape, but we may well be separated in the process. Before we are—" Karel dipped a hand into an inner pocket, then pushed himself away from the wall.

Moving swiftly among the other members of the party, he handed each man a small object. "Each of you is now in possession of a magical token that will allow you to identify Prince Adrian if you come within sight of him. It should also serve to show you where to seek the Prince, once you are close enough."

Murat looked at the thing that had been placed in his hand. It was a tiny wooden cube.

Karel observed his puzzled look. "Part of a toy the Prince enjoyed in infancy," the wizard wheezed. "Trust me, trust the power I have given it."

Murat could feel the heaviness in his soles and ankles. He did not doubt this wizard's pledges.

Rostov stuffed his own bit of toy impatiently into his belt. He was not yet ready to give up on fighting. "What if we leave the Swords out of it entirely, wizard? And if the demons could be distracted. Could you stand against him then?"

"Stand against him, one on one? No, I cannot." Karel's face and voice were bleak. "No magician in the world, I think, can do that . . . and besides, I tell you that he does come with a host of demons. We must escape him, if we can. Here."

With a gesture, and a twist of magic, Karel did something to the wall beside him. Murat could not see just what, but whatever was done caused several stones to vanish, or move aside, opening a way into some inner recess of the Temple.

"Animals can't follow us in here, sir," the sergeant reported. Even if the newly opened entrance had been big enough, the dark passage beyond it certainly was not.

"Then leave them! Too bad, but it must be."

In a few moments the men were all inside what Murat took to be a kind of secret passage, a dimly lit narrow tunnel through constricting brickwork. They were following Karel through this, at a surprisingly swift pace, when the assault of Wood's creatures came down on them all, almost unexpectedly.

This was no mere whiff of demonic presence at a distance, but the awful thing itself. The attack fell first upon the mind and soul, rather than the body. Despite the fact that the physical masonry around him remained firmly in place, Murat had the sensation that the world was collapsing over his head.

Even worse was the inward sickness, taking possession of the bowels and bones. A fear that seemed to turn the guts to jelly . . .

The men were crawling now, rather than walking, with Karel still in the lead. The magician was muttering continuously, and it seemed that somehow he was managing to stave off complete disaster. The terrible enemy was near, but not immediately upon them.

And now the pressure of demonic presence eased a bit. Somehow, Murat thought, the old man's got them looking in the wrong place for us. So far . . .

He kept on crawling, over the body of one of the troopers, totally collapsed. The man was dead, Murat was sure of that, for he could see the flesh already shriveling, as if being dried out from within.

Another trooper died as they crawled on. Wood's onslaught came near overwhelming Karel's defenses before the Tasavaltan could guide his friends to a yet more interior level of the Twisted Temple.

When the attack of the demons first fell on them, Kebbi, two places behind his countryman in the single line, thought that his last moment had come. But in his desperation he refused to give up. Rather, Kebbi took the opportunity which presented itself, and lunged out in an effort at escape. When the wizard led them past a place where the tunnel branched, Kebbi with a gasp turned aside, and flung himself down the branch Karel and the others had not followed.

Crawling farther, he realized with a sudden surge of hope that the bond of magic that Karel had put on him had somehow been broken. The pain he had known in legs and ankles, which had increased so rapidly whenever he had distanced himself even slightly from his captors, was gone now. Karel's binding work had been dissolved, or else abandoned in the wizard's need to channel all his powers into the giants' conflict that now raged between him and Wood. The energy that had maintained the Culmians' bondage was doubtless needed elsewhere now, as the great magician fought against a greater, for his life, and the lives of his companions.

Crawling and scrambling, realizing that the physical destruction around him was actually negligible, and that the demons' attention must all be focused elsewhere, Murat's cousin got away.

Murat, as soon as he became aware that Kebbi was no longer with the survivors of the party, started grimly back into the tunnel after him. Karel, Rostov, and the troopers had all collapsed, and no one tried to stop him. If the traitor should be lying somewhere, dead and shriveled, well and good. But if he had somehow got away . . .

The Crown Prince had not gone far before he too realized that he was now freed of Karel's magical bondage.

Sensing that he was gradually leaving the battle between the demons and the magician farther and farther behind him, Kebbi kept on crawling until he saw a light.

Rostov was the first of the remaining members of the party to regain his senses. Finding himself stretched out in a small, almost lightless underground room, Sightblinder clutched in his fist, he cursed and forced himself to his feet. There was one doorway besides the one through which they had stumbled in.

Karel and the four remaining troopers were sprawled around him, all still breathing, but in various stages bordering on complete collapse. The General tried to rouse the wizard, but the old man remained practically inert; naturally the assault had fallen heaviest of all on him.

It was only at this point that Rostov realized that his two Culmian prisoners were gone.

The prostrate men seemed to be recovering, though very slowly, and none of them were able to stand unaided yet. There was nothing for the General to do but exercise patience, and in that art he had had long training. The demons were gone, and in half an hour, Rostov thought, his party might be able to get moving again.

Then came an all-too-familiar twisting in his gut, alerting him that the demons were coming back.

He could even tell the direction now. That way, through the other tunnel.

Gripping Sightblinder and setting his jaw, the General waited for his foes to show themselves.

Kebbi, pushing on alone toward the light, knew such gratitude as he was capable of when he felt the presence of the demons fall farther and farther behind him.

At about the time that presence vanished from his perception entirely, he found himself dimly able to sense some kind of threshold of magic not far ahead. He could hope, at least, that this would offer him a way of emerging from the City.

Proceeding carefully, now standing erect, he became aware of strange presences around him at varying distances. Not that they frightened him, particularly; after the demons, these ghostly half shapes were as nothing.

One moment those distant figures were insubstantial ghosts, and the next they were real forms, mundane and solid humanity.

But who?

Kebbi flattened himself against a wall in fear. As the folk approached, a dim and bulky shape came with them, and strange noises issued from it. A horrible squeaking. He had heard that demons' voices sounded like—

He could see the people clearly now. Four of them, two men, two women, in shabby garments, and they were armed with mops and brooms. The noise proceeded from the wheels of the refuse cart they pushed before them.

After that, Kebbi had little further trouble in getting out of the Temple—though on doing so he was somewhat amazed to find himself emerging from the basement door of a Red Temple quite different from the one that he had entered in the City. He was definitely not in the City of Wizards anymore.

He was certainly in some city, though. A warm and muggy place, large and heavily populated. He could see palm trees. Wherever this was, he was free.

The wizard had somehow struggled to his feet, but that was the most he could manage, and he was threatening to fall again. Supporting Karel with one arm, and with his soldiers, none more than half-conscious, huddling close to him, General Rostov waved Sightblinder at a veritable horde of hideous demonic creatures. They had come pouring in through the tunnel entrance like so many semitransparent puffs of steam or smoke. In the boldest voice that he could manage, he roared at them all to go to hell. In terms usually reserved for blundering colonels, he directed them to get their miserable, spavined, worthless carcasses out of his way, before he decided to unleash his wrath upon them.

There might have been a dozen or a score of the foul things before him, and all recoiled abjectly from his wrath. They seemed to be on the point of retreating.

From the way they were cowering now, and abasing themselves before him, Rostov was suddenly sure that they were convinced he was Wood himself.

The presence, just here and now, of their mighty human master sorely puzzled these foul creatures, and some of them raised hideous bone-rattle voices in an attempt to justify their presence; but none of them were about to dare to argue with the man they were convinced was Wood.

In another moment they were gone. And none too soon.

The General, gasping, drenched with cold sweat, sank to the floor and for the first time in forty years allowed himself the luxury of nearly fainting.

Murat lost his quarry in a maze of crawling passages, but like his quarry he eventually managed to achieve his freedom. Unknown to the Crown Prince, his experiences in finding his way out were very similar to those of Kebbi. Murat, too, emerged from a different Red Temple than the one he had so hurriedly entered.

One difference in the experience of the two men was that Murat immediately knew where he was when he came out. In his early youth he had several times visited the city of Bihari.

Within an hour after the demons had been routed, Rostov, Karel, and their surviving troopers were all more or less recovered from the encounter, at least sufficiently to travel. The wizard now resumed his role of guide, and led the party on.

Long before they found their way out of the Temple, the Tasavaltans realized that they had somehow passed into a different building from the one that they had entered in the City.

For the time being at least, Wood's force of demons had been dispersed, or had lost the scent, or were reorganizing. Against the more common difficulties and snares that one Temple or another might present to a traveler in its protected regions, Karel's own powers were more than adequate protection. He could defend his several companions too.

The searchers found to their chagrin that the trail of Prince Adrian had long since disappeared, or else it had been wiped out in the most recent skirmish. Karel doubted whether even Wood would be able to track the lad this way, if this was indeed the way the Prince had come.

Either Adrian had come this way, or more likely gone

boating downstream from the Emperor's Park . . . at some point on this difficult journey, the wizard realized that even if he and his companions failed to locate the Prince here, they might well be on the fastest possible track for a return to Tasavalta.

EIGHTEEN

THIS was the second small suburb of Bihari that Adrian, Marland, and Amelia had entered. Walking down the first street they came to in the town, Marland made another happy discovery.

He was moving, as usual, a step or two ahead of his companions when he suddenly bent down with a little grunt of satisfaction. A moment later he had picked up a small purse that someone had dropped in the street. The color of the fine leather nearly matched that of the trodden earth, and however long the purse might have lain there, he was evidently the first to notice it.

After a reflexive look around to make sure that no one had taken any notice of his discovery, the man drew his two companions aside, under an overhanging roof, where he looked into the purse. It was just starting to rain, and the few people hurrying past on the wooden sidewalk nearby paid them no attention.

Abruptly the purse was empty, and Adrian could hear the coins jingling in Marland's quick hands, though the transition had been so neatly swift that the boy never did really see anything of them.

"Well," the man said, satisfied, not at all surprised, when his quick hidden count had been completed. "Plenty. For the time being, at least. I think I'm going to be Sir Marland

from now on. A knight or baronet, from . . . well, I'll
decide later where I'm from. Probably no one's going to
worry about that, as long as they can see my money."

Rubbing his chin thoughtfully, he looked at Amelia.
"You, of course, will be my mistress. And—"

She brushed irritably at a small stream that was trickling
on her from the roof's edge, and shifted her position to
avoid it. "Oh. And not your wife?"

Warned perhaps by something in Amelia's tone,
Marland hesitated. Then he brightened, as if struck by a
new thought. "Well, why not? It would add a touch of dull
respectability to my character, and that's all to the good.
All right, you'll be my wife."

He switched his gaze to Adrian. "And you, muddy one, I
can't say I want to claim you as my son. Besides, as people
of status we ought to have a servant. You'll be my page."

Adrian nodded agreeably. It made no difference to him.
He could only hope in passing that the true owner of the
purse was not going to be destroyed by its loss. The little
leather bag looked to be of the finest quality, so he doubted
that that would be the case.

Marland's next move was to locate a clothing shop,
where he and Amelia each purchased a new outfit of
somewhat better quality than the clothing they had taken
from the chest. That had been a vast improvement to begin
with, but the garments were now showing the effects of
several days of river travel. Adrian too was at last upgraded
from his loincloth to a fairly shabby but hole-free jacket
and trousers, in keeping with his newly official status as a
respectable servant.

After that, all three enjoyed a good meal, sitting down,
though Adrian had to eat in the rear of the food shop.
Having observed the behavior of a good many servants in
his time, the Prince had little trouble in playing the role
successfully.

On emerging from the shop's kitchen, Adrian passed a
kind of notice board, contrived from the tall stump of a

large tree. Among other signs tacked to the wood he saw a poster advertising a reward for a runaway twelve-year-old boy whose description matched his own appearance as it had been back in the City of Wizards.

He wasn't familiar with the amount of reward usually offered in such cases, but this one seemed unusually generous. The agency offering the reward was located in Bihari, and its name meant nothing to the Prince.

Coincidence? He doubted it. Word of his disappearance had preceded him here. Winged messengers must have been used. Had his friends or family caused the notice to be posted, or was it more of the work of Wood?

Certainly he dared not respond. Turning away from the poster thoughtfully, the Prince decided that his cover as Sir Marland's page was going to be helpful to him, and perhaps even important.

Besides, Marland had said: "I need you in my plans." And this offered Adrian enough hope of getting at the Sword to keep him keen on hanging around.

Were other such posters about, and were Marland or Amy going to see them? Even if they did, they might not connect them with their servant. But on the other hand they might.

With everyone well fed for the moment, and with Sir Marland and his new wife now rather more than just decently outfitted, in clothes that indicated at least a moderate degree of prosperity and status, and with a servant to accompany them, it was now time to seek out suitable lodging.

For their first night in this town, Marland selected a modest inn, no better than was necessary for a man of his obvious affluence. He engaged two rooms, so Adrian had a small one to himself. This was the first time he'd slept in a bed in what seemed like months, though it was really not that long.

Draffut still had not returned, and Adrian, with mixed feelings, had about given the creature up for lost.

Next day, the three traveled on by wagon-coach, on into the big resort city itself. Adrian rode in the rear, with the baggage. He was impressed by the city's size and complexity, though not so much impressed as he allowed Amelia and Buvrai to believe.

The metropolis of Bihari boasted a number of expensive inns, some large and some small, and many of them within easy walking distance of the city's huge, magnificent, and very famous Red Temple.

The Red Temple offered its own inn for guests; accommodations more luxurious than most of the others, probably more so than any of them.

But Marland rejected that choice out of hand. He wanted to be less liable to Red Temple scrutiny once the real fun started.

As he was about to begin the process of selecting one of the other hostelries for himself and his small entourage, he suddenly announced that soon, perhaps immediately, he ought to hire a bodyguard or two. Adrian supposed his decision had been brought on by a recent hue and cry after a robber in the streets.

"Not that I really need a bodyguard," he confided to Amelia, patting his Swordhilt. In the privacy of his room, using some expensive pigment, he had whitened that black hilt to something like ivory, in an effort to add to the disguising effect of the oversized scabbard. "Not with the help I've got here. But if people size me up as wealthy, which I want them to do, then it might look strange if I travel with no such protection."

Amelia sighed. "If you're really going through with this, then we must try to do it properly. Anyway, it won't hurt to have an armed man or two on our side. We could try one of the agencies," she suggested.

The man shook his head, and rubbed his Swordhilt, as if that might help him think. "I don't know. They're likely to have Temple connections. Maybe I'd better think about it for a while."

*   *   *

The former Lieutenant Kebbi had by now melded himself with some success into the city of resorts. Pawning a ring that he had managed to conceal from his uncouth captors at the mountain inn, he provided himself with coin sufficient to obtain cheap food and shelter for a time.

Alone in the cubicle he occupied in a lodging house, Kebbi took out the token Karel had given him, and looked at it.

Since his arrival in Bihari, he had occasionally been able to feel the little piece of wood tugging at the pocket in which he carried it. And now, when he took it out and held it in his palm, it tended to slide off in one direction. He had to tilt the flat plane of his hand up on that side to keep the fragmentary toy from falling to the floor.

The missing Prince Adrian must be here, then, and not very far away.

Kebbi no longer had a chance of getting his hands on a Sword, it seemed. But he might, he thought, be in reach of something just as valuable.

Thrusting into his belt the cheap dagger he'd acquired with almost his last coin, he started out to search for the missing Prince.

Murat had no ring to pawn in the big city, and certainly no Sword of Chance, but fortune had smiled upon him anyway. He had an old friend in Bihari, a lady—some would not have called her that—he'd known two or three years ago. Daring to call upon her, even in his disheveled condition, he had the great good luck to find her home and ready to receive him. Often nobility of rank did confer advantages.

Rising from her lounge on the terrace, she surveyed him with an expression of frank dismay. "Aphrodite and Bacchus, Murat, but where have you been?"

He made a rueful little bow. "Busy with military matters."

"At least you have survived them. And does your wife—do your people know you're here?"

"Countess, it's a long story. I shall be pleased to tell it to you one day—if after thinking things over you decide you really wish to hear it. Meanwhile, if you could advance me some money, I will be eternally grateful."

It was on the tip of his tongue to ask whether he could borrow a weapon or two from her household also. But once he had some money he could buy what he needed along that line.

Murat was also aware that the token given him by Karel was leading him to Adrian.

Kebbi, hanging around in the street outside one of Bihari's more elegant inns, was required to wait only a couple of hours before he was able to identify Prince Adrian, dressed as a pageboy in the service of a couple Kebbi had never seen before. He had no idea who they might be; certainly they did not look particularly Tasavaltan. Kebbi did not know what the Prince looked like, but if he trusted Karel's token there was no ambiguity about the boy's identity. The little wooden block almost jumped out of Kebbi's pocket when the youngster passed him.

Murat, with a substantial supply of money to help him, was content to observe matters from the middle distance. Once he'd located the inn where Prince Adrian was staying —in the guise of a servant, of all things—Murat rented a room there himself.

The young Prince's masquerade was so unlikely, although apparently voluntary, that Murat decided he had better make sure just what was going on before he attempted to interfere, and restore the heir to the Tasavaltan throne to the arms of his grateful mother.

The process of selecting a bodyguard had been concluded much faster than either Adrian or Amelia had expected—no doubt Marland's Sword had given him a hint that the young redhead calling himself Elgar was the right man for the job, though he hardly looked formidable enough to deter a robber.

That task concluded quickly, Amelia decided that she merited, deserved, needed, and wanted at least one maid.

Marland, thinking the matter over, admitted that the presence of a maid would add more realism to his character of a wealthy knight. But at the same time, the gambler said he was reluctant to acquire more servants who were not in on his plot to swindle the casino; and he was extremely reluctant to let anyone else in on it.

Amelia, getting into the spirit of things in her own way, complained: "It'll look strange if I don't have a maid, if we're supposed to be so rich. You said you didn't want to attract attention."

"That's true. But how're we going to keep her from finding out what we're up to?"

"We just won't talk about it when she's around.

"Buve, do you love me?"

"You know I do. I got you out of that hole, didn't I?"

But despite Amelia's pleas, Marland put his foot down on the subject of the maid, and none was hired.

After the debate on the maid had been settled, Marland grumbled about all the shopping Amelia found it necessary to do to outfit herself properly for high society. It was not the money that griped him, but the delay, when all else seemed in readiness. But the Sword he wore on his back, and in which he had great faith, was refusing to interfere with Amelia's plans. He was forced to the conclusion that they were likely to be of some benefit to his own.

He announced to his two confederates that, before attacking the big casino, he wanted to test his gambling plan in one of the many smaller establishments within this city.

When they reached the chosen place, early in the evening, neither the Sword nor the proprietors put up any obstacles to the entrance of Sir Marland and his entourage.

All the rooms were crowded, as Marland had wanted and expected them to be. He and his two companions would attract no particular attention.

In these crowded conditions, the knight found it necessary to hand out a small bribe at the door to obtain for himself a table toward the rear of the room. In this relatively modest establishment, there were no private boxes, booths, or balconies such as those the main rooms of the big casino boasted.

Marland entered limping, presenting this as a silent explanation for his preference in seating. He also adopted the look of a man who had slightly too much to drink.

Adrian considered that this was putting things on too thick, and liable to draw more attention than it diverted. But the ploy seemed to work, and it was hard to argue with success.

Once the master was established at his table, where he sat growling for more drink, Adrian and the bodyguard who called himself Elgar stood by him awaiting orders, while Amelia made her way into the throng at the far end of the room, close to the big wheel.

For this evening's practice session, Adrian had garbed himself in what he considered the least embarrassing of the several page liveries that had by now been purchased for him.

Play at the table beneath the wheel was of course already in progress, with players joining in or dropping out continually. Amelia, who was no stranger to casinos, took an empty spot, and placed a modest bet or two, without having any particular luck.

Leaning his head back as if in thought, Marland made direct contact between his body and Coinspinner's hilt. Then he decided on his bet, and, beckoning Adrian to lean close, whispered it in his ear.

The boy worked his way forward through the throng until he reached Amelia's side. So far there had been but little change in the modest stack of chips before her, but she looked uncomfortable. And worried. And glad to see Adrian arrive.

Elgar, their newly hired bodyguard, had in accordance with good professional practice taken his stand toward the rear of the room where he could supposedly keep an eye on everything. Since being hired, the man had purchased a good sword, but he still did not impress the Prince as being especially formidable. Still, as experienced fighters kept warning him, appearances could be very deceptive in such matters.

Looking around when he had the chance, the Prince, following Marland's teaching, thought that he could pick out one or two of the ubiquitous house magicians. These people looked somewhat bored, but still faithfully on duty to make sure that no would-be cheaters had any success against the house.

Marland, in sending Amelia his first chosen category—odd—of this practice run, also ordered Adrian to remind her to keep on mixing up her bets—that is, not always to use the winning, Sword-guaranteed number or category immediately, but to save it for later, so that no careful observer of the process could immediately be sure that the bets sent in by the man were invariably winners.

Adrian faithfully passed on the bets he was given. But it occurred to him how easy it ought to be for him to cross up Marland, by simply passing the wrong information to Amy. By the time the man found out, it would be too late for him to do anything about it—not too late for the Sword to do something, of course.

Murat, having followed his quarry to this casino, kept himself in the background and continued to observe. But what he saw only left him more puzzled than ever. Some kind of gambling scheme, evidently; but why should the heir apparent of Tasavalta choose to take part in it?

The Crown Prince still refrained from any effort to contact Adrian or anyone else in the party, to which Kebbi, of all people, had now somehow managed to attach himself.

Marland played for less than an hour, staking only small amounts, and then signaled his people he was ready to quit for the night. His theory of how to beat the house had been, as he considered, gloriously vindicated.

When he broke off the game he was a few thousand pieces ahead—not winnings enough to draw very much attention in a place like this. But he now had enough in his purse to stake himself solidly in the big game, day after tomorrow.

That night, in the inn, Marland was quietly jubilant. Once Elgar was safely out of earshot he announced to his two confederates that he had decided to make only a few minor changes in technique as a result of this preliminary study.

Amelia told him that was good. But she still looked as worried as ever.

NINETEEN

TALKING to Marland and Amelia, Adrian learned that the big casino in the Red Temple of Bihari was widely known as Sha's, after its legendary founder, not surprisingly a Red Temple priest. Sha's, or at least the inner rooms of that establishment, where the biggest games took place, had an expensive membership requirement, meant to keep out the riffraff.

The gambler had not been surprised by the requirement. As far as the Prince with his lack of experience could judge, he possessed a good familiarity with all important phases of the gambling business.

Not that he explained everything to his associates. On the day before he planned to break the bank, Marland, with Sword and scabbard strapped to his back, visited the Red Temple alone. When he rejoined his confederates he had little to say. The Prince wondered whether Marland, as an expert in the bottom line, might have been able to bypass some of the more expensive membership requirements by means of a little judicious bribery.

In any case, Marland in this environment hardly seemed like the same man who in other circumstances had often seemed clumsy and unable to cope very well.

Amy, who according to her own testimony had been in a

great many gambling establishments, including this one, also seemed at home here, though she continued to worry.

She did a fairly good job of concealing her anxiety. But the Prince could tell that it was still growing.

Meanwhile Kebbi was keeping his eye on Marland's Sword, waiting for the man to get careless. The more he watched Marland, the more he realized that he might be in for a long wait. Also Kebbi continued to puzzle over why Adrian, a prince in his own land, was content to act as a servant to this gambler, who obviously had no idea of his page's true identity. Prince Adrian, as far as Kebbi could tell, was in full possession of his faculties, though he was calling himself Cham. Simply taking the opportunity to run away from home? That wouldn't be unheard of, even among royalty.

The Culmian defector bided his time, waiting to learn more.

Murat, from his room in the same inn, also maintained his observation. He also wondered about Adrian's purpose in remaining here.

When the Crown Prince of Culm, who had recently used the Sword of Chance himself, was able to identify it as the odd-looking weapon now carried by the gambler on his back, he considered that he had made real progress.

Murat remained obstinately determined to restore the young Prince to his mother, as an important means of making amends to the Princess Kristin. But, if he were later able to hand Coinspinner back to his own Queen, what a coup that would be!

Rostov, Karel, and the four surviving troopers eventually arrived in Bihari, a full day after the Culmian fugitives. The Tasavaltans' arrival in the resort city had been delayed by their difficulty with demons.

Early on the evening of the day he had chosen to consummate his revenge, Sir Marland and his two helpers, accompanied by their sturdy bodyguard Elgar, took a short walk through the streets of the resort city, made their approach to the great Red Temple of Bihari, and entered, heading directly though unhurriedly for Sha's.

Marland, as on the day of his preliminary effort, had chosen this hour deliberately, knowing that the gambling tables would be already busy, but with their busiest time still a few hours in the future.

On approaching the Red Temple complex, the young Prince was impressed. This was by far the biggest such edifice that he had ever seen; indeed he wasn't sure that any building in Sarykam was quite this large.

On entering it, Adrian was inevitably reminded of the Twisted Temple of the City of Wizards, though his visit there seemed much further in the past than the two weeks or so that it actually was. Still, there were great differences between that Red Temple and this one, besides the circumstance that this one was crowded with mundane humans and that one had long been deserted by such creatures. For one thing, there was music, live and real and mundane, almost everywhere inside this Temple, whereas that one had been haunted with ghostly sounds.

Kebbi, closely accompanying his new employer, was also inevitably reminded of his recent narrow escape from the Twisted Temple, and of the differences and similarities between that Temple and this one.

Murat, on seeing Adrian and the others leave their inn again, had followed them. The Crown Prince kept well in the background, patiently observing.

Marland at last had plenty of faces around him that he could recognize, faces whose presence would have made him indeed uneasy if he had not possessed the security of the Sword. These familiar countenances were those of Red Temple priests and other employees who had been intimately involved in his downfall only a few months previously.

One gaze in particular, tonight, caused Marland to hold

his breath briefly. But the functionary, who Marland supposed might be somewhat nearsighted, looked right through him, and gave no sign of recognizing either him or Amelia.

Moments later the gambler was smiling at his own foolishness. If the Sword could extract him unharmed—as it had—from a condemned cell, a mere casino would pose no problem. With the Sword on his back now, he might have known that he was safe.

But Amelia, infinitely less sanguine, tugged urgently at his sleeve as soon as they entered the next room, and whispered that she was afraid they had been spotted.

"What makes you think so?" He hardly bothered to lower his voice.

"The croupier in the room we just left. The way he looked at us. I remember him from last time."

Marland had seen the same glance pass over them, and he was ready to assure her categorically that no recognition had occurred. On the contrary, they were practically home free already. Luck was his. He patted his woman's hand reassuringly. "I remember him too. But it's nothing. Forget it. Keep walking."

It was only natural that a good many of the dealers, clerks, croupiers, lookouts, and house magicians who had been working in Sha's then were still here now. Marland and Amelia could have called a number of them by name. But none of them were going to recognize the pair now. Marland could just feel it.

The Red Temple of Bihari, justly famous for its size and complexity, seemed to go on forever. Adrian had ceased having to play the country yokel and was beginning to gawk in earnest.

There was a strong taste of magic in the air as well. The Prince, to his own surprise, began to sense that he was no longer very far from the City of Wizards.

* * *

Marland himself had never really paid that much attention to where he was, in any physical, geographical sense. Ordinarily it made very little difference to him. The tables and games, the dice and cards, winning and losing, the risk-taking, were all he really cared about.

He, like many another gambler, had heard stories about the fabulous big game room in Sha's. Until now he had never been able to afford to enter that room, but he had determined that it would be there—though he might have been able to accomplish his goal elsewhere—that he would make his all-out effort to break the bank.

As the opulent rooms, filled with gaming tables, entertainers, customers, and food and drink, flowed by them one after another, Adrian could feel a growing sense of impending danger. There was nothing rational or logical about the apprehension, but he could not help considering, one last time, his option of abandoning the gambler and his scheme and getting away. After all, the Emperor hadn't really ordered him to stay with the gambler, or to try to take control of the Sword of Chance. That had been all his own idea.

The Prince now had a small supply of money in his pocket. He knew where he was—at least in a general way—in relation to his home, though Tasavalta was far away. And, as always, he was equipped with his own magical abilities.

But a sense of adventure held him here, and a sense that the Emperor though advising caution had somehow approved of what Adrian was doing, or what he was trying to do. Well, he still had time to decide. The sense of impending danger was not so immediate as all that.

Kebbi, meanwhile, was not having much success in formulating a plan to get his hands on Coinspinner. About all he had decided was that he had better grab the Sword as soon as he got a chance. Once he had that blade in hand, kidnapping Adrian—or anything else he decided to do—ought to be easy.

Marland, on actually arriving at the big game room, and being admitted with his party, promptly established himself in the box he had reserved. This was one of eight luxurious balconies in the rear of the huge room. All were about three meters above the floor, and Marland's was near the center, fourth from the left.

A turbaned attendant, bowing, escorted Sir Marland and his party to their box by way of a passage that ran behind all eight balconies, and was set off from them by doors and curtains. Elgar the bodyguard, at a word from his employer, assumed his station in this passage, just outside the sole entrance to Marland's box.

The enclosure in which Adrian, Amelia, and Marland found themselves was as big as a small room, containing a couch, a few small tables, and several chairs. Rich tapestries decorated the three closed walls, and a couple of candles on side tables shed a creamy light. Marland, with a sigh, pulled the most comfortable-looking chair forward to the rail and settled himself. From this position he could overlook almost the entire huge room of games, but his face and form were largely concealed by the draperies that partially covered the front of the box.

Safe from the observation of most of the room at least, and feeling ever more confident in his tremendous luck, the gambler drew his Sword. He held Coinspinner point down on the floor, its whitened hilt clutched tight in both his hands.

Amelia had gone to one of the side tables. Several varieties of wine were provided there, courtesy of the house.

"Let's have a toast," said Marland.

Looking at him, then at Adrian, she righted three of the sparkling glasses. Opening a bottle seemingly at random, she poured the glasses full, and handed two of them to her companions.

"To victory," said Marland solemnly.

Adrian sipped from his glass. He thought he had tasted better, once or twice, in the palace at Sarykam. Marland sipped at his. Amelia hesitated briefly, then gulped her wine down.

A few moments later she was on her way to the gaming table, where Marland and Adrian silently watched her vanish into the crowd.

The great vertical wheel on the front wall spun twice, after her disappearance, before Marland dispatched Adrian with his first bet of the night: a single chip upon the category black.

The wizard Karel was at that moment entering the Red Temple of Bihari with Rostov at his side. The four troopers had been left outside, watching hired animals, including a mount for Adrian, ready to move out on a moment's notice. On entering the Temple, Karel paused for a moment. It took an effort to make himself move forward once again. His magical sense had just warned him that Wood was somewhere in the vicinity.

"Heavy magic ahead," he commented in a whisper to Rostov, who walked at his side, bearing Sightblinder muffled in a sheath but ready.

"And the Prince?" asked the General.

"He's somewhere ahead also. Ah, this way for Adrian. To our right, toward the casino."

"That way too for the heavy magic?"

"That's to our left." Karel allowed himself a brief and mirthless smile. "Not needed to augment the thrills of Sha's Casino. Gambling provides its own magic, my friend. Trimbak Rao tells me that it's an especially abominable vice."

Marland had not been alone in his box for long when Elgar put his red head in through the curtains. His eyes, as they often did, focused on the Sword in Marland's hands before rising to his employer's face.

"There's someone here says he knows you, sir."

"Really? Well, send him in. It's all right, you can stay out in the corridor."

The bodyguard stepped out again. And Marland recognized the face that appeared next, though out of habit he was careful to keep his own countenance from displaying any recognition. The newcomer was Thurso, a small man with slicked-back black hair and an artificial-looking mustache; a hanger-on in Sha's and sometimes in less opulent casinos, a sometime gambler, a doer of difficult or unpleasant tasks—for hefty fees, of course—and from time to time a blackmailer.

The heavy curtain sagged shut behind Thurso. Marland supposed that enigmatic Elgar would be doing his best to eavesdrop outside. Well, let him. It was Marland who had the Sword of Luck.

"Hello, Buvrai," said Thurso, making no effort to pitch his voice particularly low.

If he had expected to frighten Buvrai by speaking his name aloud he must have been disappointed.

"Hello yourself," said Buvrai. "But you have my name wrong. I am Sir Marland, baronet of—of somewhere out in the Far Reaches, I suppose." Confident, smiling, he toasted his visitor silently in a sip of wine. He wasn't about to ask the little swine to sit down, though.

The little man standing just inside the doorway frowned, considering this unexpected response. "I know who you are," he finally said bluntly. "It'll take more than a beard and a getup to fool me. I wonder, does the house know you're here, gambling under a false name? I rather doubt it. I rather imagine they think you went to a different world, some time ago."

The curtain at the rear of the box opened, and Adrian ducked in. He stopped short, watching the men. After glancing at him they both ignored his presence.

"Do you know something, Thurso? Someone told me that was your name. I really don't give a good fart what you imagine." Marland was still smiling.

Thurso paused, opened his mouth and closed it, then with an air of determination tried again. "All right. Play it tough. I don't know what the game is and I don't care. I could use a loan, though. Say a hundred, and I go play in the other rooms tonight. I haven't seen you and I don't know you're here."

"You're right, little man, you don't know where I am, or where you are, either, come to that. Go play wherever you like. You'll get no gold from me."

The other nodded, indicating the middle of the big room before them, beyond the half-concealing curtains. "There's Tung-Hu in his little pulpit. I could go play there, and I might profit."

"If you see a good bet there, why don't you take it?"

The other, flushing, turned away instantly. But with the curtain to the corridor raised he turned back for a last effort. "All right. But don't say I didn't give you a chance. The High Priest of the Temple will be pleased to know you're back and playing, Buvrai. And that you're in the big game this time."

Marland only chuckled. When the curtain had dropped behind Thurso, he turned eagerly in his chair to see what might be going to happen. Adrian moved up to watch over his shoulder.

Soon the dark little man was visible, approaching the floor chief of security, whose raised dais gave him a good outlook over most of the room.

Just as Thurso began to mount the steps to the dais, a startled expression flashed over his face. His arms began waving, in the manner of a man losing his balance, as he toppled from sight beyond a throng of customers. A waiter who had been hurrying past carrying an upraised tray went down also, and a crash of shattered glass was audible above the room's babble of background noise. The waiter reappeared in a moment, but the little blackmailer did not.

Security began to make a fuss around the spot, and presently the heads and shoulders of two guards could be seen carrying something heavy away between them.

Thurso was not seen again. Marland glanced at Adrian, then sighed and said nothing. Adrian was still staring out over the crowd. Obviously the great majority of the people in the huge room were not aware that anything of importance had happened. With unobtrusive efficiency, servants and security people were now cleaning something up. The Prince wondered if it might be blood.

His sense of adventure was suddenly much diminished, and fear was starting to take over. He had thought himself free at any time to walk out on Marland. But now he had grave doubts that the Sword would allow it.

Carrying Marland's next bet down to Amy at the table, Adrian thought that her nerves were getting worse, though she maintained her position at the table and continued to play. A catastrophic failure of her nerves, thought Adrian, had become a distinct possibility. He wanted to say something encouraging to her, but the right words were hard to find.

Since entering the great Temple of Bihari, Adrian had been aware of all types of entertainers, almost everywhere in sight, performing for the customers or pleading for the chance to do so. Here, in Sha's Casino, the entertainers were less obtrusive than elsewhere in the Temple. Here in Sha's, so Marland had informed him, were also to be found the best house wizards in the world, and the worst chances of cheating. These wizards were superbly good at their very specialized job, which was primarily to make sure that none of the customers were ever able to cheat the house.

The legend, which the management of the casino took pains to propagate, was that no one in all the centuries of its operation had ever managed to succeed in that endeavor. Marland said that it was very possibly true.

Each day the house wizards, having made sure that their reputation with regard to their primary responsibility would remain untarnished, next did their best to keep the customers from cheating one another. In this they were often successful, though here their record was not unblemished.

And naturally this evening, after the man in Box Four started winning strongly, some of the house magicians began to take notice. It was barely possible that something strange was up. But security's preliminary look discovered nothing, no reason to harbor the faintest suspicion of Marland or his people.

The chief of floor security in the big room, the wizard named Tung-Hu, frowned, catching the shadow of a potential magical disturbance of quite a different kind. But the shadow had come and gone before Tung-Hu could even attempt to identify it.

Wood was the source. But he was able to soothe away the nervous apprehension of the house magicians almost as well as if he had been armed with one of the subtle Swords.

In the casino only Karel, and through him Rostov, were certainly aware of the Ancient One's ominous approach.

At the entrance to the great private room, Sightblinder, invisible but powerful in Rostov's fist, caused the attendants to back away in confusion. Several of them hastened to wave the General and his companion in.

On entering the big game room, Rostov thought it was high enough to allow the great god Draffut to stand upright. He also observed that the huge gaming wheel on the far wall took up most of the height with its diameter.

"The Prince is here?" he whispered to the wizard beside him, sheathing the Sword of Stealth again.

"Adrian is here. Somewhere in this room. Be ready."

Before the eccentric knight in the curtained box had been an hour at play, he, and the nervous lady at the table

who was so obviously his partner, had established themselves as considerable winners.

Observers could readily see that there was rarely time
enough for the young page, who served this couple as
messenger, to make his way from the box to Amelia's side
and back again between successive spins of the great wheel.
The great wheel made a distinctive noise, and on some
spins, when particularly great sums were known to be at
stake, the huge room grew so quiet that that noise could be
distinctly heard to its far corners.

Play continued, with the winnings of the mysterious man
in the box steadily mounting. Amy's own, unaided luck
was not bad tonight, and as usual the Sword was invincible.

Such success attracted yet again the attention of the
guardians of the house. Still the interest they were taking in
Marland was hardly more than routine; during the last
month Sha's had survived one or two bigger winners.

But when two more lucky numbers had come in for
Marland, Tung-Hu decided it would be a good idea to
listen in on what the young messenger was saying.

Word was passed down from the security chief. One of
the floor agents of the house, who circulated continually
among the crowd, and looked like nothing but another
harried player, managed to do this. He heard Adrian tell
Amy only that her next bet should be on red.

She acknowledged the message with a nod, and placed
her bet.

And red happened of course to win.

Marland was less happy at his impending victory than he
had anticipated. Coinspinner was with him, what could
possibly go wrong? The bank here, of course, had huge
reserves. But he had already mentioned to his confederates
the probability that as soon as it became obvious that he
was on a really tremendous winning streak, other bettors
would flock to ride his choices, piling their wagers atop the
winning categories or digits enforced by Coinspinner.

This, if the house allowed it to happen, would break even the biggest bank in short order.

Marland slumped in his chair, staring at the dyed hilt of his Sword. He hoped that nothing really fatal had happened to Thurso. He hadn't really wanted to kill the little bastard, after all.

A wave of noise, almost of applause, swept through the crowd in the room beyond the curtains of his box. Someone had won big.

Marland was bored.

And in fact no crisis of this magnitude had confronted Sha's in many years. Tung-Hu had already communicated with his superiors, who were seriously considering suspending play for a time. By doing this the house would risk having to write off its already very serious losses.

But for the moment the luck of the house took a twist for the better. It was Amelia's turn to place her bet unaided, and a fortune was swept away from her.

The security investigation of course was ordered stepped up. The next step called for the infiltration of some agent into Marland's box to get a firsthand look at whatever might be going on there. Somehow the draperies, or some other obstruction, always prevented anyone looking up from seeing very much.

Usually probes of this type were most successfully carried out by one of the dancing girls who roamed the Temple, performing on request or with apparent spontaneity. Besides gathering information, there was the chance that the presence of such a girl might stir up some jealousy, and rob this strange Sir Marland of the full cooperation of the lady who now represented him at the table. At the very least it might distract the gambler from his endeavors.

Tung-Hu ordered that a certain girl be brought to him at once. Somehow his orders went astray.

Without waiting for the girl's arrival, the suspicious house wizard next tried his most skillful and subtle magical method of scanning the interior of the box without making a physical approach. He could behold the result before him in a crystal globe. Yes, there was the gambler, seated, holding both hands clenched before him in a rather awkward-looking position, as if they were resting on something. But there was nothing under them. Irrelevant. Everything in Box Four looked clean. Tung-Hu's most accomplished powers assured him that there was nothing magical for him to worry about.

"Even so, it seems imperative that we investigate the matter more intensely." The High Priest of the local Red Temple himself was now standing beside Tung-Hu on the security dais. The High Priest was beginning to be desperate, though in keeping with his dignity he expressed it in a restrained way. This stranger's winnings were once more mounting to the point where it would be more than embarrassing for the casino if things went on this way.

Wood had now entered the big room, secretly, and was standing inconspicuously against a wall while he conferred with Tigris. The Ancient One had disdained to adopt any special disguise for this occasion, wearing his usual appearance of a youthful demigod.

With the hilt of Shieldbreaker under his hand, Wood was able to see and recognize at a glance Rostov carrying Sightblinder, and Karel beside him; the odd behavior of others in the vicinity of the General proved which Sword Rostov was carrying. Neither Tasavaltan had spotted Wood as yet.

Wood was also able to identify Adrian without any trouble. But now he was no longer content with the idea of kidnapping Prince Mark's whelp. Not when there were two other Swords besides his own in this room.

"We must," he whispered to Tigris, "get at least one of those two into our grasp as well."

"How, my lord?"

"As to Coinspinner, getting this mysterious man into a

special game, and then challenging him to bet his Sword, would seem to be the way to go."

"You will go right to his box, and challenge him?"

"Or somehow bring him to the table, and meet him there. Of course that will draw dear Rostov, with his Sword, as well."

"*I* could go to his box," said Tigris, "and tempt him to the table. Or to anywhere you like."

Her master, hesitating again, hardly seemed to hear her. "Or would it be better not to win the Sword of Chance again, but to destroy it now? I wasted one opportunity to do so, and now here's another; who can say if I shall ever gain another?"

Still, as before, Wood was tempted to keep the Sword of Chance and use it for himself—anyone, any being, human or otherwise, who managed to get Coinspinner and Shieldbreaker in hand at the same time would be very powerful indeed.

And Sightblinder was here, too, in the same room. The Sword of Stealth, with either of the other two Swords present, would also form a very powerful combination.

"Will you call upon the demons, sir?" asked Tigris.

"I think not. Many of them are still scattered. And I'd be surprised if the damned young whelp there lacks the power his father and grandsire seem to share against my pets."

Suddenly the master wizard was decisive. "It will be the gaming table. Save your efforts, I'll get him out of his box myself."

Adrian, coming to the table with another bet chosen by Marland, in his hurry and concentration did not at first recognize Wood among the crowd.

Once Wood had reached the table, he observed Amelia's next bet. Then Wood, having provided himself with the necessary tokens, placed his own wager in direct opposition.

There was, as on other crucial turns, a silence as the wheel spun. This time the silence was broken only by a sound as of a single drum, doubtless held by one of the musicians. Then came a gasp from the crowd. The lady had lost, a huge sum this time.

Marland, who had been watching closely, hurriedly left his seat. His first thought was that either Amy or Adrian had blundered. His second was that one or both of them were deliberately betraying him for some reason.

Only at the last moment did Marland remember to sheathe and conceal his Sword before he plunged into the crowd. He pushed his way through the crowd and toward the table.

Kebbi, seeing his employer rush out of the box in an agitated state, hastily followed.

Murat, still patiently observing from the post where he had established himself on the floor of the big room, decided that matters were somehow coming to a head, and started toward the table also.

Adrian had turned from the table when the noise of the crowd made him look back. Coinspinner's choice had lost. For a moment the Prince could only gape. Then he realized that Shieldbreaker must somehow be arrayed against Marland.

And Shieldbreaker must mean that Wood was present. A moment later, the boy saw and recognized the Ancient One among the crowd that pressed around the table.

Wood smiled evilly in Adrian's direction.

There would be no raising an elemental here. Not against this man's effortless power. Adrian now realized that he was lost. There was only one way out. There was only one way, as every heir to a warrior's throne must know, to fight against Shieldbreaker. Barehanded.

Resisting the impulse to run away, Adrian began to work his way through the crowd directly toward Wood.

Wood saw him coming, smirked at him at first, then frowned. Against an unarmed opponent, even one physically much weaker, there was only one way for the holder of the Sword of Force to win, and that was to rid himself of his peerless weapon as quickly as possible.

Adrian, having committed himself, darted forward with the speed of desperation. Wood, still fumbling to draw his Sword, could only jump aside. It was almost a panicked move, that of a powerfully built man avoiding in desperation the attack of a mere child.

Still in the act of drawing Shieldbreaker in order to throw it away, Wood attracted the full attention of the armed guards who had been steadily reinforcing the security presence near the table.

The guard nearest to Wood was extremely good at his trade. He had his short sword fully drawn, menacing this troublemaker, even before Shieldbreaker in Wood's clumsy hand had finally and fully cleared the scabbard. But against the handiwork of Vulcan, mere human skill was futile. The drum-note of the Sword of Force was sounding now, and it laid a slight emphasis upon one single beat. The guard's weapon was shattered into flying bits of steel that stung and bit at everyone they struck.

Wood paused, shuddering. Shieldbreaker was fully drawn now, hilt nestled in his right hand. It would begin, it was already starting, to meld itself into that hand. In another moment he would not be able to cast the Sword away, and it would mean his doom if he were attacked in that state by some unweaponed foe.

Meanwhile howling confusion, panic, had exploded in the room, following the blast of shrapnel from the shattered sword. Many here were armed, and weapons were now coming out. Accidental wounds were being inflicted in the crowd.

Rostov, Sightblinder in his right hand, was trying to fight his way toward his struggling Prince, but the General could make little headway against the mob of bodies. Half of the people surrounding Rostov saw him as some loved one, the other half as a dread enemy.

Tigris found herself bewildered by the simultaneous appearance of two Woods, who shouted contradictory commands. The enchantress had long known in a theoretical way what the Sword of Stealth might do to her, but the actual event was still difficult to deal with.

Before she could decide which of the images of Wood was genuine, she found Karel's magic surrounding her, the old man's craft blocking her own magic, at every turn.

Marland, stumbling amid the sudden melee around the table, tripped and fell softly to the carpet, just as the wild swing of someone's fist passed through the space vacated by his head. He was just starting to crawl, trying to distance himself from the fighting, when a surge of struggling bodies against the far side of the table tipped it over in his direction.

Missed me, he thought, *of course.* And then he saw Amy.

The fallen table, now turned completely upside down, had not missed her, and in fact she was pinned under it. For just a moment, in the way that the mind will twist things sometimes, Buvrai thought he saw his brother Talgai once again, head gray with dust protruding from the rubble of a fallen building.

But it was Amy. She lay so pale and still, prone, with the edge of the table across her back. Buvrai scrambled closer.

While a horde of people stamped and struggled around him, the guards trying to overcome mass panic and quell fights among the customers, Buvrai pulled Coinspinner from its sheath and wrapped her inert fingers around the hilt. "Amy, don't. Don't be dead. Amy, I love you." Then he let go of the Sword himself.

In the next moment he felt himself grabbed from behind, hauled to his feet in the grasp of a brawny security man.

"I recognize you! You're the one who was sentenced—" The guard broke off, let go of Marland, rolled his eyes and fell.

Kebbi, fulfilling his duty as bodyguard until he could learn from Marland what had happened to the Sword, had smashed the fellow in the head from behind with the hilt of his own weapon.

Meanwhile Wood, struggling desperately to rid himself of Shieldbreaker, tried instinctively to hack at Adrian. It was a mistake. Of course the slashes of the Sword of Force had no effect upon the unarmed youth.

Then Wood by a supreme effort managed to discard the Sword of Force just before it immovably attached itself to his right hand.

After that Wood, relying on his own powers, managed to make his getaway. Adrian saw him vanish.

Murat had hurled himself into the melee with the idea of rescuing Adrian. Then to his utter astonishment the Crown Prince suddenly beheld Princess Kristin before him—and restrained himself only in the nick of time from grabbing General Rostov with some idea of carrying him to safety.

Murat plunged back into the fray, helped lift a heavy table off a young woman who was screaming too loudly to be seriously injured. A few moments after that, the Crown Prince pulled out Adrian, still intact, from amid the struggling bodies and upended furniture.

Minutes passed before the fighting ended. When peace had finally been enforced by the house guards, the last bets were still required to be honored, by house and customers alike. On the last play the house had in fact won back a substantial portion of its night's losses. And if, according to the strict rules, any money was still due to the mysterious Sir Marland, payment would be suspended until he could be found. The High Priest breathed a sigh of relief when it became apparent that the suspension of payment might well be permanent. Rumors now rapidly spreading from several sources indicated that the man calling himself Sir Marland was really someone else.

As order was being finally restored in Sha's, Adrian was just outside, getting into the saddle of a riding-beast.

Escorted by an accomplished wizard, a determined General still armed with Sightblinder, and four Tasavaltan troopers, the Prince was preparing himself for the long journey home to Sarykam.

For some minutes now there had been no sign of either Murat or Kebbi, and neither Adrian nor his escort expected either Culmian to make an appearance now.

Karel had been the last Tasavaltan out of the casino. Before very quietly taking himself away, the old man had searched as best he could, with eyes and magic, for both Shieldbreaker and Coinspinner. He had had no success. Wood or Tigris might have recovered Shieldbreaker, he supposed—but if so, why had they fled the scene?

And Coinspinner? Sighing, the old man reflected that the Sword of Chance had most likely simply taken itself away again, no one knew where. Or had someone else simply picked it up in the confusion? There was no way to be sure.

FRED SABERHAGEN

THE BEST IN SCIENCE FICTION

THE TOR DOUBLES

Two complete short science fiction novels in one volume!

THE BEST IN FANTASY

THE BEST IN HORROR

☐	52720-8	ASH WEDNESDAY by Chet Williamson	$3.95
☐	52721-6		Canada $4.95
☐	52644-9	FAMILIAR SPIRIT by Lisa Tuttle	$3.95
☐	52645-7		Canada $4.95
☐	52586-8	THE KILL RIFF by David J. Schow	$4.50
☐	52587-6		Canada $5.50
☐	51557-9	WEBS by Scott Baker	$3.95
☐	51558-7		Canada $4.95
☐	52581-7	THE DRACULA TAPE by Fred Saberhagen	$3.95
☐	52582-5		Canada $4.95
☐	52104-8	BURNING WATER by Mercedes Lackey	$3.95
☐	52105-6		Canada $4.95
☐	51673-7	THE MANSE by Lisa Cantrell	$3.95
☐	51674-5		Canada $4.95
☐	52555-8	SILVER SCREAM ed. by David J. Schow	$3.95
☐	52556-6		Canada $4.95
☐	51579-6	SINS OF THE FLESH by Don Davis and Jay Davis	$4.50
☐	51580-X		Canada $5.50
☐	51751-2	BLACK AMBROSIA by Elizabeth Engstrom	$3.95
☐	51752-0		Canada $4.95
☐	52505-1	NEXT, AFTER LUCIFER by Daniel Rhodes	$3.95
☐	52506-X		Canada $4.95

Buy them at your local bookstore or use this handy coupon:
Clip and mail this page with your order.

Publishers Book and Audio Mailing Service
P.O. Box 120159, Staten Island, NY 10312-0004

Please send me the book(s) I have checked above. I am enclosing $_____
(please add $1.25 for the first book, and $.25 for each additional book to
cover postage and handling. Send check or money order only—no CODs.)

Name _____

Address _____

City _____ State/Zip _____

Please allow six weeks for delivery. Prices subject to change without notice.

ANDRE NORTON

☐ 54738-1	THE CRYSTAL GRYPHON		$2.95
☐ 54739-X			Canada $3.50
☐ 54721-7	FLIGHT IN YIKTOR		$2.95
☐ 54722-5			Canada $3.95
☐ 54717-9	FORERUNNER		$2.95
☐ 54718-7			Canada $3.95
☐ 54747-0	FORERUNNER: THE SECOND VENTURE		$2.95
☐ 54748-9			Canada $3.50
☐ 50360-0	GRYPHON'S EYRIE		$3.95
☐ 50361-9	(with A.C. Crispin)		Canada $4.95
☐ 54732-2	HERE ABIDE MONSTERS		$2.95
☐ 54733-0			Canada $3.50
☐ 54743-8	HOUSE OF SHADOWS		$2.95
☐ 54744-6	(with Phyllis Miller)		Canada $3.50
☐ 54715-2	MAGIC IN ITHKAR		$3.95
☐ 54716-0	(Edited by Andre Norton and Robert Adams)		Canada $4.95
☐ 54749-7	MAGIC IN ITHKAR 2		$3.95
☐ 54742-X	(edited by Norton and Adams)		Canada $4.95
☐ 54709-8	MAGIC IN ITHKAR 3		$3.95
☐ 54710-1	(edited by Norton and Adams)		Canada $4.95
☐ 54719-5	MAGIC IN ITHKAR 4		$3.50
☐ 54720-9	(edited by Norton and Adams)		Canada $4.50
☐ 54727-6	MOON CALLED		$2.95
☐ 54728-4			Canada $3.50
☐ 54754-7	RALESTONE LUCK		$2.95
☐ 54755-1			Canada $3.95
☐ 54757-8	TALES OF THE WITCH WORLD 1		$3.95
☐ 54756-X			Canada $4.95
☐ 50080-6	TALES OF THE WITCH WORLD 2		$3.95
☐ 50081-4			Canada $4.95
☐ 54725-X	WHEEL OF STARS		$3.50
☐ 54726-8			Canada $3.95

Buy them at your local bookstore or use this handy coupon:
Clip and mail this page with your order.

Publishers Book and Audio Mailing Service
P.O. Box 120159, Staten Island, NY 10312-0004

Please send me the book(s) I have checked above. I am enclosing $_____
(please add $1.25 for the first book, and $.25 for each additional book to
cover postage and handling. Send check or money order only—no CODs.)

Name _____

Address _____

City _____ State/Zip _____

Please allow six weeks for delivery. Prices subject to change without notice.

PIERS ANTHONY

Buy them at your local bookstore or use this handy coupon:
Clip and mail this page with your order.

Publishers Book and Audio Mailing Service
P.O. Box 120159, Staten Island, NY 10312-0004

Please send me the book(s) I have checked above. I am enclosing $_____
(please add $1.25 for the first book, and $.25 for each additional book to
cover postage and handling. Send check or money order only — no CODs.)

Name _____

Address _____

City _____ State/Zip _____

Please allow six weeks for delivery. Prices subject to change without notice.